HEATHEN

RACHEL LEIGH

www.rachelleighauthor.com

ISBN: 9798585490873

Cover design by Ya'll. That Graphic.

Cover Model: Eric Guilmette

Photographer: Armando Adajar

Editing by Fairest Reviews Editing Service

*"The world is full of monsters
with friendly faces
and angels with scars."*—*Heather Brewer*

·

They say that shy people notice everything but say nothing. Maybe that's why Willa hasn't said a word to me since I picked her up ten minutes ago. She sits quietly in the passenger seat of my car with her eyes glued to the windshield. Her hands are folded neatly in her lap, and the extra effort she put into this night is apparent with the thick layer of makeup covering her face.

Her honey brown eyes are outlined in black and her lips are glossed over. Though, her normal Willa wardrobe has remained the same, an old lady sweater with white pearl buttons riding down the center, and I'm pretty sure there are cats on it, although it could be puppies. Hell if I know. Hell if I care.

I glance over and watch her body tense up. It's like she knows I'm watching her. "You excited for tonight?"

Her eyes stay straight ahead when she nods. "Mmhmm." I crack a smile. For some reason her unease makes this all the more exciting.

Sure, it's just a bet. One that I plan to win, even if there isn't anything at stake. It was simply the guys telling me that I couldn't do it, and me telling them that I could bag this chick on a teacher's desk with an audience if I wanted to.

It's no secret that Willa has always had a crush on me. Junior year she was doodling in her notebook and Zed snatched it up and showed the entire class her artwork. A big heart with my name inside of it that looked like it had been traced over at least a hundred times. I was sitting in front of her, like I had every day in English class. After that, I made sure not to lean too far back, because I'm pretty sure she used to sniff my hair. She may have even plucked a few strands and stuck them between the pages of her notebook.

We pull up to Tommy's house and that motherfucker lied. He said this would be the most epic birthday party in existence. There's six, maybe seven cars, and it looks like everyone is in the house. Just fucking great. I'm gonna walk in there with Whispering Willa and there isn't a chance in hell of blending in.

Fuck it. Maybe I should call this entire thing off. Even though I know for a fact that she'll spread her legs for me with little to no effort, I'm not sure I want between them. I'm sure the girl is a virgin, and while I'm an asshole on many levels, her v-card shouldn't go to a guy who won't even look in her direction when we pass through the halls.

Before I can even change my mind, Willa is opening her door and stepping out. "You sure you wanna do this?" I ask her, giving her the opportunity to run like hell. But she doesn't back down. Instead, she smiles. A real, genuine, happy as hell smile. Something twinges in my gut and it's apparent in this moment that I'm going straight to hell. Her fingers tangle around the cross hanging from her neck and her eyes shimmer in the light of the moon. "Unless you don't want to," she says in a hushed tone, her smile fading with the possibility of me being the one to call this whole thing off.

"Hell yeah, I do." I jump out of the car and slam the door

shut then hurry over to her side. Swinging an arm over her shoulder, I press my lips to her cheek. "Wouldn't've invited you if I didn't want you here with me." Lies. All lies. But, if I'm going to hell, I might as well enjoy the ride.

Drawing in a deep breath, I swing open the front door. My eyes dance from person to person staring at me. Zed's wearing a shit-eating grin with an unlit joint pinched between his fingers. Tommy and Talon look surprised that I even got her here.

I look down at Willa and I can tell she's nervous as hell. I squeeze her closer, warranting glares from the barbie dolls huddled together at the kitchen island. Their laughter has Willa rubbing her cross again. She's probably praying for a way out of this mess. Now that she's here, she's not going anywhere. Now that we've been seen together, I have every intention of winning this challenge. "Come on, let's get a drink." I lead her into the kitchen with my arm still draped around her.

"This has to be some sort of joke." Layla snickers with an eye roll.

I kick open the lid of the cooler. "If you girls have a problem with my guest, you can fucking leave. Then we'll see who's laughing."

"We might have to. Now that she's here, it's sure to be a drag."

Shuffling through the ice inside, I pull out a can of beer then give it a good shake before angling the opening at Layla and cracking it open. "What the hell, asshole!" she screeches while running her hands over her soaked white T-shirt. Her hard nipples greet me through the thin fabric.

I slam the half-full can down on the counter then grab a couple more beers out of the cooler. "Fuck, I'm sorry." I chuckle. "Let's go, Willa. Something smells funky over here."

"Yeah, your nasty girlfriend," Layla grumbles from behind us as we walk into the living room.

"Nah, I'm pretty sure it's your rotten pussy." I glance over my shoulder and her foot stomps to the floor while her mouth forms an O.

"Fuck you, Lars."

Flipping a finger over my shoulder, directed at her, I lead Willa over to the couch. "Move over," I say to Tommy as I knock his leg over the coffee table that sits in front of the couch. "Killer party, man." I make my sarcasm obvious.

"Yeah, about that. Figured we should keep it low-key tonight." He winks. Fucker did this on purpose. He wanted Willa's presence on my arm noticed. "In fact," he kicks his feet back up, "Zed wanted to have a word with you about the arrangement."

"Arrangement?" Willa asks.

"Holy shit, she talks." Zed chimes in as he leans forward to get a better look at us. "How's it going, Whispering Willa?" He smirks.

I grab an empty can that's sitting on the table in front of us and chuck it at him. "Shut the fuck up."

Talon grabs the can mid-air. "Oooh, someone's defensive tonight."

I crack open a beer and hand it to Willa who shakes her head no. Shrugging my shoulders, I tip it back and take a swig. "So, what's the plan tonight? Sitting on the couch twiddling our thumbs until we pass out?"

"Well," Zed springs up, "I'm planning on taking one of those ladies into Mr. Chamber's office and letting her suck my cock. You're welcome to watch if you'd like." He flips Willa's hair from behind the couch and I'm two seconds away from laying his ass flat on the floor. Before I can say anything, he heads toward the kitchen. Then I hear him say, "Come on, Cara. You look thirsty."

"Is she really going with him?" Willa asks as she watches them walk away.

"She really is. Some girls have no morals." I turn my body toward her. "Unlike you." My hand finds her leg and her eyes shoot down as my fingers caress her upper thigh. Tipping her chin up with my free hand, I look into her eyes. "You're special, Willa." Tommy starts having a coughing fit and I know he's fighting not to laugh. "Come on, let's get away from these assholes." I stand up and set my beer down, then take her hand in mine.

She doesn't put forth any resistance when I pull her up. Talon waggles his brows, and Tommy sinks further into the couch. "Have fun, you two," he says before downing his beer.

With her hand in mine, I lead her up the stairs to Tommy's room. "Where are we going?"

"Away from the noise. Away from them. Thought maybe we could get to know each other a little better."

Her hand feels so soft and tiny in mine. She's this petite thing with wavy brown hair and eyes that match. She can't be more than one-hundred and ten pounds soaking wet, and she's as plain as white bread. Well, she was. Until she caked on all that eyeliner. She looks better without it, in my opinion. She's a cute girl, I'll give her that. But she lacks everything that I've always been attracted to. "You having fun?" I ask her, though I know damn well that her response will be a lie.

"I'm having a great time." There it is. Lie. Girls like Willa have no idea what fun is. She's so sheltered. I'm pretty sure she lied to her stuck-up parents just to get out of the house tonight. There is no way in hell her stepdad, the pastor, would have let her leave otherwise. And her mom, the school librarian? Not a chance. They're uptight and look down on people like me because they think they're better than us with their holier than thou attitudes.

Willa is different. I can tell that she's miserable in her same old, day in and day out mundane life. She craves excitement. And, I plan to give it to her. If only for a night.

RACHEL LEIGH

I push open Tommy's bedroom door and don't bother to turn the lights on. There's a small glimmer of light coming from the open closet and I can see all that I need to see.

"Have a seat." I nod toward the open queen-sized bed. When she sits down on the foot of it, I join her. Taking her hand in mine. "I really like you, Willa."

Her eyes light up. "You do?"

"Mmhmm, I do."

"You sure don't act like it. Before last week, you never said a word to me."

I shrug a shoulder. "I'm shy. Like you." My fingers begin tracing the inside of her palm. "I'm glad we're finally alone. I've been wanting to do this all night." My eyes close and I lean forward to kiss her, but when I feel her pull away, I straighten up. "What's wrong? You don't wanna kiss me?"

Her head drops down and she looks at my fingers that are tangled with hers. "I do. It's just that—"

"You've never kissed a boy before?"

She shakes her head, no.

"Then I can teach you. Give you your first kiss. Do you want that?"

Her tongue darts out, wetting her lips before she nods. "Ok."

Cupping her cheeks in both of my hands, I turn her head toward me. "Close your eyes." When she does, I press my mouth to hers. Prying her lips open with my tongue and sliding it inside of her mouth. She tastes as sweet as she looks. Using my hands as a guide, our heads move gently as her mouth opens and closes, her tongue finally perking up and dancing with mine. "There you go," I mutter into her mouth.

Dropping one hand, I slide it between her legs and give her inner thigh a gentle squeeze. I can feel her body tense up and I bet she's creaming in her panties right now. I know that I'm hard as a fucking rock. I didn't think she'd turn me on this

6

much, but there is something about her lack of experience that has me wanting to teach her everything I know, and then some.

Leaning to the side, I pull her down with me as we drop onto the bed. With our mouths still connected, I roll her onto her back and climb on top of her. "You're doing so good."

"I am?" she asks, seeking my praise and approval.

"Fuck yeah, you are." My open palm slides up the length of her leg then beneath her sweater. Her waist is just as smooth as her hands. Satin-like, and I can feel a trail of goosebumps cascade from my touch. Both of her hands wrap around my neck and her legs part, inviting me in. "Do you want me to show you more?"

"Ok."

My hand slithers farther up her shirt, beneath her bra, cupping one of her breasts. Small, but perky. I begin rolling her nipple between my fingers as she grinds herself against me. She fucking wants me so bad. I can probably make her come with her clothes still on. I press my cock into her, grinding back.

"Lars," she whispers, "can I touch you?"

"Hell yes, you can." Is that even a question? She's making this easier than I thought she would.

Arching my back, I reach between us and pop the button on my jeans and slide her hand down my pants. Her dainty fingers shiver as she wraps them around my cock. I slide my hand down her leggings and, to my surprise, she's completely bare, and as I suspected, her pussy is soaking wet. My fingers circle around her clit and she lets out a subtle moan, curving her back and forcing herself into me. She's a horny little thing.

"Let's get this stuff out of the way." I sit up and tear off my shirt, tossing it to the floor. She looks up at me with doe eyes and her bottom lip between her teeth. Shit, she looks pretty fucking sexy right now. Who would have thought?

I give the bottom of her shirt a tug and she sits up, allowing me to take it off. Then she unclasps her bra and lets it fall between us. "Fuck," I mumble as I take in the view. Her pink buds are sticking out, hard and hungry. "You sure you want this?"

She nods, so I take my pants off, followed by hers. I can feel her body tremble as my fingers skate down her stomach to her open legs. I trail my index finger up and down her pussy. "Have you ever been fingered before?"

She nods her head, yes.

My eyes widen. Something ticks inside of me. "You have? Who's touched you?" My words come out much harsher than I planned.

Her cheeks flush, and she pinches her eyes shut. "Just by myself."

My body relaxes. "Damn, that's hot." I enter her slowly. Little by little, until my finger is all the way in. I slide it out just as slowly. Then back in. "Does that hurt?"

"No."

Dropping my head down, I drag my teeth over her collarbone. "Do you want more?"

"Ok."

A girl of few words, but I can guarantee she knows exactly what she wants. I slide another finger in and I can feel her stretch around me. She's so fucking tight. Picking up my speed, I pump faster, and she lets out a whimper. I lean forward and look at her. "Still ok?"

Her eyes are still pinched shut as she chews on her bottom lip. "Mmmhm." Maybe she's lying. Or maybe looking at me will remind her that she's making a big ass mistake letting me touch her.

"Can I put my dick inside you?" Man, that sounded so fucking terrible. Not at all how I wanted it to.

Her eyes shoot open. "I…I don't know, Lars. I'm not sure if I'm ready for that."

I raise a brow. "How about just the tip? I'll stop if it hurts." It's a lie, really. Once she gets a little, she'll want it all.

She hesitates for a bit. Breaking eye contact and glancing over my shoulder. "What if someone comes in?"

My fingers pump inside of her, and I can feel her swell around them. "I locked the door. No one is coming in here."

More hesitation.

"Ok. But just for a second."

Damn. I didn't think she'd agree this easily. Now that she has, my heart is fucking pounding in my chest. It's not the first time I've taken a girl's virginity. I have no idea why I suddenly feel like I shouldn't do this. She's so soft and timid. Moral and kind. But, I barely know the girl. I have no emotional attachment to her. Why the hell am I doubting myself?

"Lars?" She grabs my attention. "Are you ok?"

"Yeah. Yeah, I'm fine."

Just fucking do it, dumbass. She's ready and willing. Wet and waiting.

Fuck.

Before I can even make a decision, her hand stretches down between us. She takes my cock in her hand and lines it up with her entrance. Her hips raise, practically begging for it. So, I give her what she wants.

My head slides in and her hands slap my shoulders. Her fingertips digging into my skin. "You ok?" I ask, again.

She nods, so I push in more. Giving her the shallow part of my cock. She moans in pleasure as she bucks her hips up, forcing more of me inside her. I begin sliding in and out. "You're so damn tight." Without meaning to, I look into her eyes. She looks right back at me. Full of wonder for the future and what this means for us. What this means for her. That's

9

what I see. Those are the questions I imagine are running rampant through her head.

Nothing. We have no future. When I'm done here, I'm taking her home and I'll probably never talk to her again.

I should stop.

But, I don't. Instead, I give her all of me. She cries out in a mix of pleasure and pain, but I keep going. Faster. Harder. "Fuck." I groan. It feels so fucking good inside her. I couldn't stop now even if I wanted to.

She grabs me by the head and pulls my mouth to hers. Kissing me, as if it's the first and last time, before I spill inside of her.

Slowing my pace, I pull out of the kiss.

"Thanks," I tell her.

"Thanks?"

"Yeah. Thanks for giving me your first."

1

Three Months Later

Sooner or later, everyone is smothered in a blanket of consequences when they choose the wrong path. We did just that. We saw an opportunity, and we took it and ran with it. We made our bed, and now we have to lie in it and hope that we still have our freedom when we get out.

Marni just got her tattoo. She's one of us now. She gets to stand in line and when it's her turn, she gets to pull the trigger on whoever she wants and we will all have her back. That's part of the deal. No matter what, we stand together from start to finish and everything in between.

I pull up to the house that I once called home and the garage door is closed, but I don't need to see vehicles to know who's here. Chances are, there's only one person home. The people I call my parents are probably on some sort of lavish vacation in France or basking in the sun on the beaches of Maui. Don't know, don't care. I moved out a few months ago when Dad moved his new family in. One month later, he married my bitch of a stepmother, Lynn, and decided that I was simply an inconvenience in his perfect life.

Every once in a while, I drop by just to pay a visit to my new sister because she requires my attention to keep her in line.

"Madison," I holler before the door even closes behind me. The walls have been painted since I was here last. Dad didn't waste any time letting Mommy Dearest wipe away the memories of his former wife—also known as my mom. "In your room, right fucking now," I shout even louder. I could smell her fruity body spray as soon as I walked in, so I know she's here.

The door slams shut and I kick my shoes off and head down the hall to the staircase. My socks glide across the waxed hardwood floors. "Madison," I singsong, "I know you're here." As I make my way up the stairs, the sound of her pop music gets louder. *Taylor Swift, of course.* This girl is obsessed. I'm not sure who she's more obsessed with, me or the pop princess.

Without knocking, I swing her door open. "What the fuck, Lars?" she huffs with her legs spread wide open and her purple dildo still stuck inside of her. I step in her room and close the door behind me. "What the fuck did I tell you about blowing up my phone all day?"

"But I missed you," she says, with her elbows pressed into the mattress on either side of her. She leans forward and begins sliding the dildo in and out while watching me with her lips curled up. I make a beeline to her with a heavy brow. Without even saying a word, I grab the rubber wand and pull it out. With my eyes on her, I trail my tongue up the length of the dildo, licking her sweet juices. "I was just about to come, so if you wouldn't mind." She leans forward with her legs still spread and tries to grab it from my hand.

With my free hand, I give her body a shove and push her down on her back. Crawling on my knees, between her legs, my face hovers over hers. "Since when do you do anything for yourself?" I plunge the dildo in her so hard that her entire body jolts upward, but I don't stop. Gripping the end tightly in my hand, I drive the full length inside of her continuously, causing the top of her head to ricochet off the headboard.

"Holy shit, Lars," she cries out. Her eyes roll back in her head as her back arches to gain friction. Just when I feel her body tense up, I pull the dildo out and drop it on her stomach. "What the hell?" She grimaces.

"It's about time you start taking care of yourself." I brush my finger over her nose with a smirk.

"Fuck you, Lars!" she screams as I stand up.

"In your dreams, Sis."

I turn to walk out, but she grabs my attention. "Oh, I've been dreaming about it ever since the first time you fucked me, and every time after that. Should I remind you that I could make it happen again if I wanted to?"

Just like that, I spin around, and I'm on top of her again. My jaw ticks furiously as I grit through my teeth, "Don't fucking threaten me, Madison. I'll tear you to shreds."

"Oh yeah," she seethes, "before or after you spend twenty years in prison?"

I don't humor her with a spoken response. Instead, I grab her by the throat and squeeze. Not as hard as I should, but enough to get her attention. My mind says to just fucking do it, end this madness. But my conscience isn't there. Not yet.

"One word. Josh," she mutters with my fingers still snaked around her neck. She doesn't fight me off; she just lies there with a fucking smirk that I wanna dig my teeth into and peel off her face.

Lucky for her, I'm in need of some reprieve. Which is why I came in here in the first place. I seem to have forgotten that because every time I look at her fake tan and face full of over-priced makeup, I wanna vomit. The girl's a fucking earthquake. She'll sneak up on you and shake the hell out of you while laughing her ass off in the process.

Stretching my hand down between us, I pop the button on my jeans. Her eyes light up, like the whore she is. If only she were a whore somewhere else. She's hungry for cock, but it's only mine she wants to fill her up. My stepsister is infatuated with me. Not just a high school crush. She's full-blown, crazy obsessed. And she's got me wrapped around her boney little finger.

I unzip my zipper and don't even bother taking my jeans all the way off before I shove my cock inside of her. Her fake nails dig into the skin of my shoulder blades as I rock myself in and out of her pussy. Grabbing her neck again, I squeeze tighter with every thrust. "Is this what you want, you little slut?"

Grabbing the back of my head, she pulls my mouth to hers. As much as I hate Madison, she's satisfying. She's got the perfect body. A tight pussy and a mouth that can suck the cum out of me like no other. That's why I keep coming back. That, and the fact that if I don't, she'll tell everyone what she saw that night.

The night me and the guys stuffed Josh's dead body into the back of a car. As usual, she was stalking me, putting her fucking nose in my business, and now she has me by the balls.

2

It's eleven o'clock in the morning when I roll outta bed. Since my dad and his gold-digging wife are out of town, I crashed in my old bedroom. It's probably best. Marni says she's forgiven me, but how could she fully? I held a gun on the girl and fed her to the lion. Part of me knew that she would be ok, but to be honest, I wasn't completely sure. I just knew that I couldn't let Zed open his mouth about what he stumbled upon —that I fuck my stepsister behind closed doors.

What started off as just fooling around, has turned into this full-blown mess of emotions on her end. It was innocent. Well, as innocent as it can be. We screwed a few times and it was nice, but then she started sprouting these feelings for me. She got crazy possessive. Watching me from afar, texting me nonstop.

When I tried to stop it a couple weeks ago, she told me that she had proof that me and the guys were a part of Josh's death. I told her we didn't kill him, but she doesn't believe me. The truth is, even we don't know what the hell happened to him. Now, she has me on a short leash and while I get laid whenever I want, if I so much as look at another girl, she flips the fuck out and begins making threats.

She can blackmail me now, but soon, she'll be the one begging for this to end.

My FOOTSTEPS ECHO through the empty hall and I would like to think that they were cleared just for me, but in reality, I'm late for class. I do all of my schooling online because I hate being here, but since I've fallen behind, there is one class that I have to take in person and I hate it with a passion. At least it's the last period of the day, so I don't have to drag my ass out of bed too early.

"Glad you could join us, Mr. Titan," Mrs. Rhys says when I walk through the curtain onto the stage.

"Yeah, I was busy with a math test," I blatantly lie.

"Please have a seat. Willa was just about to start her audition duet with Trent," Mrs. Rhys says as she looks out at the rest of the stagehands who are sitting quietly in the front row.

Pretty sure she was insinuating that I join them, but instead, I grab a stool to the left of me, spin it around and sit down right on the stage. This should be interesting.

Mrs. Rhys clears her throat. "Lars, please join the rest of the class."

Looking back and forth from her to the crowd, I keep my ass planted. "Actually, I prefer to listen from up here." I twirl my finger around my ear. "It helps to get a feel for the sound." I totally just pulled that out of my ass, but I'm not too keen on getting sandwiched between Allergic Alan and the chick who doesn't stop talking about her scholarship to Julliard.

Mrs. Rhys' eyebrows pinch together, but she doesn't say a word. Instead, she turns to face a flustered Willa who is standing front and center. Willa is many things, but the center of attention is not one of them. She's quiet and shy, a Bible hugger who has the self-esteem of a potato.

I lean forward, getting comfortable, and press my elbows to my knees, causing the legs of the stool to move a few inches. The sound of the metal against the linoleum floor draws Willa's attention. Her eyes shoot to me and when they catch mine, I don't see the shy girl in a knitted sweater, I see orbs of fire and fury. Pure hatred.

Yeah, she hates me. Naturally so. I took the girl's virginity —stole it rather—then stood by idly as my friends blasted a video of the entire thing to all our classmates. Everyone assumes that I shared the video, since my asshole friends sent it from my phone. So yeah, she hates me.

The way her brown-sugar hair cascades around her face leads me to believe that she does so to purposely hide herself. She's a pretty girl, don't get me wrong. With a complexion that's flawless, a cute little chin dimple, and small but perky breasts, she definitely has potential. But for some reason, she prefers to live under the radar. Except for in this moment. In this class, she wants to shine.

I smirk. "Sorry about that."

Her eyes roll back to her audience, and I wait for the background music to begin, but there is none. Her melancholy is the only sound as she begins singing "A Tale as Old as Time" from *Beauty and the Beast*.

Holy shit, Sweater Girl can sing.

She looks over at me as she continues.

Why the hell is she looking at me like that? My eyebrows pinch together as our gazes hold and she keeps on with the song that she's apparently singing to me. I always knew she was a little strange, but this is downright uncomfortable.

Finally, she turns back to the crowd. Her delicate voice is packed full of emotion and I'm pretty sure the entire class is moved by her performance. Hell, I think I even felt something tickle inside of me.

Trent joins her side and takes her by the hand as they turn to face each other, and he joins her in on the final line of the chorus.

I have no idea what this play is even about, other than a girl who falls in love with a beast. I've never watched the movie and don't bother watching them practice. I'm usually backstage for the hour-long class working on sounds. Don't even participate in the evening rehearsals because that wasn't part of the arrangement.

Counselor Goodman said to show up three days a week and participate and I get the grade. The end. I'm not putting any extra effort into this, and I certainly don't have the heart for drama club. Willa and Trent can have the spotlight. The little elves can have their moment flocking around on stage, pretending that fame is just around the corner. I just need to finish this shit so I can graduate.

When Willa wraps up the song and everyone claps, I join in on the cheer. Clapping my hands together so loudly that it drowns out the sound of the others. "Bravo," I shout. My voice is laced with sarcasm. I slide the stool back and get to my feet as Willa shoots daggers in my direction.

When I walk behind the thick red curtain, I assume I'm alone, until someone grabs ahold of my bicep. I thrust my arm back in a knee-jerk reaction as my fists clench. "What the hell are you doing?" Trent's voice is extra gruff and masculine and it makes me laugh. Trent Peters is anything but a tough guy, though it seems he's all about putting on the mask of a beast for the girl. He's this tall and lanky dude with a bowl cut and braces, and I'm pretty sure he doused himself in an entire bottle of Axe Cologne.

My thumb points over my shoulder. "Was sort of thinking I might come back here and take a nap."

"No. I mean, why are you in this class? Is it just to taunt her? To make a scene?"

Instinctively, I chuckle. It starts out hushed, but escalates quickly into full-blown laughter. "Who? Willa? You fucking kidding me?"

"No. I'm not kidding. I'm onto you, Lars. Stay the hell away from her."

I try to stop the laughter. I really do, but is this kid for real right now? Planting my palm gently on his chest, I give him a little shove. "Don't fuck with me, dude. I'm not in the mood." I've got Madison hot on my ass. Things with the guys and Marni are still a mess. And to top it off, the cops have widened the search for Josh, and we still have no idea where the hell Zed took him.

When Trent takes another step toward me with balled fists at his side, I put him in his place by shoving him harder. His ass hits the floor as he slides beneath the curtain.

The thudding of footsteps comes closer and the curtain is ripped open. "What's going on back here?" Willa's frail voice cracks as she extends her hand to Trent, before turning her attention to me. Her forehead crinkles in an array of lines. "Did you push him?"

There's no use in lying. "Sure did." She begins huffing and puffing over him as she tries to pull him up and I sweep the air with my hand and continue to the oversized recliner that has my name written all over it.

"Wait a minute." Willa scurries to my side like a puppy. "You can't just go around pushing people, Lars." Her eyes blink repeatedly and it's something that I've noticed she does a lot. I'm not sure if it's a nervous reaction, or if she just needs glasses. She's like a timid little mouse and her voice squeaks even when she tries to be angry. I say try, because I don't think she's capable of full-blown anger. If her sweet voice and the cross around her neck don't scream purity enough, the perched robin on the corner of her baby blue sweater sure as hell does.

One of the buttons in the middle of her sweater is undone, so I begin to pop it back in place. "I can and I did." I look up and her cocoa colored eyes beam into mine as she shivers under my touch.

In a delayed response, her hand swats mine away. "Don't touch me."

Throwing my hands up in surrender, I grimace. "Just trying to help. Wouldn't want anyone trying to sneak another peek under that sweater of yours." That was cruel. Probably went too far. I'm sure the memories of that night are still in the fore-front of her brain. I've pushed them aside and almost forgot about the entire thing until I joined this class a couple weeks ago. Seems my dick still reacts to the wallflower because the minute I saw her on that stage for the first time, I remembered what it felt like as I stretched her pussy and popped her cherry. Tight, wet, and so inviting.

"If you'd like to help. Go apologize to Trent." Her arms cross over her chest, as if she's shielding her covered breasts from me.

"Nah, I'm good. Got shit to do." With that, I walk away. This time, she doesn't follow. I turn around a couple times to make sure, but she's now kneeling at Trent's side while he plays victim.

Dropping my ass into the recliner, I kick my feet up on a box in front of me and stretch my hands behind my head. I watch as Trent feeds Mrs. Rhys his sob story, and I'm pretty sure my comfort in this chair is about to end abruptly when she glowers at me from across the room.

"Lars," she hollers, "a word please."

Fuck my life.

Kicking the box away, I get back up. Slow and steady steps lead me over to the circle gathered around the little pussy and his posse of drama nerds. But what pisses me the fuck off is the shit-eating grin on his face that he dishes out as he takes Willa's hand in his. I'm not sure why it irks me, but it does.

"Class, please go back out and start from scene one while I speak with Lars and Trent."

Once the room clears, Mrs. Rhys demands answers. I could throw Trent under the bus and tell her that he started this shit, but he'd deny it, and she'd believe him. Instead, I play nice. "I'm sorry, Trent. Didn't mean to push you." I pat him on the back with extra force, causing him to gasp. "Is this settled?"

"Don't let it happen again or you're out, Lars. I mean it." Mrs. Rhys threatens, but I take it with a grain of salt.

I hold up two fingers. "Scout's honor."

When she disappears in front of the curtain, I step up to Trent. "This isn't over, Choir Boy."

3

LARS

You'd think that I'd be the first one out the door when the bell rings, but I'm actually the last. The thing is, I don't like people. I prefer to avoid interaction with others as much as humanly possible. There are only a few people I trust, and not many that I tolerate. Trent just added himself to my shit list. Right next to Zed. The guy used to be my best friend, until he turned on me, blackmailed me, and threatened me. I've come to realize that he'd throw me under the bus just to save his ass.

Talon and Tommy, on the other hand, they've earned every bit of my trust. Marni is getting there, but I'm still not sure that her intentions are pure. I mean, who falls for a guy who was only using her in the first place? I'm still not convinced that she won't try to turn the tables on us to protect her dad.

Once I'm convinced the hall is clear, I pull the lever on the recliner in the dark room and head for the door. Just when I turn the handle, it swings open with no force on my end. "Lars, what are you still doing here?" Willa asks, as she tugs the straps of her backpack tightly to her chest.

"Leaving." I slide past her, but she grabs me by the arm.

22

When my eyes skate down to where her graceful fingers are wrapped around me, she pulls away abruptly.

With her eyes held tight to her feet, she uses a hushed tone. "Can I talk to you for a minute?"

Glancing down at my nonexistent watch, I sigh. "I've got somewhere to be."

When she turns and walks back into the theater room with her head hung low, I feel like the world's biggest ass, so I go after her. But my phone vibrates in my pocket before I even make it in the door. I pull it out and read the text from Talon, telling me to hurry my ass up or they're leaving without me.

Glancing from my phone into the darkness of the room, I stuff it back in my pocket and continue down the hall. Probably should have heard what she had to say, but I'm sure she just wanted to ask me to be nice to Trent, so it's pretty pointless anyway. The guy put his hands on me first. I was defending myself, plain and simple. He knows better. Hell, the entire school knows better.

Picking up my pace, I hurry to my car. We're tracking down a couple leads today to try and find out where Zed took Josh. It's a long shot, but we can't give up until we find him— before someone else docs. There is so much incriminating evidence out there that could get us all in a shitload of trouble. We never could have anticipated that Zed would turn on us like he did.

Pulling up to Talon's house, I only see Tommy's car. I kill the engine and get out to check the garage, just to humor myself, because I'm pretty damn sure they did, in fact, leave already. When it slides open, That fact is confirmed. "Mother-fuckers." Digging my phone back out, I call Talon, but it goes straight to voicemail.

My attention is jerked away from my phone when I hear the sound of a vehicle coming down the driveway. I end the call, and for a moment, I think they're coming back to pick me up. That is, until I realize it's not them. Staring back at me behind the windshield of his car is none other than Anderson Thorn, Marni's dad.

This is just great. Not only did they bail on me because I was ten minutes late, now I have to endure the wrath of this cocky bastard. He doesn't even hesitate to jump out of his black SUV, leaving his door open. "Where the hell is my daughter?" he barks, as he stalks toward me with a menacing scowl on his face. I watch his feet move quickly as he comes at me.

Sticking my phone back into my front pocket, I shrug my shoulders. "No idea. I just got here."

As he comes closer, I notice his jaw ticking ferociously. "Don't fuck with me, boy." His fingers tangle around the collar of my shirt and he pulls me so close that I can smell the stench of bourbon roll off his tongue. "Tell me where my daughter and that nitwit, Talon, are, right fucking now."

Attempting to shove his hands off me, I fail. "I told you, I just got here. I have no idea where Marni and Talon are."

My words only provoke his anger further. He pulls me closer and for a moment it feels like my feet have left the ground. "The cops were snooping around my warehouse this afternoon. I want proof that this is all laid to rest. That this boy's body won't surface on my front porch."

"What kind of proof are we supposed to give you?" I ask him. How are we supposed to prove that Josh's body is laid to rest, someplace it will never be found, when we don't even know where the hell it is?

When he finally releases his grip on me, I brush off my shirt. His demeanor changes. Shifting from erratic to unusually mellow. "I wanna know what the hell you guys did with Josh. This needs to end right fucking now."

I could tell him that we have no idea, but there's a good

chance he'd kill me right here and now. He'd probably get away with it, too. "He's buried. No one will find him."

His chin tips up and his eyes narrow in on me. "Where?"

Fucking A. Where the hell are those guys? I can't believe I have to deal with this shit right now. Sweat drips down my back as I rack my brain, trying to come up with something that will appease this man. Lake Ruin? With his car? No, that would just make him more anxious. The car has already been found. They've had divers searching ever since. "Briarwood," I spit out, without even giving it a second thought. "He's buried in the basement of Briarwood." That's where he should be, anyway.

Cocking a brow, he questions me further. "Briarwood? As in that old Asylum off Highway 55? Why the hell did you guys bury him there? That's Talon's property. Jesus Christ, are you guys trying to get us all locked up for life?"

"No one will find him. He's underneath a slab of cement. We're good. It's over. You'll never even be considered a suspect."

"Is it? Because what happens when they find new evidence that I don't know about? They found his car. Got a tip that he could be at the warehouse, fortunately that was a dead end. But what's next? Search parties are out day and night." He shakes his head. "I won't rest until I see for myself."

Fuck. Fuck. Fuck. "Let me talk to the others and I'll give you a call."

"If the cops start investigating me and I lose everything…." he pauses, "doesn't matter. You've got forty-eight hours to bring me to him, and once you do, I'm taking control. I'll get rid of that fucking body for good. I have to leave for a business trip in two days and I'll be gone for three weeks. I want this shit settled before I go. Rally together, have a little heart-to-heart, I don't fucking care. But I'm taking matters into my own hands like I should have in the first place." His hand sweeps through the air as he turns back toward his SUV. "Forty-eight hours, or I'm coming for all four of you. And I'll be taking my daughter with me."

I stand frozen until he pulls away. I'm pretty sure I held my breath for those entire sixty seconds. Once his taillights fade into the distance, I throw my face into my hands. "Fuck," I shout, kicking the toe of my shoe into the cement. This is a damn mess. It's not enough that Josh's car is being torn apart for evidence. That the entire fucking town has been searching for him day and night, meaning he could turn up at any moment. But now, we've got Anderson fucking Thorn on our asses.

When I pull my phone back out to call Talon, an unknown number flashes on the screen. Hitting ignore, I end the call. If it's important, they'll leave a message or text me like a normal person. Then I shoot Talon and Tommy a group text.

Me: Shit just hit the fan. We need to meet up. Where the hell are you guys?

As soon as I hit send, a voicemail comes through. I hit play.

"Lars, it's Willa. Can we meet up and talk? It's important. Please call me back."

4

It looks like Christmas threw up on Redwood as I drive through the small town. The sun is beginning to set and every lead the guys followed turned up a dead end. With no daylight, there is no way we are finding Josh tonight—if we ever find him. We only have one option left, and they aren't gonna like it one bit, but we have no choice. We have to get on Zed's good side.

Pulling up to Briarwood, I see Tommy's car. When I get out, I can immediately smell the burning wood. Of course. I'm hashing it out with Anderson and these guys are back here having a bonfire and partying it up. Rage consumes me as I walk around the dilapidated building. "Are you fucking kidding me? This is what you call being productive?" I stalk toward Talon as all my blood rushes to my face. "Do you have any idea what I just dealt with? Of course you don't because you assholes left me." I look around from face to face, and I'm taken aback by a familiar one. "What the hell is she doing here?" I gesture toward Madison with my eyes on Talon.

"Hey, brother. Good to see you, too," Madison says as she tips back a can of seltzer wine.

Nervousness washes over me and I'm not sure I can take much more tonight. Part of me wonders if I need to just pack up my shit and run far away. I've dug myself so damn deep that I have no idea how I'll ever make it out of this a free man. "I was just telling your friends that it would be nice if we could all get to know each other better. I've been in Redwood for almost a year and I've never even hung out with you guys."

Snatching a can of beer from Tommy, I look over at Madison and grin. "Yeah, that's because you're stuck up and we prefer to distance ourselves from fake bitches. Now if you don't mind, I need to talk to my *friends*. Go back to the mall, or maybe the plastic surgeon who fucked up your nose."

Her hand slaps to her chest. "Ouch. That might hurt if I had a heart." The imposter smile she was wearing quickly diminishes and a snark glare washes over her face. I've gotta get her out of here before she says something stupid. I wouldn't put it past her to tell these guys that she knows the truth. Even if she doesn't have proof, her statement would point a lot of fingers at us. Slamming the beer in my hand, I toss the can beside the blazing fire and stalk toward Madison.

Grabbing her by arm, I pull her away from everyone. "What the hell are you up to now?" I whisper-yell.

"Nothing. Just wanted to hang out with you all. That's not a problem, is it?"

"How did you even know they were here?" I ask with my fingers still tangled around her forearm.

Her shoulders waggle. "I followed them from town. Is that a problem?"

My phone sounds in my pocket and Madison's eyes shoot to it. "Are you gonna get that?"

"Later."

"Why later? Who is it?" she asks, as she begins trying to stuff her hand in my pocket like she's a jealous ex-girlfriend.

I shove her hand away. "Get the fuck off of me." But she doesn't stop.

"Who the hell is it, Lars?" This is what I deal with on a daily basis. Constant patrolling from my stepsister because she's an obsessed psycho.

"I don't know. I said I'd get it later." I give her another shove and she stumbles back, falling on her ass. Everyone looks in our direction and Marni's eyes widen in horror.

"Lars! Did you just push her?" She hollers as she hurries to our side. Yes, I just pushed her because she's not the sweet innocent girl she's making you all think she is. But, I don't say it. Instead, I extend a hand to try and help her up.

I'm not surprised that she ignores it and plays the victim. Instead, she lets Marni help her up. Wrapping her arm around Marni's waist, she's led back to the fire. Halfway there, she looks over her shoulder and throws me a sadistic smile. She's playing a game, and every single one of us are her pawns.

"Talon. Tommy," I yell then signal toward the building with a nod of my head. Talon gives Marni a look before following my lead. I guess that's what it's like to be pussy-whipped. Is that what I am? Am I pussy-whipped by my fucking stepsister? A girl I hate. The way she's glaring at me through the fire with flames in her eyes, I'm certain that I am. My phone sounds in my pocket again and I'm about to lose my shit. I end the call and send Willa a text on a whim.

Me: What the hell do you want, Willa?

This damn girl won't stop blowing up my phone. Not even five seconds later, she responds.

Willa: Can you meet me at Miner Park, please? It's important.

I don't even respond. I don't have time for this.

I'm a few feet ahead of the guys when I pull open the rusty old screen door. It slams shut behind me as I begin pacing back and forth in the dark entryway. My shadow casts on the floor as a sliver of light from the fire shines through the door. When it rips back open and Tommy and Talon step inside, my feet continue to move as I talk. "You fuckers left me."

"What's the big deal? We didn't find anything, anyways," Tommy says.

"The big deal is that when I got to your house, we had a little visitor. Yeah, that's right." I stop pacing and face the two of them. "Anderson Thorn showed up."

Talon looks out the door at Marni then back at me. "No?" He questions me like I'd make this shit up.

"Yes. He's making threats and demanding shit." I spit it all out in one breath and keep going. "It's fucking bad, you guys. He's livid, and in return, he gave us forty-eight hours to show him where Josh is. And the real kicker, he wants to get rid of the body himself. We're fucking screwed."

Talon holds his hand up to stop me. "Would you calm your ass down. We're fine."

Tommy has taken over my space on the floor and is pacing back and forth shaking his head. "No. Lars is right. We're screwed. I fucking knew we should have just left Josh in the road when we saw him." He stops suddenly. Turning to Talon, anger takes ahold of him. "This is all your fault. You had this grand idea to take his daughter and now look where the hell we are."

"We need to get Zed back," I tell them. "We need to earn his trust and make things right with him." As much as I don't like it, because I'm not sure if I'll ever be able to trust him again, it has to be done.

Tommy nods his head then snaps his fingers. "Yes. We have to. It's the only way."

Talon bites back, "Have you all forgotten that Zed fucking hates me. All this time that I thought he was my friend, he just wanted to get me back for giving his mom those pills."

He has a point. Sophomore year, Talon developed an

unhealthy addiction to pills and started working for a dealer to make ends meet when his parents cut him off. This was all before he was given a hefty trust fund that set him up for the rest of his life. He sold some pills to Zed's mom and she intentionally overdosed on them and died shortly after. We all thought that Zed forgave Talon when he got clean and made his amends. It seems that Zed didn't forget, or forgive.

"You need to make this right, Talon. You started this war and you need to fix it."

"What could Zed possibly want from us?" Tommy asks the question we're all wondering.

"Who the fuck knows. The point is, we have to either get Zed on our side and tell us where Josh is, or we have to eliminate Anderson before he gets to us."

Talon scratches at the back of his neck and levels his eyes to mine. "You mean kill him?"

"We do whatever we have to do."

Turning his head over his shoulder, he looks out at Marni. "No. Not a chance. We'll find a way to get in Anderson's good graces and we'll tame Zed at the same time. This isn't over; therefore, we still have a chance."

"Alright. Guess it doesn't hurt to try. Give Zed a call." I push past him and walk back out the door to get my delightful stepsister. "I've got other shit to deal with right now." She's another fucking problem. If she thinks she's going to play a larger role in my life, she has another thing coming.

With my eyes laser-focused on hers, I strut toward her and grab her by the arm. "We're leaving."

"I just got here." She jerks away. "Marni and I were just talking about throwing a party this weekend. What do you think?"

"What do I think?" I laugh. "I think you're delusional. Now let's go."

"What's your problem, Lars? She just wants to hang out with us. She's new here and doesn't have many friends."

Yeah, for good reason. She doesn't know how to be a friend. She's a manipulative little snake. But, I don't say it. Instead, I play nice. "Fine. You all hang out here. I have someone to go meet." That snaps Madison's attention away from Marni really quick. Madison is all up in my business, and if she thinks for a minute that I could be meeting up with a girl, she would lose her damn mind. In her head, I belong to her.

"Where are you going?" Her eyes sadden and I can see her heart rate accelerate through the thin fabric of her baby pink T-shirt.

"Oh, just meeting up with an old friend. You stay here. Enjoy yourself and I'll see you tomorrow." It's a semi-lie. Willa has been blowing up my phone because, apparently, there is something she needs to talk about. Not that I have any idea why Willa would need or want anything from me. We're not even friends. Hell, we're not even enemies. She just sort of exists in this world. I turn around to walk away. "Later, Marni." Tommy and Talon are still inside. Hopefully hashing out a plan. And of course, the smacking of flip flops comes trudging up behind me.

"Wait. I'll come with you," Madison says as she hurries to my side.

"I thought you might." I glare at her and I hope she knows that she's not going anywhere with me. No. I'm putting this bitch in her place right fucking now.

Sticking close to my side, she attempts to grab my hand when we are out of sight of the others. I spit, "What are you doing?" Then jerk my hand away. When she chuckles, I stop walking. "Madison, this isn't funny. You can't just show up places like this. It's suspicious."

Her fingers slither around my neck and she pouts. "How is

it suspicious? I'm the new girl who needs to make some friends. No one has a clue that you've been fucking your sister behind closed doors."

When she tries to kiss me, I tilt my head to the side then unlock her fingers behind my neck, one by one, dropping her hands to her side. "About that. It needs to stop."

"Come on. You know you like it just as much as I do?"

I begin walking to my car again, and she's right back at my side. "I have to go. Take your car and go home. I'll be there in an hour. We need to have a serious talk."

"Where are you going?"

"Don't worry about it," I tell her as I pull my phone out of my pocket and get ready to text Willa back. I wasn't planning on meeting up with her, but I needed an out. I can't let Madison hang out here. If she tells everyone that she watched us stuff Josh's body into the trunk of a car, she'll use it against them, too. She's like the female version of Zed. Possibly worse.

Before I can even get in the car, Madison snatches my phone from my hand and begins thumbing through it. It was opened to my conversation with Willa and panic ensues. Just as I go to grab it from her, she takes off running like a fucking child with a cookie. "Madison!" I shout, "Give me back my damn phone."

"Who is this?" she asks with her eyes glued to my phone. "Who the hell is Willa?" How does she know who it is? I didn't save her number. She begins reading off the message. "*What the hell do you want, Willa?*" Lifting her head, she looks at me. "What does this girl want with you?"

Walking toward her with my hands at my side, I approach slowly. Then like a tiger, I pounce—grabbing my phone from her death grip.

"Wait a minute. Willa. Isn't that the girl in the video? The virgin?"

"If you go straight home, I'll come see you later." I lie. If she thinks there's a chance I'll come see her, she'll go home.

Heading for my car, I don't hesitate or look back at her before jumping in. Locking the doors first, I shift into reverse and peel out. There's a good chance she'll go straight for Miner Park since she read the messages, so I call Willa.

I'm not surprised when she picks up on the first ring. "Hey, Willa. Still wanna meet up?"

"Want to? No. Need to? Yes. I'm already here."

"Change in plans. Meet me at the abandoned warehouse past the high school."

"Warehouse?"

"Yeah. The one that Axel Thorn used to have the fights at."

The call goes silent when she doesn't respond, and then it hits me, she probably has no idea what or who I am even talking about. I almost forgot that I'm talking to Willa Mack. A straight-A, straight-laced, straight-up saint. "Follow the road past the high school until you get to the end. You can't miss it." With that, I end the call.

My mind starts to wander to a dark place. What if she's pressing charges? When the video first leaked, I thought for sure she would, but her parents wanted to keep things as quiet as possible and just let it blow over. It took a couple weeks, but eventually it did. Of course, that was at the end of the summer when she could still hide out in her house or at her family church and avoid any insults or vulgarity. Apparently a couple weeks ago, her mom fled town and no one has heard from her since. Willa now lives alone with her stepdad, the pastor, and is raised right by the Lord.

I wonder if people have been giving her a hard time now that school started back up. It's been three months but surely some still remember. God, I wanted to strangle those assholes for doing that to me—to her.

I'll never pretend to be a good man. I've done very bad things. I've got skeletons in my closet and blood on my hands. I've struggled to feel emotion since I was a kid. I seem to lack a moral compass because regret, anger, and pain don't come easy to me. The biggest emotion that I lack is empathy. I do feel bad for what happened with Willa, so I like to think that's a start at me beginning to feel something. But, the events of that day are not what started my downward spiral. My detachment from others started when I was nine years old.

It was the middle of summer and I was supposed to be keeping an eye on Colby, my four-year-old brother, while Mom took a shower. The neighbor kid came over and we got caught up in video games. I didn't even realize what happened until Mom came downstairs and it was too late. Colby fell in the pool and drowned.

It was all my fault. It doesn't matter what anyone tried to tell me, I killed my little brother. Mom blamed herself and I think Dad did the same. '*Who lets a nine-year-old boy babysit?*' That was what he kept repeating that day. Over and over and over again. Mom and Dad divorced a year later. Apparently their marriage couldn't handle the grief. I grew an 'I don't give a fuck' attitude, and the rest is history. We never talk about it. Not just me and the guys—my family doesn't talk about it. It's like Colby never existed, and in my heart and mind, he never did. We sort of just continued to live our lives without him. Sometimes I'm not even sure that I'd call this living. Most days I feel like I'm just surviving.

Pulling up to the warehouse, I immediately spot Willa. Her car is backed in and her petite little body hides behind the steering wheel. I drive up next to her. Close enough that I'm hoping we can just stay put and roll down the windows. Really don't wanna get out.

I roll my window down and gesture for her to do the same. "What's up?" I ask. Her eyes blink rapidly and her lips are curled up in a friendly smile. I've only said two words to the girl, yet she looks like she's on the verge of tears even while wearing a smile. "Listen, Willa. If this is about that night. I've said I'm sorry and I thought we moved on from this."

Her head shakes, no. "It's not about that. Well, it is. But not exactly." She doesn't look at me when she speaks. I'm pretty sure I intimidate her and I'm not sure why that bothers me. I prefer most of the world look at me as a tyrant, but for some reason, I want her to look at me differently.

Resting my arm on the windowsill, I watch and wait. "Alright then. Spit it out."

She rubs her hands together then folds them in her lap. "I'm not really sure how."

Sweeping my hand in a circular motion, my brows raise. "Come on, Willa. I ain't got all day." There it is again. The jackass in me that speaks before he thinks. It's no wonder she's fearful of me. I'm an impulsive asshole. Sure, some deserve it, but not Willa. She's as pure and as kind as they come. Frail and pale as snow, with a cross around her neck. After everything I did to her, she's still sitting here choking on her words because I make her uncomfortable. Most girls would be slinging my dick back and forth with their windshield wipers.

"I'm…" she pauses. Looks at me, then her eyes move back to her lap. "I'm pregnant, Lars."

I don't think I heard her right. I lean forward, offering her my ear. "Come again."

Her head lifts and her eyes meet mine. "I'm pregnant." A single tear slides down her cheek as my mind repeats the words over and over again.

I'm pregnant. I'm pregnant. I'm pregnant. That's what she said. She's lying. This is her way of getting back at me. Laughter erupts from deep in my stomach. "Good one. I'm not falling for that shit. Look, if you're still pissed about that night, we can talk about it. But don't start spreading rumors."

"I'm not lying. I *am* pregnant, Lars. And it's your baby."

"You show me a paternity test and then we'll talk." I shift my car into reverse, but she starts talking, halting my movements.

"You were my first. And my last. I've never been with anyone else. It's your baby, Lars."

My hand holds the gear tightly. "Ok." I nod. "Humor me. How far along are you? Have you gone to the doctor?"

"It was almost three months ago, so I'd guess like eleven weeks, maybe. And no, I haven't gone to the doctor."

"If a doctor hasn't confirmed it, then how do you know?"

"Lars, I'm pregnant. I wouldn't make this up. A friend bought me a whole bag of tests and they were all positive."

"A friend? What friend?" I didn't know she had friends.

"Vi Moran. She can be trusted. Don't worry."

"Vi Moran, as in Josh's sister?"

She nods.

I grip the gear even tighter. So tight that all the blood has drained from my knuckles. "Go to the doctor and show me proof, then we'll talk." Impulsive jackass returns as I slam my foot on the gas. My tires spin rapidly, before finally getting some traction and getting me the hell out of this place.

My mind is in this hazy fog that doesn't allow me to even finish a complete thought.

No way. She can't be.

There is no way in hell that I can be a dad.

No fucking way. She's lying. She has to be.

God, she better be. For the first time in my life, I want to be lied to. I won't even be mad at her for this prank. She just can't be pregnant with my baby.

5

LARS

I didn't go home. Wherever home is. Is it Talon's house? Dad's place, with Cruella Deville and her wicked daughter? I drove three hours north and ended up at some ritzy hotel with a fridge stocked full of liquor and a king-size bed. Left the air on all night—even when my teeth began to chatter—just because I could. There was no one here to tell me it was too cold or too hot. No one to tell me how bad I'm fucking up. How I'll never amount to anything, or how my choices are leading me down a dark and lonely path.

With my back pressed against the headboard, I tip back my bottle of breakfast and stare at the black screen of the tv mounted on the wall. While I have been drinking nonstop since I arrived, I've also done a lot of thinking. Haven't really come up with any great ideas that will get me out of this mess I'm in, but my mind hasn't shut off. It definitely wasn't from lack of trying. You'd think half a fifth of whiskey would do the trick, but it didn't.

Looking at the bottle of vodka in my hand, I realize this one won't fix my problems either. My hand slaps around at the end table until I find the top then I twist it back on.

My phone's been off since last night when I stopped myself from making a big mistake and I really don't wanna turn it back on, though, I probably should. Regardless of the pity I'm taking on myself, there's shit that needs to be dealt with.

I hold the button down until it powers on, preparing myself for whatever might be headed my way when the missed calls and text messages appear. Before this whole situation with Josh, I never had calls. I hung out with the guys, went to the gym, partied, and life was good. Now, everything is falling apart. Our circle has been broken, and I'm not sure it will ever be repaired. We're all at the mercy of Zed. And there's a good fucking chance that I'm going to be a dad, whether I like it or not.

Just as expected, a string of messages come chiming through. Buzz after buzz. There's Madison, Talon, Tommy, Dad, Mom, and Willa. I tap Willa's name first. I saved her number last night in the heat of the moment, after typing up a dozen different messages and deleting them all. They went as far as asking her to get an abortion, but as much as I'm not ready for this, I know that's not an option. At one point I think I was even going to ask her to marry me. Also not an option. Hence, why I shut my phone off.

The truth is, I don't have those feelings for Willa that a guy should have when he's having a baby with someone. It's not that I think there's anything wrong with her. Sure, she's awkward, quiet, and basic, but it's not about that. Whatever she once saw in me isn't reciprocated. I won't run away from my responsibilities, but I'm also not sacrificing my happiness by being with someone for the sake of a child. It's not fair to either of us.

Is that cold? Probably. Am I cruel? Without a doubt. I don't mean to be, but one thing I've learned in the past couple of weeks is that it's time to start watching out for myself. Aside from Talon and Tommy, I can't count on anyone at this point.

Willa: Someone was outside of my house last night. Did you tell anyone?

Willa: Whoever it is keeps driving back and forth in front of my house. I'm getting creeped out.

Willa: Can you call me, please?

I don't even have to question who it was. Sorry, Willa. Now that you're in my life, Madison is coming for you. There is no way in hell she will let us have our secrets.

With that said, I've decided who I want my revenge on. It won't be deadly. No. She won't get hurt. But she will feel the sting of sweet pain as I blow up her entire world.

It's after dark by time I get back into town. It took me a good two hours to get out of bed, an hour in the shower while I tried to sweat out the alcohol, and five minutes to relieve myself of some built-up tension. I still haven't listened to the messages from the guys. My eyes skimmed one text that said Zed hasn't returned their calls. If he hasn't returned their calls then nothing is fixed. If nothing is fixed, we're still sinking.

I'm not sure where I'm headed, but for some reason, I end up on Hayworth Drive in front of the church. Willa's church. I know she's here. She's always here. Bible study, choir practice, youth group. I wasn't kidding when I said the girl is a saint. Her car is also parked in front, so there's that. The next thing I know, I'm getting out of the car and slamming the door shut. Still smelling like a brewery, I zip up my leather jacket and smooth my hands down my black holy jeans—no pun intended.

Cupping my hand over my mouth, I breathe out and sniff. Just the scent of my cinnamon gum. Even if the whiskey was still lingering, Jesus drank, so they can't judge me. My fingers wrap around the u-shaped handle and when it doesn't sizzle at my touch, I feel confident that I won't burn when I go in. I open the door and walk inside. I've been in the church before, but it's been awhile. I should have known I'd be opening up to a room full of tables and chairs, and of course, about thirty people staring at me. I hold a hand up and wave at all the unfamiliar faces. "Hi. I just need to borrow her for a minute." I point to a flustered Willa.

The sound of chair legs scraping against the floor darts my attention to Pastor Jeffries, who is on his feet. His eyes narrow at me and I don't think God would be happy with the look he's throwing my way right now. "Young man, you have some nerve showing up here." He whisper-talks as he jerks me by the arm and out the door I just walked in.

"Woah, Pastor. Chill the he..heck out." I correct myself, just in the nick of time. "I just need to talk to Willa." He gives my arm a shove and he's lucky he has God on his side because I'd be unleashing the devil if he were anyone else.

"You stay away from my daughter."

"Stepdaughter," I retort, but quickly eat my words because it seems to do anything but calm him.

"Willa *is* my daughter and after what you did to her, you have no business even coming to this church."

"Hmm, I didn't know churches discriminated against sinners. What's going on tonight? Open Bible study?" I arch a brow. "Maybe I wanna join. Ya know? Let Jesus in and all that jazz."

"Even Jesus can't save you, son." He pats a hand to my shoulder and attempts to spin me around to face my car that's parked right in front.

"Now, what kind of pastor talks like that?" I push past him and pull the unlatched door back open. When I step inside, it's like deja vu when everyone looks back at me. Ignoring all but one person, I walk over and take one of the two empty seats at the end of the joined tables. They're all lined up to make a

RACHEL LEIGH

square with an empty space in the middle. The smell of the room floods me with memories of Colby's funeral. I'm not sure if it's the smell, or the attention laser-focused on me. That day, everyone watched me as I sat quietly with my hands in my lap and my head hung low. I still remember seeing Willa at the funeral. In fact, the memory of her sticks out like a sore thumb. Even then, she carried this calming aura. The difference is, today my head is held high. I have just as much of a right to be here as all these other people. They sin. They fuck up.

Willa is sitting directly across from me. Her eyebrows are pinched together and her cheeks are tinged pink. When Pastor Jeffries walks back in and takes the only empty seat beside me, I let out a breathy huff. "Where were we?" he asks, looking Willa dead in the eye.

"The Christmas Pageant. We were agreeing on a time-frame for each set." Willa chokes out as she taps a pen to an open notebook.

I guess I'm not at Bible study after all. When Pastor Jeffries begins talking to the group, I catch Willa's attention and mouth the words, "Can we talk?"

In small but rapid movements, she shakes her head then rolls her eyes away from me. We need to talk, damnit, and she needs to tell me the truth. My hand slaps softly on the table. Not hard enough to get everyone's attention, but enough to grab hers and a few others. "Yes." I mouth again, then nod my head toward the door.

"Willa Jean. Please handle this and then come back inside. Alone." Pastor Jeffries speaks sharply.

When her chair slides back and she stands up, I do the same. She's fast as she makes her way through the door. Her long navy blue skirt drags on the floor and her flip-flops smack against the bottom of her feet as she walks.

Tugging her beige cardigan tightly around her, she looks down at her feet as she speaks. "What are you doing here,

42

Lars?" Her voice is calm and collected and I'm starting to wonder if this girl has the capability of getting mad.

"We need to talk about this. Were you lying?"

"Not here. We can't."

"Do they know?"

She raises her voice. "Lars! Please just stop. Go home and we can talk tomorrow."

I take a stance and cross my arms over my chest, just as she is, and step up in front of her. I raise my voice even higher. "No. I'm not leaving until I have answers."

Looking at the door in panic, she grabs me by the arm and pulls me down the cement steps. "Would you be quiet? Everyone will hear you. I'm already going to be in enough trouble because you showed up here." Her hand flaps in the air. "You can't be here, Lars."

"Fine. How much longer is this meeting?"

"We're almost done. I'll meet you at Miner Park. Just go." She gives me a shove toward my car.

Taking steps backward until my back hits the car, I watch her stand there, waiting for me to leave. How could a girl like her fall for a guy like me? She's so angelic and sweet. I'm nothing but a fuck-up. Yet, for years she watched me and waited for me until I came for her, and when I did, I stole her innocence and ran like hell. I guess that's what the devil does after all—preys on the weak and pure.

Spinning around, I walk to the car. When I look up, she's gone. Just like that night. I drove her to her house and told her I'd call her later while I bragged to the guys in a group text about accomplishing my mission. The door slammed shut and by time I realized she was out the car, her porch light was off and she was behind the closed door.

Shifting in drive, I take off. The small space in the car begins to feel suffocating. I tug at the collar of my shirt then roll the window down, letting in some fresh air. Tapping the call button on the dash, I speak out loud, "Call Tommy."

It rings twice before he picks up. "It's about damn time. Where the hell have you been?"

"Something came up that I had to deal with."

"What could be more important than making sure we don't spend the rest of our damn lives in prison?"

I could tell him that I'm already in my own personal prison, but I need to have that conversation with Willa first. "Just some shit. Don't worry about it. Where do we stand? What's going on?"

"You need to call him."

Flicking the blinker up, I look both ways at the four-way stop before taking a left to Miner Park. "Who? Anderson?"

"No. Zed. He won't talk to Talon for obvious reasons. He's ignoring my calls. You two have always been the closest. We think he'll reason with you."

I let out a sarcastic chuckle. "Zed. Reason with someone? Not a chance."

"Fine, then I guess we just wait until this all blows up in our faces."

He's got a point. Zed and I have always been pretty close. That was before he turned on me and used my sexual relationship with Madison against me. Right before Halloween, Zed got shitfaced and decided to crawl through my window like he always does. I should have known better than to leave it unlocked. He dropped on the floor the same time my boxers did while I was standing in front of Madison with my dick in her face.

At that time, I was more pissed that he cock-blocked me. He swore that he'd never say a word. Until he threatened to do just that if I didn't bring Marni to him. So I got a gun and pointed it at her while I drove her three hours to Briarwood. It was one of my bigger fuckups, but it won't be my worst—I'm sure of that.

I can already feel the heat of the flame and the last thing we need is for this shit to blow up any more than it already has. "I'll call him." I've got a few minutes before Willa will be here. We need to try anything at this point. "Hey, I have to finish dealing with….something, but when I'm done, I'm heading back to Talon's. We need to have a meeting. It's my round and I'm ready for the games to begin." I hit the end call button on the dash and shift the car into park in front of the gazebo at Miner Park.

My finger hovers over the call button, then back to my lap. I press it before I can talk myself out of it. "Call Zed."

"Where are you?" he says after the first ring.

I'm a little stunned that he even answered. Now that he has, I'm not sure if I should be angry or express a need to reason with him. "I've been around. Where the hell are you?"

"You wanna talk then meet me somewhere. I'm not doing this shit over the phone."

"Name the place. I'm there."

"Lake Ruin behind Miner Point. Thirty minutes."

I look at the clock on the dash. It would take me at least ten minutes to get there and Willa still isn't here. This could be our only shot to talk to Zed, so I have to do it. "I'll be there." The call drops abruptly.

Where the hell are you, Willa? My eyes dance around the empty park. Pinching the bridge of my nose, I slam my other hand on the steering wheel. She should have been here by now. *Fuck it.* I shift into reverse then pull away.

6

LARS

M y eyes dance from the clock on the dash to the road. I've got twenty-five minutes to meet Zed. Once again, I find myself in front of the church. Only this time, her car is gone. I didn't pass any cars on the way here, so she can't be headed to the park.

Pulling out my phone, I shoot her a quick text then start driving again. When she doesn't respond, I end up in front of her house. Sure enough, she's here. She fucking stood me up. The audacity.

Pastor Jeffries already hates me. What have I got to lose? Leaving the car running, I get out and shut the door. All the lights are on inside and I can hear someone talking as I walk up the stone path to her small house.

Willa doesn't have the luxuries that some of us do. Her parents are successful, but not in the way that most people view success. She's had a normal family life, with parents who work regular jobs. From the outside looking in, it is a good life. At least it *was* until her mom left. Everyone claims that she was having an affair, but it's hard to imagine the pastor's wife, a librarian, having an affair unless it was with God.

Willa was raised well with a good head on her shoulders. Here I am, the devil incarnate standing on the pastor's porch because I knocked up his daughter while trying to prove to myself and others that she'd give me her virginity. I took it and I ran. Karma's a fucking bitch.

The closer I get, the chatter of the people inside gets louder. No longer talking, someone is shouting. A man. It's Pastor Jeffries and he sounds pissed.

The TV is turned up so loud that Alex Trebek drowns out their words, but something is going on in there. Just as I ball my fist, ready to knock, a loud thud freezes my movements. Pressing my ear to the door, I try to listen.

"You stay away from that boy, he's the damn devil. You hear me?" Pastor Jeffries shouts.

"Get your hands off me."

"You listen to your father, damnit!"

"You're not my father," Willa cries out.

My eyes widen and my heart begins thudding fiercely in my chest. He better get his hands off of her.

His voice rises to more of a scream. "I am your father. Don't you ever say that again. I'm the only father you have and you'll do what I tell you to. If you think you're gonna run around this town and be a little slut just because your mom's gone, you're in for a rude awakening."

"Ouch! That hurts. Stop."

An elephant on the other side of this door couldn't stop me as I barge through it without a clear head. A musty smell floods my senses. Like an antique store. Everything is brown. The walls, the flowers on the old couch, the carpet. It feels like stepping into my great-gran's living room when I was four years old.

"Get your fucking hands off of her now!" I shout as I charge at the two of them. He has her wrists pinned over her head against the wall. Tears trail down Willa's cheeks and something inside of me ignites into a full-blown rage as I take the old man down. With my hands wrapped around his throat, we crash into an end table that breaks. My head slams against a lamp and although I can feel the warmth of blood soak my hair, I feel no pain.

"Lars, stop!" Willa screeches. "Please. You'll make it worse." Her hands wrap around my arm as she tries to pull me up, but I'm focused on my fingers that snake around his neck. Something doesn't allow me to stop as I squeeze harder and harder. My mind goes blank and my thoughts are irrational. When I get to this state, nothing good can come of it. *Stop, Lars. Just fucking stop.* I try to talk myself down from the ledge before I jump and there's no going back.

"Lars, please." Willa kneels next to me, her voice calm and...comforting. I look over at her tear-stained cheeks and my grip lessens. "He's not worth it." She pulls my arm until we're both standing up. Her fingers slide down into to my hand as our eyes stay locked. "Come on."

Snapping myself out of the trance I was in, I let her lead me out of the house. My staggered breaths begin to steady when we step outside. "What the hell was that all about?" I huff. We continue to walk before Willa stops and lets her hand free from its clutch around my arm.

"It's complicated. You should go."

"No." I shake my head. "I'm not leaving you here with that animal."

"I can't go with you, Lars. It will just make things worse."

"Willa," I say, as I place both hands on either side of her shoulders. I wanna ask if he hits her. If he's always this cruel to her, but what place do I have to ask such a personal question? "We still need to have that talk." I tilt my head toward my car. "Come with me. It won't take long."

Glancing from me to the house while she chews on her bottom lip, she shivers. It's mid-December and she's standing here barefoot in a T-shirt and a pair of fuzzy pink pajama pants. I tear the sweatshirt over my head and wrap it around her shoulders, surprising us both. "What are you doing?" she asks.

"You're cold. Now, come on. I have to go somewhere. We can talk on the ride." I wrap an arm around her and try to coerce her to the car, but she still puts up resistance.

She looks down at her feet. "But, I don't have any shoes."

"Don't need any." I give her a pull again, and this time, she obliges. I've always known that Willa can be easily persuaded. It's not just me. She's been pushed around her entire life. Now it appears that school isn't her only battlefield. I had her home life pegged all wrong. There's a war going on inside that house, and for some unknown reason, I feel like I need to be her shield. I'm just not so sure that's a good idea, because who will protect her from me? Good intentions or not, I'm my own worst enemy and I've been at war with myself for the past nine years.

Once we're inside, I crank up the heat and Willa tightly hugs my sweatshirt. "You ok?" I ask her.

She looks over at me and smiles. It's the same smile she wore that night. The genuinely happy one. It makes me wonder if it was as fake then as it is now. "I'm fine."

"Do you always smile through pain? Because I'm not sure how you can be fine after what I just walked in on."

"It was nothing. He just gets upset sometimes."

"Sometimes? So this wasn't the first time this has happened? Does he frequently pin you to the wall and scream in your face?"

When her head turns to face the passenger window and she squeezes the sweatshirt tighter, I assume I've gone too far. It just doesn't make sense. It's Pastor Jeffries. A man of God and someone I always assumed was one of the kindest people in our town. There's no doubt that I've felt judged by him, but he's also well aware of what I did to his daughter. Amongst other shenanigans growing up. Such as drinking behind the church because we figured we'd never get caught back there.

"It's ok. I don't let it get to me. I'm planning on moving out before I have the baby, anyways."

"Oh yeah? Where ya going?" She turns to look at me, and nervousness washes over her face. Once again, she's chewing on her bottom lip. "Well? Where do you plan on going?" I stop looking at her and hope that maybe she will relax a bit without my eyes on her.

"Far away from Redwood. I plan to leave and never come back."

My foot slams on the break so hard that both of our heads jerk forward. "What the hell do you mean you're leaving Redwood? Have you forgotten that you're having a baby? A baby you claim is mine?"

"I know," she says the words so calmly that I wanna shake her and tell her to stop being so damn calm and nice. "When I told you that I was pregnant, you never let me finish talking. You just took off and left me sitting in the parking lot at the warehouse. I *am* leaving Redwood."

"Like hell you are." I huff, before pressing the gas and continuing the drive.

"Yes, I am."

"Noooo, you're not. Jesus. Quit acting like a child."

She chuckles. "Me? You're the one acting like a child. You think you can just dictate everyone's lives because your family has money and power. Or because your friends are scary."

"My friends are pretty scary." My head shakes. "That's beside the point. I'm not trying to dictate your life. You're having a baby. You're not just gonna take off and move away where you have no help. Who will support you?"

"I don't need anyone. I've taken care of myself my whole life. Why would I need anyone now?"

This might be harsh, but it's true and it needs to be said. "Willa, you have no fucking money. You won't survive on your own."

"I know I won't," she says again, just as calm and collected. "That's why I need your help. This baby is just as much yours as it is mine and it's only natural that I'd expect you to support him or her financially."

"If this baby is mine, as you claim it is, I have every intention of doing the right thing." My voice rises unintentionally. "I just need you to tell me what the right thing is because I don't have a fucking clue, Willa."

"I need you to give me enough money to leave and never come back."

Something unfamiliar ripples through me. "No," I say, without hesitation. She's not leaving.

"No?" she questions.

"For the last time, no."

"Lars," her voice becomes tranquil and desperate, "I can't stay here. I just can't. If Rick finds out that I'm pregnant, he'll force me to have an abortion and he'll…I just can't stay."

"He'll do what? Hit you?" I look over at her, but she avoids eye contact. "Is that what he does? Is he abusive?"

"He's just very unpredictable and I'm not safe there," she chokes out. "Tell me you'll help me leave, Lars. I'm giving you an out. I'll never ask for anything else from you again, I swear. No one even has to know I'm pregnant."

Unsure of how I feel about this, I remain quiet. I can feel her eyes burn into the side of my face but keep mine on the road.

I take a sharp left down the beaten path that leads behind Miner Point and hope like hell that I make it without getting stuck or bottoming out.

Willa looks around, taking in the surroundings. "Where are we going?"

"I have to meet up with someone really quick. It won't take long." Tapping the brake, I slow the car down as we both bounce in our seats from the uneven terrain.

Bringing Willa out here isn't my best move, but it was a last-minute decision to get her away from her stepdad, Rick. I know damn well that Zed is going to question this shit if he sees her, so I need to keep my car back and her face hidden.

"This is Lake Ruin. Where they found Josh Moran's car. This place gives me the creeps."

You and me both, Willa. You and me both.

We're on the opposite side of the lake where we pushed the car over, but being here brings back harrowing memories. It feels like yesterday when we were so sure we'd get away with our illegal acts. We're not caught yet, though. Hopefully I'll leave here with some reassurance that we never will be.

Willa leans forward in her seat. "Is that Zed King?"

Pressing the brake, I stop the car far enough away that Zed can't see inside and Willa won't be able to hear our conversation. "Stay here. I'll be right back." Grazing her fingertips on the cross that dangles over her shirt, she drops back in the seat. I leave the car running and climb out, shutting the door behind me.

When Zed starts heading in my direction, I hold up a hand. "Stay there. I'm coming."

"Who's that?" He tips his head with his eyes on the car behind me. I look back and notice that the dash light hasn't timed out yet. I'm a fucking idiot.

Inside, Willa sits with her eyes zeroed in on us.

Turning back, I look at him. "It's nobody." Zed still looks the exact same, aside from a little stubble on his chin. Still has that crazed look in his eyes and tick to his fingers as they hang at his side.

"Doesn't look like nobody. Looks like Willa Mack. What

the hell are you doing with that girl? Doesn't she hate your ass after what you did to her?"

"Forget about her. I wanna know what the hell your deal is? What the fuck is going on with you, Zed?"

Looking over my shoulder, he completely ignores me. "She's trouble, man."

"Willa and trouble don't even belong in the same sentence."

"I bet she's just as screwed up as her old man. Fucking entitled prick. He thinks that just because he's a pastor we all have to bow to him." He looks right through me as he talks. A dead stare on Willa.

Snapping my fingers in his face, I break his gaze. "I said forget about her."

"Wanna make another bet?" he smirks.

"Fuck no, I don't wanna make another bet." I don't even have to think twice about that one. "The last time I did, you assholes blasted my win all over the damn town. I wouldn't trust you with my dog, and he died three years ago."

A sinister smirk dons his face. "Actually, it was only me. I just let Tommy and Talon take some of the credit, or blame rather." Taking a step forward, his smile grows. "It'll be a good one."

"What the hell do you want, Zed?"

"I'll tell you where Josh's body is right now if you let me have a little taste of your girlfriend."

"She's not my girlfriend." I grit through my teeth.

"Madison isn't gonna be happy about this. You running around with Willa is sure to piss her off. So, just give Willa to me and we can prevent Madison from tearing her to shreds."

"You really are delusional, aren't you?"

"What? You don't think she'd want me? Come on, if she let you take her v-card, surely she'll give me seconds."

All the blood rushes to my head as my hands plant firmly

against his chest and I shove him backwards. "Stay the fuck away from her."

Regaining his balance, he steps up to me. Nose to nose. "Or what?" When I don't respond, he pushes further. "Or what, Titan? You'll kill me? You don't have it in you?" My fists ball at my side and I bite down as I try to gain some self-control. "You kill the innocent, not the guilty."

I'm not even sure when he went down. All I know is my fists continue to fly through the air, one punch after another, as blood falls freely from my white knuckles. Zed's arms cover his face as he attempts to block me, but the punches keep landing.

"He fell. I didn't fucking kill him." I scream loudly, but all I can hear is the sound of my knuckles meeting his body. I'm not sure where they land, but the numbness in my hands tells me that I'm making contact. My heart beats violently in my chest as the words he said replay in my mind. *You kill the innocent, not the guilty.* "I didn't kill him. He fell in the pool." I repeat again. "He should have been more careful." I shout so loudly that the words echo through my own ears and vibrate in my chest.

Gentle hands wrap around me and that calming voice that I always want to ruffle up rings through the deafening screams inside my head. "Stop, Lars. He's not worth it." She repeats herself. "He's not worth it." She's so tranquil and unaffected. But this time, I welcome her calm. Getting to my feet, I turn and look at her blank expression. So unaffected by my outburst and the blood that drips from my fingers. She takes my hand in hers and leads me back to the car. I don't even look back as Zed lies there on the cold ground—speechless, motionless.

Willa leads me over to the passenger side of my car and before I even realize what's going on, she opens the door. I snap out of the trance I was in and look at her. "What are you doing?"

"I'll drive. You're too worked up right now."

"No, I'm fine." I push past her, but she grabs me by the

forearm. My eyes skate down to where her fingers tangle around the bare skin of my arm, then back up to her eyes. They widen as they stare back at me and her grip on me releases abruptly.

"I'm...I'm sorry." Her body twists around and she slides in the passenger seat, suddenly looking fearful and scared.

"It's ok." I press my palms to the door frame and my head droops forward, so I can see her face. Though she's not looking at me. She's watching Zed as he climbs to his feet and dusts himself off. "You really wanna drive?"

"He's coming." She grabs the seatbelt and fastens it. "Get in. Hurry. He's coming." She huffs in a panic.

Slouching down, I level with her. "Don't be scared. I'd never let Zed hurt you."

A surrealness washes over her and her head turns slowly. "You mean that?"

"Absolutely." I stand back up and shut the door.

She keeps a watchful eye on Zed, who is standing about twenty feet in front of the car. He looks zombified and unnerved, but we both know this isn't finished. I came here for a reason. Rounding the car, I make my way back over to him. "You ready to talk about what we came here for?"

"You cut my fucking head," he says in a monotone voice.

"You're lucky I didn't cut your throat."

"You like her, don't you?" he chuckles. "Lars Titan, falling for the pastor's daughter. I was curious how far my words would carry before you reacted, and now I know. You like her."

"I'm not falling for her. She just needs my help. Now, enough about Willa. What do you want?"

"It's simple really. I want my revenge."

"It's not your turn."

"Then make it my turn. Unless you want cops showing up

at all your houses and a body hidden in one of your basements, you'll make it happen."

If that's all he wants, we can make it happen. I'm a little fearful of what he has in store and I sure as hell hope the good lord has mercy on whoever he's after, because Zed is ruthless. No matter who or what it is, we made a deal, so all four of us have to do our part, even if Zed doesn't deserve our help. The pact remains, four acts of revenge, we stick together from start to finish and everything in between. "Let's say we did, who's your target?"

Tipping his head forward, he stares straight past me. "Her."

I turn around and look at the innocent girl sitting in my car. "What do you mean, her?"

"It all starts with her." He pats a hand to my back and walks away. Slowly fading into the dark. I stand there frozen until I hear the roar of his engine. Once his brake lights come on and dirt kicks up behind him, I look at Willa who is watching me with wonder. A flawless girl with a realness about her. She doesn't pretend, nor falter. I just told her I'd never let Zed hurt her. Now I have to make a choice. Her or them.

7

WILLA

Lost. That's the best word I'd use to describe Lars Titan. Born with a silver spoon in his mouth and the body of a Greek god, he's never had to want for anything. Yet, he stands out there idly with his hands in his pockets and a gazillion thoughts running rampant in his mind. He talks in circles and never finishes a conversation. Barely smiles, and almost always has his fists balled at his side. Like he's on the verge of fighting the world because he feels like it's against him.

I don't know much about Lars, but I know enough. I've watched him for years. I've caught glimpses of his blank stare enough times to know that he puts on this show of a perfect life. His life isn't as perfect as he wants us to think it is. In fact, I'm pretty sure he lives in his own misery.

A guy who practically had me on my knees begging to be noticed. He just stepped over me and kept on walking—but not before kicking me and laughing about it with the entire town. Joke's on him. Yep, Lars was born with a silver spoon in his mouth, but now he gets to feed me from it.

Lars walks quickly to the driver's side and climbs in, shutting the door behind him and wasting no time to drive us out of here. "Sorry about that. Just had to take care of some unfinished business with Zed."

Stretching over the seat, my fingers graze the cut on his head from his first brawl of the night with Rick. He shrieks at my touch, and I retreat quickly. "Sorry. You need to clean that up, though. It looks sorta deep."

"It's just a scratch. I'll be fine."

"Is everything else ok?"

"Yeah. Just some shit we've been dealing with. How are you? You good?" He glances in my direction. The light of the dash casts off his gorgeous face and I have to remind myself that the devil was once an angel. His beautiful exterior no longer masks his black heart. I see right through it.

"We really need to finish our conversation from earlier."

"Yeah. About that. You really think that leaving Redwood is the best plan?"

"I don't think. I know. I have to leave. Staying is not an option." He'll never understand. He'll also never know why I need to leave. No one can ever know. I have to get as far away from here as possible. Rick will never allow me to keep my baby, and I'll never allow him to try and stop me.

"Come back to Talon's for the night. Sleep on it and we can talk more tomorrow."

I chuckle unintentionally. "Me? Stay at Talon Porter's? Not a chance."

"You got a problem with Talon?"

I absolutely have a problem with Talon. As a matter of fact, I have a problem with all four of these guys. Naturally, I hate them all. After the humiliation I went through, just so they could get a good laugh. Anyone would hate them for what they did. But I don't say it. "No, no problem. I just don't feel comfortable staying there. Just take me home and we can both sleep on it."

"You can't go home. Are you forgetting that your stepdad attacked you?"

"He didn't attack me. He was just mad. He gets like that sometimes. I'll be fine. I've dealt with him for years." I don't mention that I keep a knife under my pillow. Or that I had to use it once.

"Are you sure? It doesn't seem safe. What if next time he hurts the baby, or you?"

"He won't hurt me. I swear. I have to go home, though. If I don't then he'll call the cops." He's done it before. Played it off like a concerned parent. Fortunately, my own reputation precedes me and everyone in this town thinks I'm a good girl. It's not a lie. I am good, at least I try to be. But someone taught me not too long ago that being nice only makes you appear weak. What these people don't know is that I grew a backbone and I'll never let anyone break me again.

"Alright. If you're sure."

"I'm sure. Can we talk after class tomorrow?"

"How about if we meet at the park after dark? Make a plan for what's coming."

"You mean, a baby?" I look over at him. He raises a brow in question. "A baby, that's what's coming." I don't think he fully grasps what I'm trying to tell him. It's like he doesn't believe that I'm pregnant, or he doesn't want to.

"Yeah. That's what I meant. We can talk about the baby." He pulls up in front of my house and turns his body toward me. "But Willa, this has to stay between us for now. All of it. We can't let this news spread like wildfire. People can be….harsh."

"I know. I haven't told anyone and I don't plan to. I told you, I'm leaving Redwood."

"That also means that we have to carry on like normal for a while. Ya know, keep our distance like we usually do."

"Ah, ok." Makes sense now. He doesn't want to be seen fraternizing with the pastor's quiet stepdaughter. I push open the door with no hesitation. "Don't worry, Lars. Your reputation is safe." Then I slam it shut and walk briskly up the path to the house.

I don't even turn around to look at him as my heart shatters into tiny pieces. What's left of it, anyway. The other pieces are still lying in Tommy's bed from the last time he broke it. Some are scattered around this house from the months of abuse I've had to swallow. Pretty sure Mom took a few chunks with her when she fled and left me here to endure the wrath of her monstrous husband. I've laid in bed often wondering how Mom couldn't possibly know what goes on between the walls of this house. Maybe she just didn't want to admit it because admission would mean guilt on her behalf. Doesn't matter, anyway. All hearts break. I just have to smile through the pain, pretend like nothing is wrong, and bide my time until I can get as far away as possible.

Gulping down the lump in my throat, I close my eyes and say a silent prayer. *Please, God. Please let him be asleep.*

Holding my breath, I listen intently. It's so quiet it's eerie. Even my heartbeat sounds like thunder ripping through the room. Tip-toeing ever so gently, I startle myself by the creak of the old floorboards as I pass through the dining room. Pushing open my bedroom door, I step inside. Shutting the door, then locking it, I make sure the deadbolt is secure.

Rubbing my hand over my belly, I whisper, "Soon. This will all be over soon."

I'M sound asleep when a gentle tapping noise startles me awake. It starts off like the tap of rain against the glass window, but quickly escalates into a repetitive pounding that has me up and on my feet quickly.

Stepping closer to the window, I watch for any type of movement behind the closed curtain. Taking the end into my hand, ready to pull it back hastily, I gasp when a dark shadow darts past the window. Ripping it open, I look left and right to try and catch a glimpse of the perpetrator, but whoever it is, is long gone. Was it just my imagination? I run my hands over my face and keep my eyes fixated on the lawn. Afraid to blink out of fear of missing something, or rather, someone. No. It wasn't my imagination. Someone was definitely out there.

Pulling the curtain closed, I climb back into bed. With my back pressed against the cold metal bars, I keep my eyes wide open. Afraid to close them, worried that I'll fall asleep and wake up to someone at the end of my bed.

Glancing over at the old clock on my nightstand, it reads two-twenty. I watch as the minutes tick by and the next thing I know, I'm waking up to the buzzing of my alarm. Slapping my hand to it a few times until it stops, I immediately get out of bed and walk back over to the window, pulling the curtain open.

Was it all a dream? Watching, waiting, looking for some sort of evidence that I didn't imagine it, my eyes catch something on the glass of the window. A handprint—but it's not just any handprint. It's coated with chunks of dirt and debris and it looks like whoever did it, dipped their hand in mud before slapping it on my window. Chills slither down my spine as I try and wrap my head around who would have come here, and why. Though, it's terrifying, it's also reassuring that I'm not losing my mind.

8

LARS

Meeting up with Zed last night wasn't a total waste of time. Even though his requests are irrational, we have a start. As of right now, the ball is in our court and we don't have to worry about a body turning up—at least for the time being.

"Willa Mack?" Tommy says as he shakes his head in confusion. "Who the hell could he possibly be after that he can get to through Willa fucking Mack?"

"It's Pastor Jeffries." Talon chimes in from behind the couch where we sit. Tommy and I both turn around to look at him. His expression is bleak as he recants himself. "I mean, I assume it's Pastor Jeffries. Who else would it be?"

Tommy chuckles. "Why in the world would Zed, or anyone for that matter, have beef with a damn pastor?"

"Ya know. The guy is a sort of douche. Last night—" My words trail off when I realize what I'm about to say. They can't know that I was with Willa. They'll start asking questions that I'm not ready to answer, because I don't even know the answers myself. "Last night I saw him outside of the church and he was yelling at Willa. Looked pretty pissed." It's not all a lie. He did yell at Willa, but it wasn't outside the church. It was in her living room while he had her arms pinned over her head and pressed against the wall.

Tommy kicks his feet off the coffee table in front of us and gets up. "Well, I've gotta get to school. You guys talk about the next phase of our plan—whatever our plan is—and we'll catch up tonight." He focuses his attention on me and smirks. "You going to your ballet class today?"

Grabbing a pillow sitting next to me, I chuck it at him. "Fuck off. It's drama class. No one fucking dances." Not exactly true. There's actually a lot of dancing and singing and all-too chipper faces. I'm not sure how people can be that damn happy all the time. It's a struggle for me to even fake a smile, yet everyone in that class is always smiling and happy. Everyone except for Willa. She's always so sad. I always thought she had the perfect life, but I'm starting to wonder if her internal scars match ours. I suppose that, deep down, we're all a little broken, battered, and bruised. Those who pretend they're not, are doing just that—pretending.

"Dude." Talon snaps his fingers in my face. "Where the hell did you go just now?"

With wide eyes, I snap out of it and realize that Tommy has already left. "Huh?"

"I said your stepsister just pulled up. Get rid of her so we can finish this shit before I have to meet Marni at her dad's."

Standing up, I walk over to the window and sure as shit, Madison is stepping out of her pearly white Aston Martin that my generous father bought her for her birthday. "Fucking great," I mutter under my breath.

"What's up with that girl lately? She keeps popping up all over the place."

"She's psycho. That's what's up." I tear the door open and step outside. My bare feet hit the bone-dry porch and I hurry over to the steps to stop her from coming any closer to the house. The last thing I need is for her to get comfortable here. This is my safe haven. I come here to get away from her and everyone else that I have no interest in being around. "What do you want, Madison?"

"You." She replies point-blankly.

"Don't you have class?"

"I do, but I'd rather see you. Thought maybe I'd skip the first period and we could *talk*." Her fingers trail up my bare arm, but I slap them away.

"We have nothing to talk about. Go to school." I turn around to walk away in hopes that by the time I get to the door she's gone. My fingers linger around the handle, and when I feel the weight of her body come up behind me, I spin around. Clutching her shoulders, I pull her close. "Are you fucking stupid, Madison? I said go!"

Completely unmoved by my outburst, her fruitless expression digs deeper into me, pulling out a newfound rage and fury, and for a moment, I consider shoving her down the stairs. It wouldn't kill her, but it would paint her a nice picture of how she makes me feel inside.

"I just wanna spend some time with you, Lars. Why are you being so cruel?" Her words come out seductive and sweet, when she's anything but.

"This has to fucking end." I give her a gentle shove. Just enough to backstep away from her before I do something I'll regret.

"I hope it never ends." Her cold fingers slither up the front of my shirt. My back steels as she presses her chin to my collarbone. "In fact, I want us to last forever."

My eyes close and my jaw locks. Holding my hands out on either side of me, I refrain from touching her. "This is going too far."

Stepping closer, if that's even possible, her mouth ghosts

mine. Her tongue darts out, sweeping across my bottom lip. "Is this about *her*?"

I tilt my head back and look into her turquoise eyes. "Who?"

"Willa. I know you were with her last night. What I don't understand is why. It's not like you could possibly be into that girl. She's practically married to God. And you, well, you're a murderer. It won't end well."

My heart rate suddenly excels and sweat begins to pool at my hairline. I grab her by the arm and pull her to the end of the porch. Gritting through my teeth, I whisper, "I've told you over and over again that we didn't kill Josh. Now quit fucking saying that."

"Uh huh. You said what you said, but I don't buy it. Why else would you go through the hell of scooping his dead body off the road?"

"As I've also told you time and time again, it's not your damn business." Drawing in a deep breath, I try to reason with this unreasonable girl. "Look, I'll give you all the money you want if you just move to Colorado with your dad and never set foot in Redwood again. Name the price. It's yours."

"It's not money I want." Her hand stretches down between us and my body jolts when she gets a firm grip on my dick. "I want this, and this." Her opposite hand pats my chest. "That's all."

I've given Madison every inch of me, aside from my heart. She's consumed my thoughts more times than I care to admit. I've fed her my dick more times than I can count. And, I've tasted every part of her body in return. But she will never have my heart. She's not even in it. What started off as fun and games and a little crush on my stepsister has developed into pure loathing. She's never going to give up.

Talon pulls open the door, and I jerk away from Madison before he steps outside. "Everything ok out here?"

"All good. I'll be in, in a sec," I tell him.

Cocking a brow in concern, his eyes dance back and forth between me and Madison. "Alright. We need to finish that conversation before I leave. So, hurry up."

Once he's back inside, I do what I have to do to rush her out of here. "Fine. I'll come see you tonight. We can talk about the future." The word 'future' always appeases her. Right now, I just need her gone.

She presses a chaste kiss to my cheek. "See you in class." Then she spins on her heel and walks away.

In class? We don't have any classes together. Brushing it off, I go back in to talk to Talon. I can't fight this battle with Madison on my own any longer. It's time to come clean.

"What the hell was that about?" he asks as he sits on the couch, lacing up his black boots.

"Madison knows." I spit it out with zero hesitation or thought behind it.

His laces drop and he gets to his feet. "What the hell do you mean Madison knows?"

Pacing the floor behind the couch where he stands, I attempt to explain. "She followed me and Zed that night. She saw us put Josh in the trunk of the car. She thinks we killed him. No matter how many times I tell her we didn't."

"What the fuck, man?" He snaps. His fingers grip the sides of his head and he fists his hair. "Why the hell are you just now telling us this? Fuck!" he shouts even louder.

"I didn't wanna stir up unnecessary shit. Thought I had it all under control. She's fucking crazy, Talon. Really fucking crazy." I stop pacing and face him. His face is pale as he drops down onto the couch.

Circling around it, I drop down next to him. "I fucked her. Multiple times."

His head twists around and his eyebrows shoot to his forehead. "You fucked your sister?"

"She's not my sister. Everyone needs to quit saying that shit. I knew the chick two months before our parents got married. The point is, she's become obsessed with me. She follows me. Threatens to turn us in if I don't do what she wants."

His hands slap to his legs. "Well, what the hell does she want?"

"Me." My head drops into my hands and I rub my temples aggressively. "We need to stop her. I'll use my one shot on her. This just has to end. I've got too much shit going on to deal with her."

"Alright."

"Alright?" I question.

"Yeah. If that's what you want, then that's what you get. We made a deal. We've got you, man." He slaps a hand to my back. "No questions asked. Consider it done." He begins tying his laces again.

I breathe out a sigh of relief. There's one truth I gave them. A little weight off my shoulder. Eventually, I'll have to tell them about Willa, but not yet. The more I think about it, maybe her leaving wouldn't be such a bad idea. Then I think about the baby. I don't wanna be a dad, but if I don't have a choice, I want to try to at least be a good one. I want more for this baby than what I had growing up. I'd probably fuck this kid up, anyway. Maybe it would be better off without me. Willa will be an amazing mom, no doubt. I might just need to let them get as far away as possible so that they can be free of this town and of me.

Grabbing his phone and keys from the couch, he heads toward the door. "Now we just have to deal with Zed. I say we agree to help him. We have no choice. We'll stop Madison and help him with his revenge against the pastor at the same time."

"What makes you so sure that it's the pastor he's after? What if it's Willa?"

"Just a hunch. But if it is Willa, then she better say a prayer because ready or not, here we come." He pulls the door open. "I have to meet Marni, but don't worry, man. This all sucks ass, but we're in this together."

Once he's out the door, I sink farther into the couch. What if it is Willa that Zed wants?

I'll have to break the pact.

It's my duty to protect her now. No matter what the cost. As much as I hate it, Willa and her baby are my responsibility now.

But first, I need to make sure that baby is mine.

9

I could stand in the middle of the crowded hall of this school and scream at the top of my lungs, and I still don't think anyone would notice me. I suppose it's better that way. If they did notice me, they'd quickly realize why they never did before.

I'm nothing special. Nothing much to contribute to society, aside from rehearsed Bible scriptures that I've repeated in my head countless times.

I can count on one hand how many times I've put makeup on. Haven't done more than brush my hair since I was a kid, and that was only because Mom did it for me. She'd drag that brush through my hair so aggressively that I thought for sure I'd grow up with bald spots. To my surprise, I have a full head of luxurious caramel colored virgin hair. Never dyed, and never scorched with a straightener or hair dryer.

Hugging my books tightly to my chest, I travel down the halls like an invisible ghost. A squadron of freshman girls with Crayola-colored faces and bright clothes walk toward me. Five of them. Lined up in a planned parallel line, taking up the entire space of the hall. I'm smack dab in the center. I try to swerve to miss them, but the taller and thinner of the girls nudges her shoulder into mine. Without even cracking a devious smile, they continue on their way. Yep, I'm veiled by the misfortune of being a loser.

My heart jumps into my stomach and I instantly begin to sweat when I see Lars. With one hand pressed against a locker, the corner of his mouth tugs up in that sexy way it always does. Squeezing my books tighter, I pray, *please don't look at me.*

There was a time that I prayed to be noticed by him. I still get those weird giddy feelings and butterflies in my stomach when I see him—probably always will. He was the first boy I ever loved. But, he was also the first boy to ever break my heart. Scratch that. He was the first boy to ever rip my heart from my chest and play monkey in the middle with it while I stood there in tears because I just wanted to be invisible again.

The first couple of weeks back to school after summer break were tortuous. I thought that after a few days, people would forget, but that wasn't the case. It seems to have all blown over now and I'm back to being Sweater Girl, or Whispering Willa, as they like to call me.

As I draw closer, my heart beats violently in my chest, rattling my rib cage. When he doesn't even lift his head, sickness pools in my stomach as I wonder why he doesn't notice me. I'm so messed up. I beg not to be noticed and then I drive myself crazy wondering why I'm not. I suppose I thought that after everything that happened over the last couple days, he'd at least acknowledge me with a wave or a smile.

Passing by, I notice that beneath his arm is a petite blonde with glowing skin and a crop top that shows off her belly button ring. She's beautiful. Of course he's flirting with her. Why wouldn't he? I was just a bet. He never actually noticed me. Still doesn't.

Feeling sick and pitiful, I keep walking. As if there were an invisible string from him to me, my head turns and I glance over my shoulder. My heart melts in a puddle when his eyes catch mine. Something holds my gaze on his as I continue to walk forward. Gorgeous green eyes, a slender nose, dark hair with natural highlights, perfect white teeth, and a chiseled jaw that wears a little scruff. He conforms to being a misfit so well. Dressed in black jeans that run into his black boots. A white T-shirt that hugs tightly to his toned, bronze skin. And tattoos that paint a picture of his life.

Still staring, he cocks a smile. But it's not meant for me. It's for the girl who's got her hand on his waist giggling. Just as the string snaps and he looks back down to her, I feel the smack of the cold brick wall to my head.

"Ouch," I shriek as I rub the top of my head. Looking around, I see if anyone noticed. And of course they did. You see, I am invisible until I do something stupid like trip over my own feet, walk into a wall, or give my virginity to one of the most sought after guys in Redwood. Then I become the center of attention. Jada Montgomery is keeled over laughing at me as her and her posse all point and find humor in my clumsiness.

"You ok?" Trent asks, as he comes hurriedly to my side.

"I'm fine. Just another day." I brush it off and turn in the appropriate direction to the theater room.

"You sure? That's a pretty big goose egg you've got there." His fingers glide over my forehead and I shriek at the pain.

Feeling it for myself, my eyes bug out. "Oh my gosh, is it noticeable?" This is just great. I have the second part of my audition for the lead role of Belle today, which means all eyes will be on me. That's my luck, or lack thereof.

"I mean, it's big." He tells me. I'm not sure if he's trying to be reassuring, but he most definitely is not.

Trent is a good person, and a good friend. He looks at me the way that I used to look at Lars. He's probably the only person on this planet who sees something in me that I don't see in myself. Beauty and adoration. I wish I could give him more than just my friendship, but old wounds have to heal before I can offer anyone a piece of my heart.

"Willa." I hear my name called from behind us. It's an unfamiliar voice. I turn my head and see Lars' stepsister Madison jogging toward me. "I saw what happened. Are you ok, sweetie?" she says in a tone that one might use to talk to a toddler.

"I'm ok. Thank you for asking." This girl gives me bad vibes.

"Oh, good. I was worried about you. Here," she grabs my books from my hands. "Let me carry those for you." She turns her attention to Trent. "You can go now. I've got her." Her tone is demeaning and harsh.

"We..I..we're going to the same class. We always walk together." He tells her as he stutters over his words, making it apparent that he's highly intimidated by the girl.

Madison shoots a thumb at Trent and chuckles. "Is this guy your friend?"

I stop walking. Getting defensive, I huff. "Yes. Is that a problem?"

The aggression in my tone must have thrown her for a loop. All of my classmates would be surprised to learn that I am, in fact, growing a backbone thanks to their sly remarks and threats, as well as the fact that they've seen me entirely naked on video and admitting that I finger myself from time to time. Holding up a hand, she raises her brows. "No problem at all. Just making sure he wasn't bothering you."

Since when does Madison Bishop give a damn about me? And why is she treating me like a child?

Hooking an arm around mine like we're old friends, she gives me a pull. "Well, come on. We'll be late."

I try to stop her movements, but she keeps on walking, taking me with her. "Don't you have to get to class?"

"Mmhmm. I switched classes. Now let's go. I have an audition for the role of Belle in three minutes."

Pausing my steps, I look at her for confirmation that I heard her correctly. "You're auditioning for the part of Belle?"

Excitement leaks from her pores. "I am!" she beams. "I have no doubt the part is mine. Three years of singing lessons and a member of drama club since middle school, how could I not?" She giggles.

Something churns inside my stomach. Like lava spilling out and rushing through every inch of my body. "You're auditioning for the role of Belle?" My voice cracks and I realize that I sound like a sad child.

"Of course, I am." She laughs again. It's high pitched and rings loudly in my ears. "With my experience, I belong in the spotlight." She stops, turns to me, and raises her brows with a fake pity that makes me nauseous. "Wait, is that the role you wanted? I'm so sorry."

"No. Of course not." I lie. "I don't have much experience other than church choir and—"

"Good. Because sweetie, you're far too shy for center stage." Pulling me again, we continue to walk while her hold on my arm burns through the fabric of my knitted sweater. "You'd be an amazing Enchantress."

Enchantress? The Enchantress has a silent role.

I didn't even know Madison was joining the drama class. She's the second one to drop in mid-semester. Lars being the other.

It's probably better this way. I didn't even want the stupid part. Ok, I did. Even though I have no intention of being here after Christmas break or for the musical, I wanted to prove to myself that I could get it. Sort of a holy grail and 'watch me do this' before I fled town. I wanted it so badly, but there is no way I can compete with Madison. She's boisterous and outgoing. Beautiful and well-liked. I'm just...me.

We walk backstage and I force a smile on my face. Lars is already kicked back in the recliner while minions dance around him trying to do his job with the sound. As soon as his eyes land on us, he springs up from his comfortable position. "Madison, what are you doing here?" he spits out. Leaving me to assume he wasn't aware of his sister's schedule change.

"Told the guidance counselor that I wanted to pursue my dream of acting and she got me right in. You can thank your dad and his generous donation to the drama club."

"I'll be sure to do that." His eyes dance back and forth from me to Madison, who still has her arm clutched around mine. Pointing a finger between us, he asks, "What's this? When did you two become friends."

Remaining silent, I let Madison talk because, honestly, I have no idea what her sudden interest in me is.

"It's recent, but I think it's the start of a beautiful friend-ship." She smirks, forcing me to smile back at Lars.

I don't have many friends, and personally, I don't want any. Even if I did, Madison Bishop would not be anywhere near my list of people who I want in my life. Sure, she's popular, but she's also condescending and I get the feeling that she knew exactly what she was doing by stealing this part. I'm not the fool that most people take me for. My silence shouldn't be misconstrued as stupidity. I choose my battles wisely and a stupid high school play is the least of my concerns.

Although, a friendship with Madison could benefit me. I have a hunch that these two don't get along. Maybe it wouldn't be so bad to have her on my side.

"We are soooo glad to have you joining us, Madison." Mrs. Rhys beams with eagerness as she places both hands on Madison's shoulders. "I've heard so many great things about your performance at your last school. Meet me out front and we'll get started with the opening chorus for your audition."

I've heard so many good things about your performance at your last school. I mock Mrs. Rhys in my head in disgust. I might as well just join the stage crew because I'm toast. And I don't mean the role as a toaster. I doubt I'd even get that.

Madison leaves with Mrs. Rhys and Lars comes up beside me. My heart swells when I see the pity in his eyes. He knows what's going on and now he's going to pretend that he feels sorry for me. When I go to speak, I hold up a hand. "Just leave it alone. I didn't want the part anyways." Tears well in my eyes and I turn away quickly before he can see them. It's ridiculous, why am I so emotional over this? It's a play. This is high school. It's not important. I've fought off monsters and had my body stolen by thieves, but I'm sulking over the loss of a role.

I pull open the door and rush out into the empty hall. My eyes are dead set on the girls bathroom as I hurry to it. Pushing open the door, I let it close behind me before locking myself in the back stall. I don't even pay attention to the fact that it's filthy as my back slides down the wall. Swallowing down the lump in my throat, I begin to cry.

I hate this school. I hate this town. I hate everyone.

And they all hate me, too.

It's us against the world, sweet baby. They can take my dignity, steal my part, and hold my body hostage, but they will never take you away from me. Ever. I'll die first.

When the door squeaks open, I grab some toilet paper that's hanging from the holder on the wall. Ripping it off, I begin patting my eyes and hold off on exiting the stall until they finish their business and leave.

"Ya know, Willa." My heart drops when I hear his voice. *Why is he in here?* "You have just as much of a shot as she does. I heard you sing. You're really good."

"You shouldn't be in here." I choke out as I sniffle and wipe the snot from my nose.

"Neither should you. You should be out there, claiming your role and showing everyone why you deserve to be Belle."

He doesn't understand. "You don't understand. I'm not like you, Lars. I'm not like Madison, or Talon, or Marni." People don't notice me and no one cares what I have to say. I'm unseen, unheard, and nonexistent.

"You're right. You're not. You're better than us." The door squeaks open and I wait until the air is still before getting to my feet.

Drowning my sorrows, I stop at the mirror and take a quick look at the girl staring back at me. With red-rimmed eyes, I fake a smile at myself in an attempt to trick my brain into thinking that I'm happy. I've always heard that's a thing. Sometimes it works; sometimes it doesn't.

Pushing the bathroom door open, I step back out into the hall. "Trent stepped down." My heart jumps, taking my body along with it.

"Why aren't you in class?" I ask Lars.

Pushing himself off the wall that his foot was kicked up on, he walks alongside me. "Trent stepped down from the audition. Rhys wants me to take it."

I don't mean to laugh. But I do. "You're kidding me? You? In a play? As a lead role. Good one, Mrs. Rhys."

"I'm dead serious."

"Trent wants this more than anything. There's no way he'd step down." I stop walking and drop my tone down a few octaves. "What did you do, Lars?"

"I didn't do a damn thing. You think I want this? No fucking way."

"It doesn't make any sense."

"You're right it doesn't. But as of right now, no one will step up and take the part."

"Then you have to do it. The show must go on."

"Spoken like a true actress." He bites his lip and it does something to my insides. Shooting tiny bolts of lightning through my entire body. "I'll make you a deal. I'll audition, if you do, too."

My head shakes instantly. "No. I can't compete with Madison. She was born a star. I'm just..I'm just stardust."

"We're all stardust, Willa." He throws an arm around my shoulders and leads me back into class. Even with everyone watching, he keeps his arm around me and for a brief moment, I feel proud—acknowledged. I feel seen.

That is until I see Madison. She's front and center. The melody begins and she taps the mic in front of her. All eyes are on her, including Lars. Without even looking at me, he whispers, "It's your call. Do we have a deal?"

She begins her solo and it's good. I knew it would be. She talks a big game, but she's backing it up. Not only does she have the beauty, she also has a perfect pitch. The only thing lacking is the emotion. Her vocals are spot on, but I don't feel the passion behind it.

The music stop and so does she. Everyone claps, including Mrs. Rhys, who thinks she deserves a standing ovation. Though, she's the only one standing. "That was lovely, Madison," Mrs. Rhys says, before turning her attention to the class seated behind her. "This is the last call for auditions. Is there anyone else who would like to audition before my decision is made?"

Lars steps forward and speaks up. "Scene two. You know, the one where I cue the fireplace sounds. Willa and I would like to give it a shot."

"What? No." Madison huffs while she stands in the middle of the stage.

I grab him from the back of his T-shirt and give it a tug. "What are you doing?"

"We had a deal. Let's do this." He takes my hand in his and leads me out to the stage. My hand trembles in his and it feels like this is all happening too fast. I'm not a spontaneous person.

Everything I do is generally well-thought-out and planned for. I'm not ready for this. Sure, I've had every line and song in this play memorized since I was eight years old, but there is no way that Lars knows this off the top of his head. I've never even seen him with a script in his hands.

"Do you even know the lines?" I mutter under my breath.

"I do now." He pulls out a paper from his back pocket that's rolled up like a newspaper.

I'll never understand why he's doing this for me. This is a side of Lars that I haven't seen before. I'm not sure anyone has. I still hate him for what he did to me. But right now, he's reminding me why I once loved him in secret.

Madison comes to my side and leans forward, whispering in my ear with a clenched jaw. "You agreed you'd be Enchantress. What the hell are you doing?"

"I never agreed to anything," I say in a hushed tone. Lars smirks as if he knew that this would upset Madison. Is that why he's doing this? Because of their sibling rivalry?

Madison stomps away and takes a seat next to Mrs. Rhys, making her displeasure apparent with a pouty face and her arms crossed tightly over her chest.

Lars sidesteps and faces me. Puffing out his chest, he forces a stern look on his face, much like a beast, and I can't help but laugh. "Lars, you're supposed to be injured, not beastly," I whisper with a cracked smile.

He straightens the papers in his hands. "Oh, right." He begins reading over them then grabs his arm. "Uggh, my arm. It hurts," he shouts, all too loudly.

When I just stand there, sorting through lines in my head, because the one he just said is not anywhere in the play, he turns the paper toward me. "Umm, let me see. Just hold still." I pretend to dab at the invisible wound with an invisible washcloth.

"Ouch." He shrieks.

"Well, if you'd hold still it wouldn't hurt so bad."

"You should have never run away. If you hadn't, this wouldn't have happened."

I look up and our eyes catch fire. I begin to choke. "You frightened me. That's why I ran away."

Holding my gaze, he continues without even looking at the paper. "You shouldn't have come. You should have stayed away." Wait. That's not a line. My eyes widen as we both stand there frozen. He looks at the paper. "Temper," he whispers.

"You need to learn to control your temper."

"I'm learning. Be patient with me," he says quietly. That's not in the script, either. I turn to look at the crowd who is dumbfounded. Mrs. Rhys looks like she's ready to end this entire thing.

We just stand there, totally screwing this up. Skipping a few lines that are lost in my memory right now, I continue, "Thank you for saving my life."

The corner of his mouth pulls up into a smile. One that's not part of the play and one that I won't forget anytime soon. "You're welcome."

It's safe to say that Lars will not be performing as Beast. It's also safe to say that I no longer want this part without him.

"Well, that was a disaster." Lars chuckles as he walks hurriedly off the stage. I follow behind him, but he doesn't join the class. Instead, we go behind the curtain to the sound room.

"I hope you weren't expecting the part because you most definitely did not get it." There's no point in pretending. I'm pretty sure he didn't want it anyway. "Now tell me the truth, why'd you do it?"

His shoulder shrugs. "I wanted you to get another chance. Stay fresh in Mrs. Rhys' mind since your original audition was yesterday."

"And you just assumed that I'd do it if you did?" Of course, he did. He knows exactly what to do and say to get me to do what he wants.

"I had high hopes. Let's just leave it at that. But, even though I bombed it, you still rocked it. So, you're welcome," he says, slyly.

"Are you sure this has nothing to do with Madison? Seems like you two have a little quarrel going on."

"It's no secret that I can't stand the girl. But no. I did this for you, Willa." His butt drops down on the leather recliner that is practically molded to fit his body. He's always in it. Always such a slacker. I'm beginning to think he's more than that, though. More than just a rebel—he's got a heart—a rebel heart.

"While we have a minute to ourselves. I really think we should finish our conversation from yesterday. You said to sleep on my plans, and I did. I'm still planning on leaving Redwood."

His eyes widen and his body shoots up. "You can't leave."

Tilting my head, I cock a brow. "Why not?"

"Because you're needed here." He says the words so casually that he expects me to just understand what they mean.

"I'm not needed anywhere. Let alone in Redwood."

"You'd be surprised." His fingers lock behind his head and his eyes close. "Wake me up when class is over."

Without digging further into this, I just chalk it up to Lars being Lars. He speaks in riddles and leaves every conversation unfinished. He will talk to me and I will get that money. One small act of kindness doesn't make up for the hell he's put me through. I refuse to let my heart go there. I refuse to let him hurt me again.

10

"You actually got on stage and acted out a scene." Tommy laughs, again.

"I was helping someone out while doing everything I could to stop Madison from getting the part."

"Talon filled me in on that mess. So, your way of stopping Madison is by making sure she doesn't get a role in a high school play. Did it work? Can we move on to the next person?" He spews sarcasm and I wanna slap him.

"Shut the hell up. No, we can't move on. Have you heard any talk around school about her? Anything I can use against her?"

"Nope. I try not to pay attention to the rumor mill. Got my own shit to deal with."

"I need you to keep an eye on her. Something tells me that Madison has a lot of secrets up her sleeve. We need anything we can work with."

His chin drops to his chest with annoyance. "Seriously, man? Your plan is to just dig something up on her and threaten her?"

"Her and Zed are the main problems in my life right now.

Doesn't matter the extent of my plan, what matters is that the problem is eliminated. I could just kill her. Does that sound easier?"

Shaking his head, he agrees with me. "Fine. I'll see what I can find out."

"Ya know. I've been a puppet to both you and Talon, and now Zed, too. My time is coming and you fuckers better be ready to bend over backwards for me."

I hold up my fist to him. "You got it, man."

If I can get Madison away from me, that's one less thing I have to worry about.

Her joining class and expecting us to take the lead roles together was a bit too much. I also don't think she was expecting me to suck so badly. In her dreams, she was Belle and I was her Beast.

I didn't want the part. Wouldn't even accept it if it was offered. I did it partly because I did, in fact, want to stick it to Madison. She's a royal bitch and knew damn well that Willa was in the lead for that role. She notices that Willa has been getting a fraction of my time and she's ready to pounce. All the more reason to keep my distance from my Bible hugging baby mama.

Talon walks into the living room, stuffing his phone in his pocket. "Zed's coming tonight."

Tommy looks stunned. "Seriously? How the hell did you pull that off."

"Told him that we have his back. The Rebels are reuniting whether we like it or not. He's done some fucked-up shit, but if we want this nightmare to end, we have to pretend we've moved on from what he did."

"I'm not so sure I can do that." I state the obvious. "I'm not sure any of us can ever really move on from what the fucker did to us and I don't know how the hell you are evening willing to pretend after what he did to Marni."

"Look. We all know Zed is fucked-up. Shit, we're all fucked-up. But he's holding our future in the palm of his hand and he's ready to squeeze. We have to try something. Maybe once he gets his revenge on whoever it is he's after, he'll have a fresh start."

"Is that what you got? A fresh start?" I ask. It was only a month ago that Talon killed his dad. A man who abused, tortured, and scarred him for life. We don't call it murder—we call it justice. He deserved everything he got.

"You have no fucking idea. Driving away from my old man's burning vehicle, the clouds parted, the sun shined, and it was like the weight of the world was lifted off my shoulders. You all saw how I was. I was almost as bad as Zed. Now look at me," he points both fingers to his face, "I'm fucking smiling. Who'da thought?"

Marni joins us, wrapping both arms around Talon and resting her head on his chest. "I like to think that I have some-thing to do with that smile."

"It's all you, babe. All you." He perks up. "Speaking of, has anyone heard from Anderson again?"

Looking around from face to face, we all shake our heads. It won't be long until Anderson is making an appearance again. He said forty-eight hours, and it's been forty-six. "I'll give him a call. Let him know we have this all under control," I tell them.

I'm not really sure that we do, but we're about to find out.

LYING on the bed with my boots still on, I realize I've stretched the hole in my black T-shirt to triple its size. My thoughts keep going back to today, when Willa ran into the bathroom and cried. Sure, I wanted to oust Madison and piss her off, but

Willa deserves that part. Madison is like a fucking leech that refuses to go away.

Tommy pokes his head in the door. "He's here."

Looking down at my shirt, I notice that I practically shredded it. Tearing it off, I drop it to the floor and snag another solid black tee off the dresser.

Here we go.

With no hurry behind my steps, because I'm not anxious at all to see this shithead again, I walk down the stairs as I pull my shirt on and stretch my arms through the sleeves. Trailing my hand over the banister, I listen intently to the conversation that's already being had.

"But what does Willa Mack have to do with any of this?" Tommy says.

I stop. Frozen in place.

Zed begins speaking, "She's my Marni. Talon used her. I'll use Willa."

Talon laughs. "And you think you and Willa will just fall in love like Marni and I did? Never gonna happen."

Like a stampede of buffalo in my chest, my heart hammers inside. My fingers clench tightly around the banister as my short nails dig into the wood. Splinters embedding beneath my nail beds.

"This isn't about love. This is about revenge. My revenge. No questions asked. You don't need to know who I'm after and you don't need to know why. All you have to do is what I say. When it's done, you'll get the body and I'll disappear."

"And my dad?" Marni asks.

"He'll never be a suspect. None of us will. I have a plan. Are you in or are you out?"

Still on the steps and out of sight, I continue to listen.

"Looks like you've left us no choice. Where do we start?" Talon says.

"I've already started. Almost three months ago. We take down the girl to get to the main target."

"Just fucking say it, man. We all know that you're after her dad. Why won't you just say it out loud?" Tommy huffs.

Zed's feet hit the ground and I can see his shadow as he springs from the couch. "Why the fuck would you say that? He directs his attention to Talon and shouts, "What the hell did you tell him?"

Talon throws his hands up. "I didn't say a damn thing. It's obvious, though. I mean, who else does Willa have in her life that you'd want revenge on? Surely, it's not her mom."

Moving down, one step at a time, I zero in on Zed. "What did you mean your plan started three months ago?" My fists ball at my sides, and I can feel blood trickle from one of my splintered fingers.

"Ah, there he is. It's been awhile, Lars. How ya been?"

"Shut the fuck up. I just saw your dumbass last night and if I had my way, I'd never look at your ugly face again. Now tell me, what the hell did you mean?"

He shrugs his shoulders. "The video of course. I mean, did you think it was just for fun? I have a plan, unlike you. How's your sister doing, anyways?"

"I don't know what you're talking about?" I play dumb.

Talon shakes his head in guilt. "I told him."

"You what?" I spit out. "You fucking told him?"

I don't even know how I'm friends with these guys. Oftentimes I have to remind myself that I've known them since grade school, because you'd think I just picked em' off the side of the road with how much they surprise me. "Why the hell would you do that?"

"The pact, man. We stick together."

"He killed the pact. We all know it." I point at Marni. "It died when he raped your girlfriend and blackmailed me into holding her at gunpoint." Marni's face flushes at being called out. And I feel bad, but damn, are they all forgetting what he did?

Talon walks at an amble pace to my side. "Come with me." He gestures toward the kitchen. "What the fuck, man? We talked about this."

Weaving my fingers through my hair, my jaw ticks. "I can't fucking do it. I can't pretend." I look him in the eye. "And I'm telling you right fucking now, if anyone touches Willa—if that psycho goes anywhere near her—I'll gut him, and this time, I'll hide the fucking body."

"It's all temporary. This is the only way. Can we count on you?"

"I'm not making any promises. I need to know what his plan is because I'm dead serious. Willa is out."

"What the hell is your deal with that girl, anyways? First the performance and now this. You got a thing for her?"

"Hell no." I huff, with an airy chuckle. "A thing for Willa? Not a chance."

"Ok then. What's the big deal?"

"Yeah, what's the big deal, Lars?" Zed smirks as he leans against the frame of the entryway and crosses his ankles.

Grazing my tongue over my top teeth, I refrain from lunging at him. "Don't worry about it. Nice cut by the way." I tip my head with my eyes to the gash on his forehead.

He kicks one foot off the other and steps toward me. "Oh, I'm gonna worry about it, because she's my pawn. Has been for a while now. You were just my stepping stone to her." He laughs and it's loaded with sarcasm. "Come on now, you got her first. Let me have her second."

Unable to refrain any longer, I barrel toward him. Wrapping my arms around his waist, I swing one leg behind his and push, taking him straight down to the floor. He's intentionally trying to get under my skin, and it's working. My fingers wrap around his throat and I squeeze like hell. Zed's strong, but I'm much stronger.

"Stay the fuck away from her," I shout. His eyes bug out and it fills me with a sense of relief when I imagine him dying beneath me. I've never killed anyone, but I'm all about making this world a better place by eliminating this asshole.

An arm locks around my neck and pulls me backwards. I lose my hold on Zed's throat but shove my thumb into the wound on his forehead before I'm completely pulled off of him.

"Fuck," he bellows. "I just super glued that bitch shut last night. Thanks a lot, douchebag."

Talon holds my arms tightly behind my back as I try to break free. "You're lucky I didn't give it a twin."

"Seriously, this shit again," Tommy says as he walks in with a bag of chips.

"Really, Tommy? You're fucking eating?" Talon says from behind me.

"What? I didn't have dinner. What's going on here?" He looks over at Zed who is sitting with his back pressed against the refrigerator. "Dude, what happened to your head?" Blood drips down his face and across his lips. Zed darts his tongue out and licks it from his lips.

"I fell." His voice rises. "What do you think happened? Your rabid friend attacked me. Again."

Tommy looks at me like he's my fucking father. "Why'd you do that?"

Drawing in a deep breath, I once again question my own sanity when I chose these guys as my friends.

Zed speaks up. "Because he's protecting Willa."

"I'm not protecting her," I shout. Though, I am protecting her. I didn't realize it until I was on those steps, but I have to protect her. The thought of any of these guys, or any guy for that matter, touching Willa stirs something dark inside of me.

It's this indescribable feeling that makes me lightheaded and nauseous. My heart races. My palms sweat. I can't wrap my head around it. She's having a baby. Even if it wasn't mine, we don't fuck with a pregnant girl.

Talon chimes in. "You sort of are."

"Mmhmm." Tommy retorts as he stuffs a handful of chips in his mouth.

"Damn straight he is. And we wanna know why," Zed says.

Fuck. I've gotta get the hell out of here.

"You all figure this shit out. I've gotta go." I head to the door, grabbing my leather jacket off the back of the couch on my way out. I have to leave this house. I can't be here.

As soon as I step outside and close the door behind me, I fill my lungs to the point of pain. Exhaling quickly, I keep moving to my car.

Without any idea where I'm going, I get in and drive.

11

"Oh Willa Jean," Rick, my stepdad, singsongs as he inches closer and closer to my locked door. "I know you're in there."

I don't respond. I never do. I sit quietly with my arms cradled around my legs while I rock back and forth on the bed.

The Lord is my light and my salvation—whom shall I fear? The Lord is the stronghold of my life—of whom shall I be afraid? I repeat the verse in my head. *The Lord is my light and my salvation—whom shall I fear? The Lord is the stronghold of my life—of whom shall I be afraid?*

"Willa Jean?" he says again with a gentle knock to the door. "Daddy needs to talk to you." The whooshing sound of his belt ripping through the loops of his pants has me holding my breath, while my heart beats at an unprecedented rate.

Hugging my legs tighter, I bury my face into the tops of my knees. *The Lord is my light..*

"Willa Jean!" he shouts louder. My entire body jumps so quickly that I knee myself in the mouth. Sucking in my bottom lip, there's a metallic taste on my tongue. "Open the damn door or I'll break it down." I suck harder, feeling the blood seep into my mouth.

Swallowing hard, my throat aches as a lump lodges in my esophagus. I eyeball the window, but quickly remember what happened last time I escaped it. He was waiting for me on the other side. Like a villain in a horror movie, he stood there ever so casually while I dangled from the sill. Then his arms wrapped around my legs and he pulled me to the ground. The rest is a blur because I prefer it that way.

Holding my breath again, I listen.

Nothing. No sound of his heavy breathing. No footsteps.

Leaning forward, I try to look through the gap between the door and the old hardwood floor for a shadow or any sign that he left. Coming up on my knees, I shudder when the springs of the mattress squeak. My body freezes, the air still in my lungs from my last inhale.

Once I hear the clanking of metal on metal at the door, I jolt up. Fleeing to the window.

He's coming in.

I have to get out.

He's coming in.

Fidgeting with the lock, I finally get it unlatched. I slide open the window and punch out the screen. But I'm too late.

"Now, where do you think you're going, young lady? We haven't said our bedtime prayers."

"I just—"

"Just what?" His voice is husky and stern and it sends alarms ringing through my head. "Just thought you'd sneak out and go see that boy who fucked you this summer?"

"No." I shake my head while staring out the window. "I just needed some fresh air."

Where are you, Mama? Why aren't you here? Why did you have to leave me?

I close my eyes when I feel his presence draw closer. A

breeze hits the side of my neck, before he sweeps my hair to the side. His calloused fingers scratch along my collarbone. "I thought I told you to stay away from that boy?"

"I have been." I choke out the lie, but it's pointless. He won't believe it anyway.

"You screwing him again?"

"No. I swear, Rick...err, Dad. I haven't done anything with him. It was just that once. I promise." Rick doesn't like it when I call him by his first name. He calls me his little girl and demands that I call him Dad. He's not my dad. He's nothing like my dad. My dad was a good man. Rick is a sick and sadistic monster that people worship as if he is their God.

"Turn around."

My head shakes, no. I can't look at him. It's too hard to look at him.

"I said turn around," he roars as he spins my body so that we're face to face. I pinch my eyes shut tightly.

The Lord is my light and my salvation—whom shall I fear?

His palm presses to the top of my head as he pushes me down. I collapse on my knees and tears spill down my cheeks.

The Lord is the stronghold of my life—of whom shall I be afraid?

My stomach turns at the sound of his zipper coming down. The weight of his pants drops to my knees and his fingers clench my cheeks. "Open up, little girl." When I don't, he pinches harder, prying my lips apart by shoving two fingers inside my mouth and pushing down on my bottom teeth.

I dig my nails in the palms of my hands so hard that it's all I can focus on. Blocking out his touch and the act that I'm being forced to commit, I focus on the beautiful pain of my nails piercing through my skin. I count as I alternate hands. Squeezing one, then the other—two, three, four, five.

Once I get to forty-six, he's done.

Swallowing hard, I take what was given to me. His hand presses to my forehead and he aggressively shoves me backwards. My head hits the frame of the open window. "Go to bed. You've got school tomorrow."

Swiftly, I'm crawling on all fours over to the trash can and throwing up what just went down before he's even out the door. "Don't forget to say your prayers. The Lord *will* forgive you for your sins," he says before the door slams shut.

Wiping the back of my hand over my mouth, I curl into a ball on the floor. I notice the light of my phone where it lies on the floor. Somehow I must have kicked it off the bed when I was trying to get to the window.

Stretching my arm out, I grab it and slide it toward me. Numb of emotion with a stomach that's completely empty, I push myself into a sitting position before swiping the screen.

Lars called. But, why?

Without even thinking about it, I return the call.

"Hey," he says on the first ring.

"Can you come pick me up?"

"Yeah. Sure. Is everything ok?"

"Meet me around the corner of my house." I end the call.

There's no reason for me to stay here anymore. I'm eighteen years old and I can make decisions for myself. It's time to face it: mom isn't coming back. I need to leave now.

W ith a bag thrown over her shoulder, she leans against the stop sign beneath the streetlight. Lifting her head, she looks in my direction and begins walking to my car while I come to a rolling stop. I press the button to roll down the window, but she opens the door instead and climbs in.

"Hey. What's wrong?" I ask her. It's apparent something happened. Her puffy eyes and timid behavior are no mask for whatever she's trying to hide.

Her hands fold in her lap and she stares straight ahead. "Just drive. Please."

Giving her a minute, I don't ask any more questions. I drive in complete silence, unsure where I'm even going. I left Talon's an hour ago and drove down every road in this town before I found myself calling Willa to just ask how she was doing. She didn't answer, though. Two minutes later, she called me back, and here we are.

"I'm gonna need that money, Lars. I have to leave Redwood tonight."

"Tonight? You don't even have your car."

"I'm taking a bus. It's not my car. It's his."

"Willa, let's be real for a minute. You're not leaving Redwood tonight." I chuckle, though I don't find it funny at all.

"You should have just stayed away, Lars!" she shouts, and for the first time, I see Willa in a different light. No longer the quiet girl—she wants to be loud and heard. "This is all your fault. You pissed him off and now I'm paying for it." Tears slide down her cheeks and, in this moment, I realize something is very wrong.

"Did he hurt you?"

Her demeanor changes as fast it comes. "What? No. No one hurt me. I just...I just have to leave. Please, just give me the money and I'll go and never return. No one will ever know about the baby, I promise."

I haven't had much time to think about the baby. It's only been a couple days, but I think it's time that I start. For whatever reason, she wants to leave. Maybe I should let her. Protect her from Zed. Protect her and the baby from me and my ugly secrets.

Pulling down the dirt road, I follow it to the end where power lines stack in rows across an open field. This place has a significance to all of us. I had my first beer out here. We used to throw raging parties with huge ass fires and drink until the sun came up. There are no houses for at least a couple miles, so it's the perfect spot to have privacy.

Shifting the car in park, I crank the heat up before turning to face her. A blank stare holds to her face as she looks aimlessly out the window. I place a hand on her shoulder. "Willa. Talk to me." Her body trembles as she jerks away out of fear. "What's wrong? Why are you so jumpy?"

"I just have to go."

"What about school? What about the play?"

"Madison can have the part. It'll make her happy. As for school, I'll finish up online once the baby is born. I'll be ok."

She places a hand on her stomach then turns to look at me. "I'll take good care of her, I promise."

I shake my head in confusion. "Her?"

A smile grows on her face, raising the cheekbones on her pear-shaped face. "Yeah, I think it's a girl."

"A girl, huh?" I drop back into the seat with an audible breath. "I'm not sure I'm ready for a daughter. A son, maybe. But, how do I raise a girl knowing there are men like me out there?"

That smile she wears so well quickly fades, shooting an aching sensation into my chest. "You don't."

"I don't?"

"No." She shakes her head. "Haven't you been listening to me. I'm leaving." Suddenly she begins laughing, but it's forced. "This is your out, Lars. Take it. Trust me, you don't want a baby."

I slap my hands to the steering wheel. "Damnit, Willa. I don't know what the fuck to do."

"Take my offer. Please. You'll never have to see me again." Her phone begins buzzing in the pocket of her oversized hoodie. Pulling it out, she glances at me. "I don't know who this is."

I stretch over to look at the screen. "Is someone calling?"

"No. It's a text message with a recording."

"Well, press play."

We both look at each other when music begins playing. Familiar music. A lullaby.

Rock a bye baby.

The melody stops and a robotic voice cuts in, *"and down will come Willa, baby and all."*

The phone flies out of her hand, hitting the dash and dropping to the floorboard. "What was that?" She looks at me with wide eyes and an undeniable fear.

"I have no fucking idea," I tell her, and it's the truth.

"Who did you tell?"

"No one. I haven't told anyone."

"Liar," she screams, showing me a side of her that I've never seen before. "You're lying. Who did you tell?" Breaking into hysterics, she begins shaking uncontrollably. "Who did you tell, Lars?"

I place a calming hand on her arm, but she slaps it away. "I didn't tell anyone. I swear to God, Willa."

Her head lifts slowly and her jaw clamps firmly. "You don't even believe in God. Now tell me who you told."

I have no fucking idea what is going on. I didn't tell a soul about the baby. Hell, I've barely even convinced myself that it's true.

When I don't respond, she begins fidgeting with the door. Once it's open, I jump out the driver's side and race over to her. Grabbing her by the shoulders, I look into her eyes. "Willa. I swear to you, I didn't tell anyone."

"Someone knows. No one is supposed to know. This has to be the person who's been showing up at my house. Someone has been watching me, I can feel it."

"What about Vi? You said she bought the tests. Would she tell anyone?"

Her head shakes as she digs into her shirt, pulling out the cross attached to her chain necklace. She rubs it aggressively between his thumb and forefinger. "No, she wouldn't tell anyone. I don't think so anyways."

"Well, apparently she did, because I sure as hell didn't."

"I have to go now. Give me the money, Lars." She holds out her hand like I'm expected to just pull a few grand out of my pocket and say, 'good riddance.'

"I don't have that kind of money on me. Not enough to make sure you're set for a while."

"Forever," she says. I question her with a cocked brow. "Not awhile. Forever. I need enough to stay away forever. This is just as much your baby as it is mine. We deserve your financial support since you won't be helping in other ways."

"Yeah, well you're the one making that call. I never said I wouldn't help take care of the baby. You made my mind up for me." I cross my arms over my chest and steel my back. "Besides, I'm still not even sure it's mine."

"Seriously." She shoves me so hard in the chest that I stumble back and my feet tangle in a bundle of tumbleweed. Catching my fall, I tear it off my foot. She shoves me again. "You think I'm making this up?" And again. "You think I wanna have a baby with you? I hate you, Lars Titan. You made my life miserable. I wouldn't be in this mess if it wasn't for you and your friends." And again. Only this time, I don't move. This time I grab ahold of her as angry tears continue to spill down her face.

"Stop." I pull her to my chest. "Just fucking stop. I know you hate me. I know I screwed up. If I could take it back, I would." Her forehead rests on my shoulder and my hand ghosts her head before finally dropping and stroking her soft hair. "I'm sorry."

"How long until you can have the money?" she says in a placid tone as she sulks into the collar of my shirt.

"Give me a week." My eyes close and I inhale the sweet scent of her honeydew hair.

"I can't wait that long, Lars. I have to leave before anyone else finds out—before Rick finds out."

I'm not sure why I feel this pang in my chest at the thought of her leaving. Two days ago, I barely looked at her. But now—now, I feel like she belongs to me in some fucked-up way. Not in a sexual relationship sort of way, but in a way that I need to shield her from pain and heartache. I need to protect her from her stepdad and Zed, and even Madison.

"I'm not sure who that message came from, but I promise you that I will find out."

Her head lifts and she looks me in the eyes. "I can't go home. I can never go home again."

Why? What the hell happens in that house? What does he do to her that has her so scared of her own home? It doesn't make any sense. "Can you tell me why you can never go home?"

"Because I'm scared. But, he'll find me if I stay in Redwood. I know he will." Her eyes hold sadness, but deeper than that, they hold hope. She wants more than this life she was given. We'll say goodbye in a week and before long, she'll be a distant memory because she deserves to find happiness.

"Then you won't. I think I have an idea." I take her hand in mine. "C'mon."

"Where are we going?"

"Someplace where you'll be safe." I'm about to do something that I never thought I would have to do. I have to betray my friends. "I have to make a call real quick." Opening the passenger door, I wait until she climbs in before I close it.

I pull my phone out of my pocket and tap the first name on my contact list—Anderson Thorn.

"Pushing it pretty close, you're down to the last hour. I was just about to leave for my trip," he says from the other end of the call.

"What if I told you that I could guarantee you'll never have to worry about this Josh fiasco again?"

"I'm listening."

"I'll be at your house in ten minutes. You have a houseguest coming to stay with you." I end the call before he questions what I just said.

Anderson wants peace of mind and I can give it to him, but he has to give me something in return. He's always away on business and this is just temporary until I can get the money from my dad to help Willa leave. As a top-dog mafia leader,

Anderson has high-end security and the perfect home to hide Willa away.

WE PULL up to the mansion that sits on forty acres of desert land. A lot of people in this town come from money. You don't find many average Joes in the neighborhood, but Marni's dad is far above average. He's an extremely successful 'business' man who lives a very private life. Well, he did until we came along.

"Do you trust me?" I ask Willa, as she stares at the house in front of us.

"Not at all," she says honestly, without even giving it a second thought. I'm not surprised. She shouldn't. I don't even trust myself.

"Well, for the next ten minutes, pretend that you do because I have to leave you out here while I talk to someone."

"You're leaving me out here in Marni and Axel Thorn's driveway?"

"Just for a few minutes. I'll be right back. I'll keep it running, so you're warm. Lock it after I get out." I open the door and step outside before closing it. Running my hands down my shirt, I brush myself off then run my fingers through my disheveled hair. *Here we go.*

Taking a deep breath, I knock my knuckles to the door, but before I can even tap a second time, the door swings open.

Anderson waves me inside and looks out the door, both ways, before closing it. "Who's in the car?"

"Willa Mack. She's in some trouble and needs a place to stay."

I follow behind him as he walks into his study. He grabs a glass carafe full of bronze liquid and fills a small glass half-full.

"That's what shelters are for. What the fuck does this have to do with me?"

He extends the drink to me, but I hold up a hand. "Nah, I'm good."

"Suit yourself." He tips back the glass and takes it all in one swallow.

"You said you're leaving for a long business trip. I want you to allow Willa to stay in your house while you're gone."

"Now why the hell would I do that? The last thing I need is the pastor's daughter snooping through my house."

"There will be no snooping. If you agree to let her stay here for a week, I'll tell you everything that really happened that night."

An unpleasant look takes hold. One that would instill fear in most people. But I have his future in the palm of my hands.

"What's that supposed to mean? I already know what happened that night. I was drunk, hit the boy and left him there. You assholes recorded it and my misfortune was your gain."

"There's a bit more to it and I'll fill you in once you agree to my terms."

"I'm not agreeing to shit. Last time I did that, you turned my daughter against me."

It's true, in a sense. Marni is pretty furious with her dad. She knows that he agreed to step aside while we used Marni for Talon's game. What he doesn't know, is that he should be just as angry with her. She's known for almost a month that her dad didn't kill Josh and she hasn't said a word. At first, she wanted her trust fund, but now, I think she's just riding this out until we know where Josh is.

"Marni will come around eventually. She's just hurt. This isn't about her, though. This is about Josh. Agree to my terms and I'll tell you the truth."

"What is it you want?"

"Willa gets to stay here. I get access to the cameras. Security is on call if anything happens."

Even if he doesn't believe that I can help him, he is desperate for any way out of this mess. It's been months, but for some reason, he's on high alert right now. He raises a brow and prominent wrinkles crease on his forehead as he takes small strides back and forth in front of me. "And this will be over?"

"It will. I'll make sure the video is destroyed and all suspicion will be erased."

"Fine," he huffs, "my office is off-limits. She can stay in the guest room on the second floor next to Marni's room."

My phone begins buzzing in my pocket. *It's Willa.* I hold up a finger to Anderson and take the call. "Hey, almost done in here. You good?"

"Please hurry."

"I'll be out in a minute." I end the call, but keep my phone out. Tapping on the screen, I log into the dummy cloud account where we stored the original video. We made this account last year for fun. Every incriminating video we've ever made is in here. There are about a dozen, but I zone out as I focus on one. Three months ago. The night with Willa. I knew what they were doing—what Zed was doing. Saw the phone recording, yet I did nothing. I stood by idly while they blasted the video of us to half of the town and gave an unknown girl a reputation as *the bet.*

Snapping out of it, I tap on the uncropped video of the night Josh died. I turn the phone around and hold it in front of me as it plays.

"He might have just got hit. They might be coming back."

"Fuck!" Tommy shrieks.

"Oh my god. The car rolled right over Josh's body like he wasn't even there."

"The driver's getting out. Wait a minute. That's Anderson Thorn, Marni's dad."

"Do you think he's the one who killed him?" Talon asks Tommy.

"Nah. He looked scared shitless. No way. Someone else did this. Someone hit him and left his body out here."

"Who would fucking do that?"

The video rolls silently for a minute. I watch as Anderson's eyes all but jump out of their fucking sockets and I'm really second-guessing this decision.

Tommy's voice comes through again. *"Anderson did look scared. Like he thought he hit and killed him. Then he drove off out of fear."*

"We have a video of him running over Josh. What if we crop it and make him think he did kill Josh? We could get whatever we want."

"What could he possibly have that we want?"

"His daughter," Talon says with a mischievous tone.

Turning the phone back around, I hit pause then swipe out of the video.

"Is this some sort of sick joke?" Anderson scowls with a crimson-flushed face. "That's not the video you assholes showed me. And what's this talk about Marni." He steps closer, then takes two steps back.

Holding up my hands, I plead with him. "Let me explain."

"Yeah, you better fucking explain before I rip your goddamn head off, along with those imbecile friends of yours."

Taking a few steps back, I try to move away from his reach. "Come on, man. You were a teenager once. You know how we don't think clearly under pressure."

His voice rises as he goes ballistic. "This isn't a fucking football game you're trying to win. This is someone's fucking life. Have you all lost your damn minds?"

"I know, it was stupid. No one wanted Josh to die, but it's not our fault. Not yours and not ours."

He tips his chin up. "Who the hell did it? Huh? Was it Talon? Did he fucking kill him and try to pin it on me, while manipulating my daughter?"

"What? No. Talon didn't kill him. None of us did. The truth is, we have no idea who killed Josh. We just convinced you that you did it for our own personal gain. Got rid of him and the car and made it look like he just went missing." I try to reason with him, but it's not looking good. "You're missing the point here. You didn't kill Josh and I have proof of it. You can't be incriminated. You don't have to live with the guilt."

"Guilt?" He laughs and it's sadistic and unnerving. "I didn't feel guilt. The guy was obsessed with my daughter, you all told me so. If I had caught him out there that night, I'd have killed him with my bare hands. What rattles my fucking cage is that you all played me for the last three months. Turned my daughter against me, and for what? So that nitwit Talon could weasel his way into her heart."

"Talon has his reasons for doing what he did, but I can tell you that he would never hurt Marni. He loves her. She's safe with us."

"I highly doubt that. And now you're doing the same thing to the pastor's daughter. Using her for your gain. You sick motherfuckers."

"Willa isn't part of this. Not exactly." I'm not here because of the revenge pact. I'm here because for whatever reason she's terrified of her stepdad. So much so, that she is willing to quit school and give up everything just to get far away from him.

The squeak of shoes across the hardwood has both of us shifting our attention to the room outside of his study. "Who the hell is that?" Anderson huffs, as he hurries over to the door.

Following behind him, I see Willa standing there. Her hands are at her sides and that fear that I saw earlier has returned. "Willa, how are you, hun?" Anderson asks, as she stands there observing me.

"You ok?" I ask her.

"I just got scared out there. You took too long."

"Sorry about that. We were just finishing up." I look at Anderson. "But, we're done here, right? Willa can stay?"

After a beat of silence, he rubs the stubble on his chin and speaks. "I'll have Ruby get the room ready. She'll be on vacation for the next couple of weeks while I'm away. The house will be empty, but I'll be sure to accommodate your requests. This room is off-limits and I'll be leaving in about twenty-minutes." Stepping toward me, he leans forward and whispers in my ear, "I want that fucking video." Then he turns to Willa. "It's good to see you. Tell your parents I said hello."

"Thank you, Mr. Thorn. I really appreciate this," Willa says in a placid tone.

Anderson closes the door to his study and sticks a key in to lock it, then walks away.

"I told you I had a plan. You'll be safe here. But first, you need to tell me everything."

Her eyebrows pinch together as she questions me. "Everything?"

"I need to know who and what you're running from. If I don't know why you need protection, I can't protect you."

There's a beat of silence while she fidgets with her phone through the front pocket of her hoodie. She opens her mouth to speak, but closes it again.

"What is it, Willa?"

"Have your parents ever told you that monsters aren't real?"

I shrug. "Yeah. I think so, why?"

"They lied. Monsters do exist, and I've been living with one for the last seven years."

13

WILLA

"It wasn't always bad. For a while I loved him like a dad. We shared the love of the Lord. Said bedtime prayers at night. He gradually became erratic and unpredictable. Mostly when mom would go to work or leave for her literature conferences. But now she's gone and I don't think she's coming back this time."

"He hurt you?"

"Sometimes." I'm not sure why I'm telling him this. I don't trust Lars, but I also need him to give me the money to get away. I need his pity—he owes me this much.

"Did he...did he ever touch you, Willa?"

"No." I lie. A deep and painful lie that has my stomach twisting in knots. "Not in that way. He just gets angry and violent. That's why I can't stay any longer. He's getting worse by the day and if he finds out that I'm pregnant, he'll force me to abort the baby." Or he may even try and do it himself. I don't say that, but it's the truth.

"Ok."

"Ok?" I mimic his word, wondering what 'ok' means.

"I'll get the money and help you leave. Under one condition. I need to know where you're going. I can send you money, help out however I can."

"Ok. I can do that." I lie again. No one will know where I'm going, especially Lars.

This sweet side of him is all a facade. There was a momentary lapse of weakness on my part at school today, and maybe even tonight at the power lines. But I can't forget why I've hated him for the past three months. I'll never know why I loved him for the five years before that.

For five years he looked at me like I was scum. I watched as he pushed people around and laughed about it with his friends, but I still loved him. I was a fool. Now I get to have my own little secret while I pass that title over to him when I take his money and run.

These four guys took my innocence and made a mockery of me. The entire town turned a blind eye to the entire thing. Rick blamed me and I'd rather spend life in prison, or die, than ever have to face a punishment like that again. They began this game and they are responsible for everything I've had to endure since that night.

"Ms. Mack," A petite elderly lady says as she appears across the room. "Your room is ready, darling." She's sweet and reminds me of my gram. Snowflake hair, milky skin, and dark eyes that I'm sure have seen far more than they'd hoped for. Living in this house, how could they not?

"Thank you," I say whole-heartedly. She lowers her head and walks up the stairs. I follow behind her, and Lars follows behind me. I hope he doesn't plan to stay here. As much as I hate him, he has the capability of stirring unwanted emotions inside of me.

Opening the door, the housekeeper waves her hand and signals me in. It's breathtaking. Like nothing I've ever seen before. A king-size bed sits in the center of the back wall with white linens placed perfectly on top, not a wrinkle to be seen. I walk over and run my fingers over it in search of a flaw, but there's not one.

A matching white canopy hangs over the bed with fringed seams that dangle pea-sized crystals. I bet that the reflections of the glass beads dance around the whole room when the sun catches them. A white Persian rug lays in front of the bed on the cherry oak hardwood and a dresser that probably costs more than Rick's house is pressed against the wall.

Aside from that, it's empty, but it's perfect. The walls in my room at home aren't even visible because of all my belongings packed into the small space.

This could be my life. I can have this, and more, if I play my cards right. My baby and I will never want for anything.

Turning around to thank the sweet lady, my mouth hangs open with the words on my tongue when I notice she's gone.

"I noticed your bag looked empty, but you and Marni are about the same size. I'm sure she won't mind if you borrow some clothes while you're here," Lars tells me.

I wanna yell at him and ask him what his reasoning is for all of this. Surely I'm not here because his heart doubled in size and found a place for me inside of it.

"No, I wouldn't feel comfortable even going inside of Marni's room, let alone taking her clothes."

"Suit yourself, but the housekeeper is leaving and you only have one outfit to last you the rest of your life. Good luck with that."

"I know how to do my own laundry, Lars. In case you've forgotten, I didn't grow up with a nanny or a maid."

"Oh yeah. And what do you plan to wear while your pajamas are in the washing machine?"

"I'm sure I can find a robe somewhere in this house." I take a step toward him and place a hand on his shoulder to turn him around. "You can go now. I'll be fine. Please call me as soon as you know how long this should take."

"Woah. I'm not leaving," he says in an aloof manner. "You really think I'm just gonna drop you and go. Someone is on to you, Willa. Someone out there knows you're pregnant and they sent that recording for a reason."

"Fine. You can stay, but I just need to be alone right now. Do you mind?"

"Nope. I've got some calls to make, anyways. I don't have class until the afternoon, which you already know, so I'll see you in the morning."

I nod my head. "Sounds good."

Backtracking to the door, he stops but doesn't look at me. "You had that part in the bag. It's a shame you're throwing away your chance to prove it."

I remain silent until he closes the door behind him. Once his footsteps fade down the hall, my heart hammers in my chest as I miss him already. God, I hate that I'm so drawn to him. "Goodnight, Lars," I whisper under my breath.

PULLING the cord to the white slatted blinds, I welcome the sunlight in. My eyes skate around the room as I watch the luster of light prisms blink along the walls. Stretching my hand up, I try and catch one, but much like everything else in my life, they are unattainable.

"Willa." Lars knocks his knuckles on the door. "I'm heading out for a couple hours. Cameras are on and security is around."

"Ok. I'll be here," I respond while my eyes follow the bands of color.

"Oh, I'm making an appointment at a Planned Parenthood in Washau for tomorrow morning."

My eyes rip away from the ceiling and shoot to the door. "You're what?"

"Come on now. You're a sweet girl and all, but you really think I'm handing over my life savings without knowing for sure that you're pregnant."

Heavy steps lead me to the door as anger ripples through my core. I tear it open with one swift pull. He stands on the other side with dampened hair and tousled glistening tips. He smells really good. Like pine tar and lemon peel and his shirt is in one piece. More times than not, he's sporting the grunge look with ripped shirts and holey jeans. But today, he looks well-put-together in his—still all-black—attire.

"You still think I'm lying about this?" I grab his hand and place it on my stomach. "There's a baby in there, Lars. I'm not lying to you."

His eyes slide down to where his hand sets gently in mine, pressed against my belly button. It's still early, but I'm beginning to notice a tiny bulge. Surely he can feel it.

"I don't think you're lying, but those tests aren't always accurate. I...we need to be sure before you run away for nothing. You also need to have the necessary pregnancy blood work done and start on some vitamins."

"How do you even know this stuff?"

He holds up his phone. "Found an app about pregnancy. Lots of cool stuff on it."

My heart skips a little beat, but I take a deep breath, not letting the gesture fool me.

Even if I wasn't pregnant, I'd still be leaving. I'd just be leaving dirt poor and on foot.

"Fine. You want proof then you can have it."

"Good. It's all confidential, so you have nothing to worry about. No one will know you were there."

My arms cross over my chest and I look down, realizing I'm not wearing a bra. "And once you have your proof?"

"Once everything is confirmed, I'll help you leave."

I don't say anything. I just stand there. Stunned, shocked,

in disbelief that he thinks I'm lying to him. Me? Sweater Girl, Whispering Willa, the girl with God in her heart, and an angel on her shoulder. At least, that's the way they all see me. They don't know that the girl they thought they knew is gone. She's dead and she's never coming back. "Fine. Do what you have to do." I slam the door shut.

I'm leaving one way or another and no one will be stopping me. It's time for me to put the pain behind me and try to live a normal life.

Once Lars is out of the house, I plop down on the bed and turn my phone back on. Holding my breath, I pray that Rick hasn't alerted the authorities or sent out a search party for me yet. When I notice just a couple missed calls and a text from him that says: *Where are you?* I exhale the pent up air in my lungs. He knows I'm gone, but he hasn't gone off the deep end, yet.

14

Stepping inside Talon's house feels like walking into some sort of trap. These guys have been plotting destruction, day and night, while I've been tending to Willa. My head is in a spiral of fog and distortion as I try to prioritize and I'm not even sure what's more important right now—getting Willa out of this town so she feels safe, or making sure that none of us become suspects in a murder case. On top of that, I've still got this shit with Madison to deal with.

It would appear that Zed wasted no time reclaiming his throne and getting comfortable at Talon's house. Apparently he's staying here again and Marni fled to a hotel because she can't stand being under the same roof as him. Talon assured her this is temporary and that it has to be this way, but it's obvious where his priorities lie. I wanna fucking break shit when I think about how we're all catering to Zed just to appease him. At least he's buying it, because if he catches wind that we're just trying to save our own asses, we're all screwed.

"There he is." Zed beams as he shoots up from the couch and drops the game controller on the cushion. "You bring me a present?"

"What the fuck are you talking about?"

"My girl, Willa. I'm gonna need you to butter her up and pass her my way."

Something sinister stirs inside of me. Is he really doing this shit again? Thought for sure I made it clear that she's off-limits.

Tommy comes walking in wearing a salmon colored button-up shirt and a pair of gym shorts. He looks like he dressed himself when he was half-drunk and when he stumbles to the side, I realize that he is, in fact, more than half-drunk. "Why the hell aren't you at school?" I bellow. Out of the four of us, Tommy is the one who takes school seriously. He's an athlete, an artist, and has his future all mapped out. Lately, though, he's been different. I can't put my finger on it, but it's like he's taken an emotional beating and he's drowning his sorrows in the bottle. "Just do what he says, Lars. Let's end this shit."

"Can't," I deadpan.

"What do you mean, you can't?" Zed puffs out his chest like he expects it to intimidate me.

"I mean that I can't. Willa left town last night. Had it out with her parents and fled the state. Looks like you need to find a different pawn in your little game." I sidestep around the couch and walk into the kitchen where Talon is pacing the floor while he talks on the phone.

"Listen, babe. It'll be over soon. Go stay at your dad's for a bit. Lars mentioned that he was leaving town until after Christmas."

His eyes land on mine and he raises a brow in question when he notices the displeasure in my expression. I shake my head, no.

Holding his hand over the speaker of the phone, he brings it to his waist. "Why's that a problem?"

Zed comes flying into the kitchen and gets all up in my face again. "Where'd she go? You tell me right fucking now?"

There's a sense of familiarity when I shove my hands into his chest. "How the fuck am I supposed to know?"

"I'll call you back in a few minutes." Talon ends the call and drops his phone on the counter. "Where'd who go?"

"Willa." Zed huffs. "Lars said she took off and left Redwood last night."

"How would you even know that?" Talon asks me.

Pinching the bridge of my nose, I discern that I'm royally screwed. "Ok. You," I point to Zed, "can find someone else to use. Willa is gone. Deal with it. You wanna piss off someone close to her, find another way. And you," I point to Talon, "tell Marni that she can't stay at her dad's because he canceled his trip." It's a lie, but it'll buy me some time. "Now, before we get started on everyone else's fucking problems, let's not forget that I've got a psychotic girl up my ass who knows what we did. We need to guarantee her silence before we can do anything for Zed."

If I can get everyone to focus on Madison right now, it'll give me enough time to get Willa out of here before anyone can toy with her emotions or use her in their game. I'm also pretty sure that Madison is the one who called Willa and left that fucked-up recording last night. It won't be long until she's on the hunt for blood if she does, in fact, know that Willa is pregnant with my child. She's a loose cannon that needs to be disassembled.

"Not my fucking problem. You deal with that shit. Tommy, Talon, and I had a little chat last night and they've agreed to my terms. You find out where she went and tell me or else this entire deal goes up in flames and we all let Marni's innocent dad take the fall."

"He won't fall far. He knows the truth." There, I said it. He knows and there isn't a damn thing they can do about it.

"What do you mean he knows the truth?" Tommy asks.

Talon and Zed share a look and I repeat myself. "I told him everything. You'll have to find a new victim this time around." I turn to walk away but stop myself and make a spontaneous decision on my own. I'll probably regret this, but fuck it. "Oh, and I'm out. You all can play your games and fight your demons on your own." Flipping them the middle finger, I walk out feeling like the weight of the world was just lifted from my shoulders.

I just can't do it anymore. None of it. It's too much and I fucking quit this friendship if it means driving myself to insanity just to please everyone else. Hell, maybe I should just ditch this town with Willa and start over somewhere else.

DRIVING around town for a couple hours, I realized that I need help.

A call rings through the speaker and I take it as I turn onto Tommy's road.

"Bradley, is it taken care of?" Bradley is one of Dad's employees. He handles the nuts and bolts of the business, which means he takes care of the dirty work.

"She wants a lot, Lars. I'm talking ten-thousand dollars."

"I don't give a damn what it cost, you get someone in that office to run the test through the lab or I'll make damn sure my father fires your ass." I slam my finger into the dash screen and end the call.

It's not that I think Willa is lying, but I'd be a goddamn fool if I didn't make sure the baby is mine before handing her over thousands of dollars.

I've gotten quite attached to the modest violet, but as of right now, I don't trust anyone. I barely even trust myself.

Pulling into Tommy's driveway, I'm relieved to see that he's here. I need to talk to him, one-on-one, without outside influences. He's slightly intoxicated, but hopefully coherent enough to understand what I'm about to tell him. Tommy's the most humane one of all of us and I know that if I share a little insight to what I've got going on, he'll be in my corner.

Zed wants Willa. Well, Zed isn't fucking touching Willa.

Without even knocking, I push open the door. Tommy comes walking out of his room in just a pair of gym shorts, with his phone pressed to his ear. "Yeah, Dad. Uh huh. No parties, got it. Ok, bye." His words slur a bit, but he seems to have sobered up a tad.

"Parents outta town?" I ask him, once he drops the phone on the couch.

"Yeah and it's a damn shame that I can't even throw a party because I'm too busy wiping your asses to make sure they're clean."

Slapping a hand to his back, I try to reassure him. "It'll all be over soon. Then we'll be at your beck and call, bro."

"Whatever. I don't even care anymore. This shit just needs to end." Tommy walks into the kitchen and I follow him. He grabs a couple bottled waters from the fridge and tosses me one. "So, what are you doing here? Need more services? Got another person for me to follow?"

Twisting the top off, I take a long drink before I answer him. "Not exactly." I screw the top back on and set the bottle down on the kitchen table. "I know that you guys made this deal with Zed to make sure that he gets what he wants, but I need you to help me instead." It really sucks feeling like I'm out of this group; I've been battling all this shit on my own and I can't fucking do it anymore.

His brows dip. "So you want me to betray our friends?"

"I wouldn't call it betrayal to them as much as a loyalty to another friend."

"If this is about Madison—"

"It's not. It's about Willa."

Tommy pulls out a chair and sits down then proceeds to drop his head in his hands and let out a breathy sigh. "Fuck. I knew you had something going on with that girl. What is it? You falling for her?"

He lifts his head and watches my expression. "She's pregnant and she's still in Redwood."

A very thick silence surrounds us and the air suddenly feels heavy. He's the first person I've told this to and now I'm really regretting it.

"Holy shit, man." He slaps his hands to the table and his wide eyes convey his shock. "Pregnant?"

I nod my head. "Yeah. Pregnant."

"And it's yours?" He doesn't even wait for me to respond. "Of course it is. Why else would you be telling me this shit?"

"That's what she says."

"And you believe her?"

I shrug one shoulder. "Yes and no. I mean, I want to because, come on, it's Willa Mack. But I'm also skeptical."

He takes his sweet ass time as he chugs the rest of his water, and I'm sure it's because he's speechless. Once he finishes and crinkles the plastic in his hands, he asks, "What the hell do you plan to do?"

"She wants to leave Redwood. Told me that no one needs to know and she'd free me from responsibility if I set her up for a while."

Smacking the bottle to the table, he beams eagerly. "Well, fucking do it, Lars. You're eighteen years old. You can't have a baby."

"Yeah, but she's eighteen, too. Do I really just send her on her way to live alone and take care of a baby by herself?"

His eyes bug out and he nods. "Yes. Yes, you do."

I thought Tommy would at least understand, but apparently, he doesn't. It doesn't matter, that's not why I'm here.

"I'm still thinking about that. The reason I'm telling you this is because someone has been harassing her. Someone knows. I'm assuming it's either Zed or Madison."

"Ah, and you need me to find out? Of course." He salutes me. "Aye aye, Captain."

"No. I'm working on that. I need you to convince Zed and Talon that Willa isn't the answer. For whatever reason, Zed wants to use her and there's no fucking way I'm letting that happen."

"Come on now," he laughs. "This is Zed we're talking about. The least reasonable person in existence."

"Did they say what the plan is? What he wants with her?"

A beat of silence has me on the edge of my seat.

"He says he has a plan and swears that no one will get hurt. Maybe he just wants to talk to her."

"Yeah. Talk to her my ass. We all know what he did to Marni. Not a chance in hell. I'd kill him first."

"You like this girl, don't you?"

"No!" I shout as I jump to my feet, running my hands down my face. "She's carrying a baby, Tommy. You think I'd let Zed near any pregnant girl, or even any girl who's not pregnant for that matter. He's a monster. This damn pact has gone too far. These girls are innocent. First Marni and now Willa."

"And Madison?"

I hold up a finger and glower. "Madison is not innocent. Don't be fooled. But Willa is. She's been through enough. Not to mention, she's fucking pregnant."

"Zed thinks he can stop Madison, too."

"Yeah, and what's in it for him? Hmm? Zed doesn't do anything for anyone without a string attached."

"Consolation prize, maybe? He rewards you for letting him use Willa."

Sighing heavily, I glance at the door, ready to leave. "Yeah, that sounds more like something Zed would do." My arms fly up. "Fuck it. I guess I'll just handle this shit on my own. Thanks for nothing."

"I'll talk to them. My hands are tied, man. It's all I can do. We all just want this shit to end."

"Well, in order for Zed to use her, he has to find her." Huffing and puffing, I leave before I lose my cool and do something I'll regret.

Thought for sure that Tommy would have my back. But it looks like Zed's the ringleader and calling all the shots. Maybe our hands are tied, but I'm shredding that rope and freeing us before he tightens his grip and feeds us all to the wolves.

Once I'm in the car, I rip my phone out of my pocket and tap Madison's name. It doesn't even ring before it goes straight to voicemail. "Fuck," I shout. If I can just find a way to get her off my ass, this can be over. Offer her something she can't refuse. Force her to leave town. If only the roles were reversed and she could go while Willa stays.

I have no fucking idea what it is with Willa, but she's getting to me. She's crawling into my skin and I can feel her piercing the veins of my heart. When all of this started with her, it was a stupid bet, but the more time I spend with her, the more time I *want* to spend with her. I can't wrap my head around this nagging desire to be near her. Even if it's just to watch her from afar.

I'm suddenly noticing things I never did before. The way her rapid blinking happens mostly when she's nervous. How she has a dimple on her left cheek when she smiles that matches the one on her chin, but her right side is unblemished. Whatever this is, it's unexpected, and to be honest, it's unwanted. Yet, the idea of Zed or Madison going anywhere near her stirs something sinister inside of me. Makes me crazy and puts irrational thoughts in my head.

Trying again, I tap Madison's name over and over and over again. Climbing into my car, I keep trying. Starting the engine,

I keep trying. Voicemail. Voicemail. Voicemail. School got out ten minutes ago, she should be answering her goddamn phone.

Just as I start driving down the road, the Bluetooth kicks on, and her name flashes on the screen.

Now that I've got her on the line, I'm not even sure what I want to say. But, I play nice.

"Hey, Madison. Where are you?"

"Sitting at home. Bored as fuck. You?"

"I'm coming over. Don't leave." I end the call and shuffle through different options in my head.

I WALK UP to the front door that was once blocked with an abundance of shoes. My house was always the go-to hang out spot. We'd all come here after school, raid the refrigerator, drink endless cans of soda and play video games until curfew. It was just Dad and me and he was always busy working. My dad wasn't as absent as some parents, but he definitely favors work over family life. It wasn't always that way. It wasn't until we lost Colby that we all changed.

At the very last minute, I think I've come up with a plan. Madison pulls the door open and invites me in, as if this isn't even my house. She and her mom have made themselves far too comfortable here for my liking. Regardless, I bite my tongue. "How was school today?" I ask, making small talk.

"I missed you in drama class. Where were you? Were you with that girl?"

"Girl?" I play stupid, but she doesn't buy it.

"You know who I'm talking about." Her hands slither up my stomach and she locks her fingers behind my head. I twist my neck, looking to the right and avoiding eye contact, as she tries to kiss me.

"If you're worried about Willa, you have nothing to worry about. She moved."

Her hands unclasp and she turns my head to face her. Her eyes light up. "Yeah, so people are saying. But we both know she's still here."

Pushing her back a few steps, she pouts while I observe her. "What's that supposed to mean?"

Unable to keep her bony fingers off of me, she reclaims my personal space and cups my face in her hands. "You can fool everyone else, but I know she's in Redwood. I also know that you're falling for her." She bops my nose. The same way that I did to her a few days ago.

"It is you, isn't it? You've been harassing her? Leaving her sick voice messages, creeping around her house."

Her forehead wrinkles in confusion, but she's not confused at all. She's playing stupid. "I have no idea what you're talking about."

"Stay away from her, Madison. I'm warning you."

Suddenly looking like she's on the verge of tears, she buries her face in my chest. "Why don't you love me like I love you?"

I attempt to pry her off of me, but she's like a leech. As I push her shoulders back, she tightens her grip on me.

"Given enough time, I think you could love me."

"Well, unlucky for you, we will never get that time." I peel her fingers off of me one by one, squeezing her left hand tightly before doing the same to the right. Once I have them both secured, I give her a push back. "I'll never love you, Madison."

Glowering, she comes charging at me. She plants her fists in my chest over and over again. "I hate you, Lars. I hate you, and I'm gonna make you pay for this." More slaps to the chest as I grab her wrists and she breaks out in an all-out ugly cry. "I hate you." Once I steady her, she stops crying and her mood swings abruptly. "I'm sorry. I don't hate you. I love you." With fluttering eyelids, she smiles while tears still roll down her cheeks from the other side of her personality I just witnessed.

Making an attempt to keep my calm and be as straightforward as possible, I try not to unleash her crazy. "You don't love me. You love the idea of me. Two different things."

"I really do. You're like sunshine behind the clouds and the rainbow after the storm. You're my soulmate, Lars. And soon you'll see it. Soon we'll be together and no one will take you away from me."

This is getting really fucking bad. She's getting worse by the minute. Madison doesn't need to just move out of Redwood, she needs years of psychiatric help.

"Mrs. Rhys said she's announcing the roles for the play after Christmas break. I know we got the parts, even if you did do that awful audition with Willa. I know you're just trying to be nice to her, right?"

"Yeah," I shake my head and roll my eyes, "just trying to be nice. Look I've gotta go."

I go to leave, but she grabs me by the arm. "Stay with me. Please."

Jerking my arm back, I continue on my way and hope like hell she's not following after me. When I hit the staircase, she hollers, "We'll be together soon, Lars. I'll love you forever."

Taking a deep breath, I chalk this up to another wasted trip. It's safe to say that Madison has lost her damn mind. Tommy chose sides. And I have no doubt that Madison is the one stalking Willa. She admitted she knows she's in town. The clock is ticking before she finds out that Willa's staying at Anderson's. Unless she already knows.

 LARS

A s soon as I get back to Anderson's house, I head straight upstairs to check on Willa. It's unfathomable how heavy this girl weighs on my mind these days. I've been convincing myself that I'm not falling for her, but as I second guess every other thing I feel or do, I question my feelings for her, too.

My heart drops when I don't see her, and I immediately think the worst.

She left town already. Someone got to her.

When I hear the shower running, I don't even hesitate to open the door. A cloud of steam hinders my sight of the shower in the large bathroom. I don't even think she heard me come in. I drop my pants to the floor and rip off my shirt. Gripping the curtain, I slide it open just enough to step inside behind Willa.

My hand ghosts her back before I finally touch her wet skin. She jumps. "Oh my God, Lars. What are you doing?" She attempts to hide her breasts with both hands. "Get out!" she shouts.

She continues to rattle off hateful words, but I don't even hear her. All I can focus on is the very noticeable bump that pushes out her belly button. She's not showing much, but she's definitely pregnant. As she spews nonsense, I lay my hand flat against the skin of her stomach. Something ignites inside of me. Something raw and real and unexpected.

"Come downstairs, Lars. Your dad and I have a surprise for you."

Tossing my school bag on my bed, I holler back. "I'm coming." My feet move so fast that I can barely keep up with them as I hurry down the stairs. "Did you get me the PlayStation?" I ask as my heart jogs inside of my chest.

"Even better," Mom says. "Come sit on the couch."

Sitting down, I fold my hands in my lap and wait, expecting them to drop a present in my hand. Mom grabs my hand and places it on her stomach.

"What are you doing?" I snatch my hand away. "Where's my Play-Station."

"You're getting a baby brother, Lars."

"I don't want a baby brother. I want the new PlayStation."

The look on Mom's face is tranquil but her smile quickly fades. "I'll have Dad pick you up the PlayStation tomorrow," she says before walking away.

"You could have at least pretended to be excited," Dad tells me with a gentle swat to the back of my head.

"Pretending means I might actually care. I don't care at all. I don't want a stupid brother. He'll just take everything away from me."

"Lars?" Willa says, snapping me out of my trance. "What's wrong?"

"Hmm?" I look up at her, realizing that I've been staring at my hand on her stomach. "Sorry, I'm just..surprised is all."

"Can we talk about this after I'm done taking a shower. This feels really awkward."

"I wanna help you raise the baby, Willa."

"You don't know what you're saying. Are you drunk?"

Taking her hands in mine, I look deep in her eyes. "I know that I talk in riddles and half of the time I don't make any sense. Hell, half of the time I don't even make sense to myself. But this is my chance to make things right. I wanna help you raise this baby."

Stepping to the side, she pulls the curtain and extends a leg to get out, but I stop her. Pulling her by the waist, our bodies crash together. I don't even give her a chance to react before I guide her mouth to mine.

Just when I think she's going to retreat or slap me, she grabs the sides of my head and forces my mouth harder onto hers. Her tongue sweeps against mine and our teeth clank together.

"You're so fucking beautiful." My fingers weave in her soaked hair.

"And you're a liar."

"No lies. It's all true." I kiss her again. I've kissed Willa before. It was forced but satisfying, nonetheless. This is not forced and it's everything it should have been that first time.

"How can I ever believe anything you say to me after all you've done to me."

Her words throw me off guard because I assumed she forgave me. "I thought we were past that."

"No. You moved past that. I'm still stuck in that day."

"I'm sorry." It's all I can say. "I'm so sorry, Willa."

Her grip slowly works loose before she's no longer touching me. Wiping the water from her face, she looks uneasy. "You have no idea the mess you made for me after that night, Lars. No idea. I'm not sure that I can ever move past that. For that reason, I don't want your help. I just need to leave." She steps out of the shower, and I let her.

Minutes pass, I'm not sure how many, but I'd guess close to thirty before I kill the water and get out. Once I'm dry, I wrap a towel around my waist.

I never expected to develop this attachment to Willa. I don't even think it's just because of the baby. There's this magnetic pull between us, but I'm starting to think that I'm the only one who feels it. She's so timid and fragile and I want to be the one to protect her. I wanna wash her wounds and dry her tears—but how can I do that when I'm the reason for her pain.

She's lying in the bed wrapped in a towel on her side when I walk out of the bathroom. Her sandy brown hair looks as black as coal as it scatters erratically across the white pillowcase. I could leave and give her some space, but I don't. I've made so many reckless choices, and I'm about to make another.

With my towel still intact and beads of water on my chest, I sit down on the edge of the bed. My weight on the mattress alerts her that I'm here and I watch as she tugs the towel tighter to her chest. "You're wasting your time," she says softly.

"Do you remember when Colby died?" I answer for her when she doesn't respond. "Of course you do. You were at the funeral. Your family had just moved to Redwood. I still remember that pink foofy dress you wore while everyone else was dressed in black. You looked like you were at an Easter Sunday service, not a funeral for a four-year-old boy."

"I picked my clothes for that day. Mom tried getting me to change, but I told her pink made people happy."

Smiling at the image in my head of nine-year-old Willa, I make the point of this story. "I'm sure it helped lighten the mood. Anyways, I was sitting there with my chin to my chest because I didn't want anyone to see the lack of emotion on my face. You sat down next to me and asked my name. I'm pretty sure I snubbed you and told you to get lost."

Her body springs up and she looks at me. "I do remember that. You were so mean. I almost forgot about that day. I guess I pushed it in the back of my memories because I always wanted to believe that you weren't really that cruel."

"I was. Still am, I suppose."

"You're really not helping yourself with this conversation. What's your point here?"

"Colby's death isn't what made me so calloused. It was Colby's birth that did that. You see, I was this spoiled fucking brat who got whatever he wanted. Once Colby came along, I wasn't a priority to my parents anymore. Colby died because of me, and for a while, I didn't even care. My mom came running in the house soaking wet with Colby's lifeless body in her arms and I kept playing my video game. Even my friends were freaking out. It wasn't until my life on that game ended that I threw the controller down and pretended to care. I say pretend, because that's what I did. There was a part of me that felt relief. And when I say part of me, I don't mean a small part. My first thought was, *I'll have my parents all to myself again.* Who the fuck thinks like that?"

"You were nine years old, Lars. Don't beat yourself up over it."

"For the last nine years, I've tried to make myself cry because I thought maybe that would mean that I was starting to care that he's gone. I'm not a kid anymore. I should miss him, but all I feel is guilt because I don't."

"Colby was only four. That was only four years that he was part of your life. It's not completely unreasonable to think that you just didn't have enough time to connect with him. You're not a bad person for it, if that's what you're getting at."

Shaking my head, I disagree. "I am. I'm not a good person. I know that. I hate that I've never been able to connect with another human. I think I love my parents, but how do I really know if I do? I've got friends, but I'm not even sure how much I care about them. Never had a real girlfriend that I had feelings for. In reality, I've never really cared about anyone but myself."

Turning her whole body, she crosses her legs and tucks the towel between them to refrain from exposing herself to me.

Her hand grips the corner by her breasts and her hair falls carelessly around her face. Her eyebrows arch. "If that's really how you feel, then what makes you think that raising a baby is what you want? If you think you're incapable of caring for another, why put that pressure on yourself?"

"You've awakened something inside of me that I've been searching for my entire life. This unnerving urge to keep you safe, to protect the baby and your body, your feelings and your heart—to be near you."

Each moment that passes leaves Willa's eyes sadder and sadder. Behind them, I see so much pain and uncertainty. I just bared my soul to her and I'm sitting here with more vulnerability than I ever knew was possible for me to feel. It's a strange feeling, one that I'm not sure I like. Racing heart, sweating palms, and a gazillion possible outcomes racing through my mind.

When she finally opens her mouth to speak, I predict what's coming, so I grab her hand. "Stop questioning everything."

"Don't do this, Lars." Her head shakes back and forth, as she gets to her feet. "Please just leave." She heads for the bathroom door.

"Would you just wait a damn minute?" I jump off the bed and jog over and throw my hand on the door before she closes it. "Why the fuck do you hate me so much, Willa?" I shout, more loudly than I planned to.

She shouts back even louder, her hands flying in the air as she speaks. "Because you ruined my life. You took this sweet and kind girl and shook things up, and in the process, you turned her entire world upside down." Her hands stop wailing in the air as she slaps them to her chest. "Me, Lars. That girl is me. You crushed me and any hopes or dreams that I've ever had." Tears stream down her face and I place a hand on her cheek, sweeping the droplets away with my thumb. "I do hate you. I hate you so damn much." Her fists knock into my chest as she chokes on her tears. "I hate you," she says again and again, before she collapses in my arms.

Knotting her wet hair in my hands, I bring her head to my chest. "I'm so fucked up, Willa." I never imagined that the girl who would ignite a flame in my dark world would be the one standing in front of me. Never felt anything toward her. Wasn't attracted to her. It was nothing for me to steal her innocence and run like hell. I'd credit this all to the baby, but I don't think it's just that, it's the baby's mom that has me in agony these days.

Just when I think that she's settled down and is ready to talk about what's next, she lifts her head and her expression goes awry. Before I can even react, her lips crash into mine.

My towel drops to my ankles and I make no effort to grab it and cover myself back up. The next thing I know, Willa is letting her towel fall on top of mine. Our naked bodies connect as if they were always meant to as our lips stay locked. Her sweetness rolls off her tongue and I can only hope that it takes away some of the bitterness on mine.

All my life, I've thought that I was numb to feeling any sense of compassion, empathy, or remorse. But Willa makes me feel so many different emotions.

Even now, as her back falls to the bed, and I brace myself gently on top of her, the static between us zaps every cell of my body and I need more—I crave more of this new sentiment. Want it to last forever and fear that she'll leave and I'll never experience it again.

Maybe I'm crazy. Maybe this is all an illusion, or even a punishment for my sins. Torture to the third degree. A blood red heart that finally beats with purpose, only to have Willa stomp on it on her way out the door. Leaving me shattered, broken, and lost—even more so than the moment I realized that I needed her in my life.

Or, it's possible that I don't need her at all. It could be an enigma. A hunger to feel like my life has meaning, when in reality, I've lost the emotional war I've waged against myself.

Sliding her hand between us, she grabs a hold of my cock. My eyes question her actions and the wry look she shoots back to me does nothing but leave me more confused. She squeezes so hard that I'm beginning to wonder if her plan is to rip it off and choke me with it. This isn't the innocent virgin I took to bed three months ago. No, this girl has wild eyes that harbor wild dreams.

Stroking with a firm, tight grasp, we stare each other down. She bites the corner of her lip and that movement, paired with her feistiness, only arouses me further. "Fuck me like it's the first time, Lars."

My eyes widen and the shock of her words cannot be contained. I've never heard Willa swear. Who the hell is this girl? "What?" I say, taken aback and almost certain that I must have heard her wrong.

"Did I stutter? Erase the memory of that night. Give me something else to remember you by before I leave."

"But, the baby?" I peer down at her stomach and realize that I was lying on top of her with my full weight. "Shit. Did I hurt you?"

"The baby is fine." She grabs my hand, curling my fingers and placing them at her entrance.

I hesitate, but slide one finger in slowly and she's soaking wet. Her hips vault up to try and gain momentum as she lets out a whimper. "I'm not a virgin, Lars. You don't have to be gentle."

She's right. She's not a virgin, because I took that title from her when I planted my seed in her and knocked her up. *Fuck. Quit it, Lars. She's lying here begging for your cock. Give it to her. Enjoy it.*

Pushing another finger in, I go deeper, feeling her drench

my hand and swell around my fingers. Her right hand grabs my head and pulls my face to hers, kissing me forcefully. My fingers continue to glide in and out of her pussy and my cock aches with need to be inside of her.

As if she reads my mind, she grabs a hold of it again and lines it up where my fingers dip inside her. I pull them out and she uses the pressure from her own body beneath me to swallow up my cock. Damn, she feels so fucking good. As good as that night, maybe even better. Her tight, wet pussy envelops my cock and I can already tell this isn't going to last long.

Trailing my lips across her neck, I kiss my way down, sucking gently at the skin of her collarbone. Her back arches, and she begins rocking beneath me. Breaking the kiss, I watch her as I fuck her.

Her lips press into a thin line and her nostrils flare as she lets out a whimper, but it's not a painful cry; it's all pleasure. She fucking loves this. I invited her into a whole new world when I fucked her three months ago; yet, she's so angry about it. How can anyone be angry about this? Not just the sex, but the attraction between us. It's thick and heavy and impossible to ignore. She feels it, too. I know she does.

"Get behind me," she says.

"You want me to fuck you from behind? But this is only your second time, are you sure?" I'm not sure how it works for girls, but I'd assume that might be too painful or too uncomfortable. Of course, I'm all for it.

"I'd like to try it. I need more. My hormones are out of control right now." She pushes me up and squirms out from beneath me.

Shrugging my shoulders, I succumb to her demands. I've always heard that pregnant women like to fuck like rabbits with all that hormonal shit going on. I guess it's true, after all.

Adjusting herself on the bed, she gets on her knees then

drops forward. The top of her head presses against the mattress with her forearms straight on either side of her.

"God damn," I mutter, as both of my hands sweep across her perfectly round ass that's staring back at me. I slide one finger down her crack then into her pussy. Her want for me drips onto the bed and my cock begins pulsating again. Fucking her with one finger, I watch as it slides in and out before I shove my dick inside of her. Closing my eyes, I draw in a deep breath, holding still before I spill inside of her. I'm not ready yet and if I keep going, I'm done for.

Her ass begins rocking back and forth as she takes control. Faster, deeper, and more determined thrusts vibrate her ass against my pelvis. "Fuck," I bellow. "You're so fucking hot." I slap one hand to her ass cheek and it only arouses her further. We move in unison. Stretching one hand out, I tangle her damp hair in my fingers and lift her head while she fists the sheet on the bed. "You like it rough, don't you?" My words come out gruff and barely recognizable.

"Mmhmm."

The euphoria takes over and I work with my mind and my body at the same time. "I should have known you weren't as timid as you wanted me to believe you were."

She seems to like it because her ass rams back into me, taking every inch of my cock. "You took me for a weak girl and made me ten times stronger, Lars Titan. You did this." Her voice cracks and I can tell she's close to coming.

Dropping her hair onto her back, I grip both sides of her hips aggressively as I ram into her tight pussy. Our bodies shake and shudder at lightning speed before I let out a raspy groan and hold my breath, releasing inside of her. She revels in the pleasure and cries out with muffled moans, and when I feel her walls pulsate and restrict around my cock, I push harder, riding out her orgasm. Once her body relaxes and her arousal pools at her entrance, I retreat, spilling everything onto the bed.

Rolling onto her back, she drops down on the bed and grabs the towel next to her to wipe up. "That was—"

"Amazing?" I finish the sentence for her. "It definitely was."

Biting her cheek, she smirks. "I was going to say unexpected, but amazing works, too."

"You've got a little kink in ya." I tap the tip of her nose. "I like it."

Her cheeks flush and it's cute as hell.

Once I get myself all cleaned up with my towel, I grab hers and toss them in the corner of the room. "I'll go find some new bedding for you." I lean forward and kiss her lips ever so gently. To my surprise, she kisses me back. I'm not sure why it surprises me, but it does.

Once I come back up, I give her one last look, before walking away. When I reach the door, she stops me. "Lars."

I turn around. "Yeah?"

"Nothing's changed. You know that, right?"

A prick in my chest has me feeling lightheaded. Instead of responding, I just leave the room. She needs more time. I get it. I fucked her up three months ago and it's gonna take more than a couple days and some kind gestures to gain her trust. But I will. In time. She brought light into my life and I refuse to let that flame burn out so fast.

I dropped some clean sheets on the bed while Willa was in the bathroom, and decided to give her some space. When I lie down in bed, I stare up at the ceiling and thoughts of her continue to circle through my mind.

She's got a hold on me. I'm falling while she's flying away.

My eyes flutter open to the sound of something, or someone rather, mauling at the bedroom door. "Willa, get up. Our appointment is in two hours and it's a long drive."

Stretching my arms over my head, I let out a yawn. "What time is it?"

"It's time to get up. Let's go."

In a fit, I tear the blankets off of me. It felt like I didn't get any sleep last night. Although my eyes shut as soon as my head hit the pillow. That bed is so comfortable, I could probably sleep my life away in it. It's nothing compared to the five-inch mattress on my twin-size bed at home.

"Are you up?" Lars knocks again.

Raising my voice with each word, I shout, "I'm up. Stop banging on the door." I'm not a morning person, and I'm pretty sure I just made that obvious.

Digging my fingers into my eyeballs, I adjust to the light before I grab Marni's clothes off the dresser. Black leggings and a purple and black Ravens hoodie. I may have decided to borrow just a couple of things. I wouldn't want to embarrass

Lars by going to an appointment with him in a pair of pink pajama pants and a T-shirt.

This appointment is so stupid. Lars knows I'm pregnant; yet, he's making me take a test. He mentioned that I'll get some prenatal blood work and a script for some vitamins, too, which I suppose is a good thing. I'm glad that he worked all that out because I didn't have any intention of seeing a doctor until I was settled in New York.

After I brush my teeth and run a comb through my hair, I head downstairs.

The smell of toast has my mouth watering as I make a beeline for the kitchen. "Mmm, are you cooking?" I hover over Lars while he butters some toast on a napkin.

"Hey, I've got a question?" he says, as he folds a napkin around the toast. "Last night, you said nothing has changed. Do you still mean it?"

"Lars, please don't do this. I don't know how many times I have to tell you that it has to be this way." I feel like a broken record. There is a huge part of me that wants to believe that Lars could be the person I used to think he was, but the memory of unfortunate events he caused are still etched in my heart.

He turns his whole body toward me, like he's been waiting for me to come down here just so he could talk about this. Was he thinking about it all morning? All night?

"I just don't get it, Willa. I was pretty sure all through high school that you had a crush on me and I know that I made some mistakes, but aren't those feelings still in there somewhere?"

Yes. They are. "No." I lie. They are in there, but they've been shoved into the back of the closet and filled with new feelings, such as shame and regret. "When I say that this is for the best, I don't just say it for me and the baby. I'm saying it for you, too. You don't want this life."

Lars snatches up the toast and some bottled waters and begins walking toward the door and it feels as if he's taking a part of me with him. I hate that he still has this effect on me. Even after everything, I'm still so inarguably drawn to him.

"Hurry up, we gotta go," he says with anger in his words as he pulls the door open to the garage. I sure hope that he drops this attitude quickly because the last thing I want is an hour long ride with a grumpy-ass.

"I'm coming." I huff with each step. "Geez, couldn't you have made this appointment in the afternoon?"

"Get used to it, sweetheart. You think babies care if you wanna sleep in?"

He has a point, but still, I find a way to argue it. Snubbing my nose in the air, I smirk. "She'll be on my schedule."

"Keep dreaming. Newborns don't follow a schedule. They wake when they wanna wake, eat when they wanna eat, and shit all day long." Instead of going to his car that's parked in one of Anderson's spaces in the ten-stall garage, he goes to an SUV.

"What are you doing?"

"We can't take my car. It's too well-known around here and you can't be seen."

He has another good point.

"Isn't this like grand theft auto or something?"

Keys clank as they dangle from his hand and he seems to have lightened his mood. "Not when you have these." He pulls open the passenger door and I slide in.

"I'm going to hell." I fuss. "Straight to hell."

"Save me a seat, cuz I'm going with you," Lars says before he closes the door and rounds the SUV to the driver's side. I'm immediately engulfed in the new car scent and the smell of crisp leather. Lars is accustomed to fancy cars and valuable possessions, but I'm sure not.

"I'm sorry," I say out of nowhere. "I'm sorry that I came

along and shook things up for you." Regardless of what Lars did to me, I have a guilty conscience of my own. I'm not as innocent as he thinks I am and the least I can give him is an apology to help ease the weight on my heart. Even if he doesn't know what the apology is for.

"I'm sorry, too."

There's an awkward silence between us and the windows begin fogging up because I'm pretty sure I'm inhaling and exhaling three times the normal breaths.

Taking a bite of my toast, I speak with a full mouth to try and break the ice. "So, how do you know so much about babies?"

"I've been doing some reading. And I had a baby brother who cried and woke me up all hours of the night and bright and early in the morning." He quickly changes the subject. "Take a nap and get comfortable, it's about an hour and a half away."

When he said he'd take me somewhere that no one would recognize me, he wasn't kidding.

Once I finish my toast and wash it down with some water, I rest my cheek in my palm and stare out the window. If someone had told me a year ago that this is what I'd be doing my senior year of high school, I would have picked them up and carried them to church. As much as I hate the pastor, I sure do miss my church family. They're the only real family I have.

Placing a hand on my stomach, I get this warm and fuzzy feeling that ripples through me. Unexpected and totally new. It's this anxious, excited, butterfly feeling. I have a new family now. My baby and I are going to be the best of friends and I'm going to be the best mommy in the world to him or her. I smile as I stare out the window. I may have lost a lot, had a lot stolen from me, but now I have something that is all mine and no one can take it away.

HEATHEN

"What'cha thinking about?" Lars asks. I lift my head with a big smile, but it wears away immediately when I remember what I'm doing to him. Taking his money and running, leaving him with a lifetime of what-ifs.

Pulling out a lie, I rest my head back down. "Just thinking of what themes I want for the baby's room."

"Oh yeah? And what have you come up with? If it's not Baby Yoda, I don't wanna know about it."

"It's *not* Baby Yoda, so I won't bother telling you."

"Humor me with a second choice."

"Bumblebees?" I say it like it's a question. I'm not sure why; it's not like I'm seeking his approval.

"No." He shakes his head. "Monkeys, maybe." He clicks his tongue on the roof of his mouth and tilts his head. "Sloths, possibly. But bumblebees are scary as hell. Got stung by one as a kid and I've hated them ever since."

"Duly noted." I chuckle. "Bumblebees are out."

Who is this guy and what did he do with Lars Titan? And why in the world am I squeezing my thighs together and wanting him to slide his hand between them?

Pulling out my phone, I turn it on and double check that the location is still off. I ignore all the missed calls and messages and begin playing Pet Rescue Saga to try and calm myself down.

My phone begins vibrating and a text comes through. Only, it's an unknown number, but just the brief glimpse of it assures me that it's not Rick or Mom.

"Who's that?" Lars asks, as he peers over and tries to steal a glance at my phone.

"Just Rick again." I lie.

Opening the full length of the text, I begin reading it.

Unknown: Hi Willa. I know I'm the last person you probably expect to text you, but I think we need to talk. Don't fall for Lars' lies. He's fed them to me,

137

too. Buttered me up and made me think that he wanted a future with me. In the end, it was all a game that he was playing with his friends. Can you meet me Saturday night so I can fill you in? I think we can help each other.

I immediately send a reply to the unknown person.

Me: Who is this?

Unknown: Madison Bishop. Lars' stepsister.

My heart drops deep into the pit of my stomach, taking a seat next to the baby. Nausea ensues and I'm not sure how to react. I don't know if she's lying to me or if I really should hear her out. She must know I'm in town still. Why else would she think I could meet up with her?

Me: Ok. Meet me at the power lines and please don't tell anyone I'm coming.

Unknown: I'll be there. I won't tell a soul. You can trust me <3

Clearing the messages immediately, I look at Lars who's side-eyeing me. "Who was that?" he asks again.

"Trent. Told him I moved." I lie again.

"What's he want from you?"

"Just wondering why I wasn't in class today. No big deal."

"You know he's got a crush on you, right?"

"Yeah, I know. But I don't have the same feelings for him."

"How do you know he likes you? Do you two hang out often?"

I can't help but think that he's just the slightest bit jealous and I sort of like it. "A few times."

"You fuck him?"

My hand slaps his shoulder. "Oh my God, Lars. No!"

"Why is that such a ridiculous question? People fuck. It's nothing to be embarrassed about. You fucked me last night," he says it so nonchalantly, like we're discussing a birthday present or something.

"Sex is nice and all, but it's not really something I care to discuss." I can feel my cheeks flush with heat and I turn back toward the window before he notices it and points it out. Because that's totally something he would do.

"So, you didn't fuck him. Did you kiss him?"

Pinching my eyes shut, I try to ignore the questions. Because, yes, I did kiss Trent once. But Lars doesn't need to know that. It was just a kiss.

"Well. Did ya?"

"Yes." I spit out and clap my hands to my legs. "Yes, I kissed him once."

When he looks at me, it feels like he's suddenly lost all respect for me. Like the sweet, quiet girl has no life. I didn't actually have much of a life, but Trent and I kissed a week before school started back up and I found out I was pregnant. We weren't together, but I'd given up on Lars and was ready to try dating someone in hopes of finding some sort of happiness. I'd never had a boyfriend before and Trent was sweet. He was also clingy, whiny, and needy, but he was nice to me.

Then Lars joined drama class and as much as I hated him then, any possibility of Trent and I being together quickly diminished. My heart was suddenly Lars' again. I didn't know it at the time, and I'm still fighting it, but it's true. He has it and he probably always will.

"How was it?" He eggs me on, not letting this go.

Biting back a smile, I avoid looking at him. "I'm done talking about this."

The rest of the ride is quiet as I stare out the window, lost in thought. My mind wanders everywhere from Mom leaving to the scars Rick left behind, all the way to leaving Lars and going to New York. The idea of never seeing him again punches at my gut.

Lars maneuvers the ginormous SUV between two closely parked cars then shifts the vehicle into park. "Ready for this?"

I stuff my phone into the front pocket of the hoodie I'm wearing and unbuckle my seatbelt. "Yep. Time to prove you wrong."

"Me wanting this doesn't mean that I think you're lying. It's just a lot of money to hand over when a stick test could have been wrong."

"Doesn't matter. We're here now so let's do it. It's no big deal." I open the door and step outside before he does. Sticking my hands in my pocket, I meet him in front of the vehicle. It feels so strange being out in public like this with Lars. People pass by us and don't even question his reasoning for being with me.

Do they think I'm his girlfriend? Sister maybe? No one knows me or my past, and it's refreshing to hold my head high without judgment. No one knows about the video, my social status, my lack of friends, or even my Christianity.

When we go inside, Lars checks us in, and I feel like a child having him handle the appointment for me. Then again, he's the one who demanded it, so he should be the one putting forth the effort.

After we're checked in, Lars shuffles through an old magazine and it's pretty much what you'd expect to see in a movie. Teenage girl and teenage boy sitting at a health clinic two hours away, waiting to get a pregnancy test. I sit with my hands in my lap, twiddling my thumbs and tapping my foot on the two-toned plank floor. There is one lady, sitting across from me, with her hand on her bulging stomach. She has to be at least seven or eight months pregnant. She looks worn out and in dire need of a nap as her toddler-aged son drives a truck across her tennis shoes.

He makes a car sound as he goes across, then back. "Vroom. Vroom. Vroom."

Lars looks at me with a grin. "You ready for that?" His eyes shuffle to the boy.

Biting my lip, I snicker, "Ready or not."

"Willa?" The nurse calls from the open door. She's wearing a pair of black scrubs and her top has bumblebees on it. I look at Lars and suppress a laugh. When he smiles back, I know that he read my mind. "How are you two doing today?" she asks, ever so sweetly.

"Wonderful. Thank you." I follow behind her and Lars follows behind me. I jump when he pokes a finger into my side and makes a buzzing sound. Swatting behind me, as I continue to walk, I miss him. When I glance over my shoulder, his hands are in his pockets and my heart doubles in size.

Being in this situation feels far too intimate for us. What if they have me undress for a pap smear? My heart begins to beat rapidly, hammering against my breastbone. What if they do a breast exam? Suddenly, this isn't feeling like no big deal.

The nurse gestures Lars into an open room and takes me around the corner to get my weight and vitals. "Step on."

Once my weight is checked, she cuffs my arm and sticks a pulse ox on my finger. "Blood pressure is slightly low but that's pretty normal. Pulse is great. Now, before we re-enter the room, I have to ask, have you been a victim of sexual abuse?"

My eyes widen and my heart pretty much stops. I sure am glad she checked my blood pressure and pulse before asking this question. "No." I lie.

"And what about domestic abuse?"

"No." I lie, again.

"Great. Follow me to the bathroom and I'll need you to pee in this cup. Once you're done, please head back to the room and I'll join you shortly."

"There won't be any exams will there?"

"Nope. Just the test and if it's positive, we'll do a quick blood draw in the lab and then you'll be done." She points to the bathroom.

"Thank you."

I do my business, scribble my name on the cup and stick it in the cute little door in the bathroom then head to the room.

Lars is slouched back in a chair with his legs spread and his face in his phone. I'm pretty sure he didn't even hear me come in until my shoes squeak against the floor. His head lifts. "All good?"

I hop on the bed, wrinkling the paper underneath my butt. "Now we wait."

The room is full of posters in front of a giant rainbow painted on the wall. One talks about the different trimesters, another talks about safe sleeping for the baby, there's one with the different types of STDs, and a domestic violence helpline number.

I almost called one of those numbers once. Sometimes, I wish I had.

The door opens and the nurse steps inside, shutting it behind her. "Your test confirms that you are in fact pregnant. Congratulations."

I'm tempted to stick my tongue out at Lars, but I refrain from the childish act.

"Here is a lab slip." She hands me a piece of paper. "The lab is through the main entrance at the end of a hallway. We'll call the number on file when the results are ready. Where would you like the prescription for your vitamins called in?"

Without even lifting his head from his phone, Lars answers, "Wherever's closest."

The nurse scribbles something on a piece of paper then hands it to me. "This is the address for the nearest pharmacy. Give them about twenty-minutes. Congrats, again," she says before leaving.

Once she's out the door, I do it. Crinkling my nose, I stick my tongue out at him. Call me childish, but he deserves it.

His pearly white teeth flash a smile and he hooks an arm

around my neck. "Come on, let's go get that needle stuck in your arm so they can drain your blood."

"Eww. That's so gross."

"You think that's bad. Wait until you push that baby out of you. I saw a video—"

I hold my hand up to stop him. "Don't go there. I prefer to go in blind." I still can't believe he's been researching pregnancy.

Snapping out of those thoughts, I remind myself why I'm doing this. It's because of what he did. But, the more time I spend with him, the memories and pain I endured begin to fade and are getting replaced by the new ones we are making. Most of the time, I completely forget. I guess part of me is beginning to forgive him, but it still doesn't change anything. I still have to go. No matter how much it's going to hurt when I do.

L ars has been gone ever since we got back from the appointment. Said he had to deal with some stuff for his dad and then he had class. Christmas break starts soon, so today is his last day at the school. The realization that I'll be spending the holidays alone leaves an unexpected ache in my chest.

Lying with my back on the bed, I start missing him. Wishing he was here. I'm probably just craving the company because I've been stuck in this house.

I've been bored out of my ever-loving mind. I've eaten my weight in food, watched three episodes of Bridgerton and took an hour-long shower.

Bending my legs while I lie there on my back in a pair of shorts and a T-shirt, an image of Lars in the shower yesterday flashes in my mind. A body that good has no business pressing against a body like mine. Lars is sculpted to perfection. He belongs with someone who matches his physical appeal, certainly not a plain-Jane like me.

If it weren't for the baby, he would have never given me a second look, aside from the night he won the bet. There's no way that Lars would ever fall in love with someone like me and I'm kidding myself to think he would. He's been good to me. But, it's only because he feels like he has to be. And I'm here. I'm available and turn to mush every time he looks at me. I can hate him one second and then he can walk in the room and my heart jumps out of my chest and into his hands.

I'm pathetic because I'll probably never stop loving him. Even years from now when I see his engagement announcement in the paper with some girl who comes from the same side of the tracks, I'll still love him.

My hand slides down my chest to my stomach, pulling my shirt up, I continue to caress myself, sliding my hand down my shorts. After so long of being at the mercy of another man, it's enlightening to have control over myself. Being able to do what I want, when I want. No pressure. No tears. No force. I'm in control of my body, and my future.

A vivid picture of Lars paints itself in the forefront of my mind. Beads of water rolling down his rigid, bare chest. His engorged cock digging into my hip while his strong hands touch me.

My eyes close as I bite my lip and rub circles around my throbbing clit. God, how I wish it was Lars touching me like this. The stubble of his chin grating against me while his tongue slides in and out, licking up my arousal. My fingers locked in his hair as I ride his face.

I dip two fingers inside of me and use my other hand to rub violently against my clit. Bucking my hips up with my eyes pinched shut, I pretend he's here. Releasing a short-winded moan, I push my fingers in deeper, but the angle makes it hard to get what I really want out of this. I want him inside of me. His full girth filling me up while I come around his cock. I wanna make him come with my tight pussy just to have the satisfaction of knowing that I gave him the orgasm. One he'll never forget.

Feeling myself get wetter by the second, I move faster and push my fingers in as far as I can, while my husky breaths become labored and unfulfilled.

The door swings open and I quickly pull my hand out of my pants. "Lars," I spit out as I straighten my shirt and sit up. My cheeks flush and humiliation takes over my entire body. This can't be happening right now.

"What are *you* doing?" He smirks. A devious one that has my stomach twisting in knots.

He knows. He doesn't even have to say it. The look on his face says it all. Not to mention his instant hard-on. Unless...unless he was out there listening this entire time. Oh my god! My feet hit the floor and I bolt toward the bathroom, fighting to avoid eye contact. "Just getting up to go to the bathroom."

He grabs a hold of my arm and stops me. "It's nothing to be embarrassed about, Willa."

Oh my god, he does know.

But there is no way I'll admit it. "I don't know what you're talking about." My eyes are locked on the bathroom door; I need to get in there before my jelly legs give out and I make an even bigger fool of myself.

Pulling me close, his lips trail down my neck as goosebumps cascade down my back. Slow and steady until they cover every inch of my body. "I told you before, I think it's sexy as hell."

Feeling my cheeks heat like a raging fire, my embarrassment is front and center for him to see.

Lars takes both of my hands and locks them behind my back as we mirror one another. He presses his mouth to my collarbone and sucks the skin between his teeth. "If you need a hand, I'm happy to help."

Warmth radiates through me as my thighs begin to tremble. Weak and off-balance, my self-control flies into the bathroom without me. He drops my hands from behind my back and my head tilts instinctively as he pushes the sleeve of my shirt down my shoulder, his lips following suit.

My eyes almost roll into the back of my head when his fingers creep underneath my shirt then trail the hem of my shorts. I can feel my arousal, from my earlier machinations, and my want for him dampening my panties while my body begs for him to tear them off with his teeth. I'm weak and in dire need of him to get me off.

When his hand descends farther into my shorts, I part my legs with ease.

"You're drenched, babe. I think we need to do something about that." He begins kneading my nub and electricity sparks inside me, sending currents through my entire body.

Giving into temptation, I lift my arms that were draped at my side and place my hands on his shoulders, unsure what to do with them. Still reeling from embarrassment that he caught me fingering myself.

With his hand shoved down my shorts and his chin resting on my shoulder while he kisses my neck, Lars takes my hand off his shoulder and brings it between us, placing it on the bulge in his joggers. My heart beats at warp speed inside my chest and I hate that I'm so awkward. I give it a couple squeezes and when I feel it twitch, I stop, thinking I squeezed too hard. "Sorry."

He lifts his head from my shoulder and looks into my eyes and I wanna tell him to put his head back down so he doesn't look at me. "For what?"

"Did that hurt?"

He laughs. "Trust me, nothing you do can hurt me. I don't even think you're capable."

Oh, you have no idea.

Just as the thought leaves my mind, his lips crash into mine and it's everything. God, he tastes as good as he looks. Like berries and mint. And his scent, Lord help me. I feel tipsy and off-balance from that alone. It's like my body takes over and my mind doesn't allow me to think anymore as the kiss intensifies. His tongue sweeps around my mouth as if it's searching for something, and I'm not sure what has possessed me, but I do the same to him.

My hands end up on the back of his head as I pull him closer, never wanting him to break free. If I could capture this moment and keep it forever, I would.

My feet begin moving in sync with his as he takes a few steps backwards, our mouths never parting.

Does he feel what I feel? He has to. That crazy pressure inside my chest. Butterflies. Fireworks. Fear. Love. Hate. It's like every emotion in existence is spilling into this kiss. Our steps stop when the back of his legs hit the bed. He lowers his back down, slowly taking me with him.

With my legs shouldering his body, his erection presses through the fabric of his pants right in front of where I sit on top of him. I feel like I'm on display and I should feel uncomfortable, but I don't.

My forearms rest around his head and in a matter of seconds, our kiss intensifies, giving me the urge to tear into him. Gripping the pillow behind him, I begin rocking myself against his erection.

"Fuck, Willa. What have you done to me?" he grumbles into my mouth.

I can feel myself smile in response. I'm doing this to him. He wants me. Not because of the baby. Not because of his guilt. I gave him this hard-on.

Feeling brave, I stretch my hand down between us and begin rubbing him. He must take it as an invitation, which it most definitely was, because the next thing I know, he springs it free and I'm stroking his length.

Something unexpected and unwanted rolls through me and

my strokes slow. It's hard to breathe and a distaste curdles inside my stomach.

His head lifts off the mattress. "What's wrong?"

"Nothing. It's nothing."

It's something. I didn't feel it in the shower or when we had sex last time. But harrowing thoughts flood through my mind and I wanna scream at them to go away. To leave and never come back. I want to unfeel Rick. Untaste his disgusting cum in my mouth. I can feel the burn of his touch on my throat. His words echoing in my ears. *Whore. Slut. Sinner.*

I want to forget it all. Why am I thinking about this? Why is this happening to me?

"Willa?" Lars says with sheer concern. "Are you ok?"

I snap out of it and wonder how long I was lost. Jumping up quickly, I flee to the bathroom. Slamming the door shut and clicking the lock. With my back pressed to the door, I slide down slowly until my butt hits the floor. My fingers wrap around my neck as I try to wipe away Rick's imprints.

Lars knocks on the door. "Hey. What happened?"

I open my mouth to speak but nothing comes out.

He knocks again. "Open the door so we can talk."

"I..I just need a minute."

God, I'm such an idiot to think that leaving would make me forget. He's everywhere. He's planted himself in my head and he'll always be there.

The handle of the door begins twisting as he tries to open it and something shifts inside of me. I get on my hands and knees and begin crawling away from the door. Turning around, I sit down against the wall underneath a window. "Go away," I shout with my eyes locked on the handle. It keeps moving. Pinching my eyes shut, I pray under my breath. "The Lord is my light and my salvation—whom shall I fear? The Lord is the stronghold of my life—of whom shall I be afraid?"

"Willa. Open the door."

I repeat the prayer silently. *The Lord is my light and my salvation—whom shall I fear? The Lord is the stronghold of my life—of whom shall I be afraid?* When he doesn't go away, I scream, "Go away!" My fingers dig into the floor at my sides. My nails dragging across it as I try to get some sort of grip. On life. On myself.

It goes quiet.

Too quiet.

"Rick?" I say out loud.

When he doesn't respond, my body stills as I try to listen for an inkling that he's trying to trick me again.

The door handle begins moving again and I'm quickly on my feet. I have to get out of here. I turn around and push the blinds up on the window then unlatch the lock. I hear the doorknob drop, and my heart goes right along with it. Shoving the window up, I push out the screen and begin climbing up onto the sill.

"Willa, what the hell are you doing?" His heavy footsteps come toward me.

"Go away!" I fling one leg over, but I'm not fast enough. He grabs me. Only, it's not Rick.

"Lars?" My voice comes out confused and like that of a child. He takes me by the waist and he sets me down on my feet, but his hands never leave my sides.

His eyebrows dip. His concern apparent. "I have no idea what's going on, but we're at least thirty feet from the ground up here and if I'd have been two seconds later—" His words trail off as he sweeps the hair off his forehead.

He doesn't have to finish, though. I know what he was going to say. I want to tell him that I wouldn't have jumped, but would I have? My entire body feels like it's shaking. "I don't know what I was doing."

Lars takes my hand in his and leads me out of the bathroom. When he pulls back the blanket on the bed, I lie down.

Feeling myself sink into the mattress as I put together the puzzle in my head. I remember running into the bathroom. I sat on the floor by the door, and then I heard Rick.

Only, it wasn't Rick. My mind was playing tricks on me. It was Lars the entire time. Am I losing my mind?

As I lie there on my side, I watch Lars, thinking he's going to leave, so I can get some rest. I'm grateful that he didn't poke and prod, although there is no way he's going to let this go. If anyone did what I just did, I'd probably assume they needed to be committed. Now more than ever, I have to get out of this town. Maybe the miles between here and there will make me forget.

When the light goes out, I tug the blanket up over my shoulder. There is still a glimmer of light from the bathroom, which is good. I hate the pitch-black. But, Lars doesn't open the door to leave. He walks toward me and lifts the corner of the blanket, sliding his body underneath it.

"We'll talk tomorrow, ok?"

I'm not sure that he can see me, but I nod my head just so we can put this to rest for the night. Flipping over to my other side, I face the wall and close my eyes, hoping to chase away this night and go to a happy place in my dreams.

The mattress begins to shift and I feel his body pressed against mine. One arm wraps around me, and suddenly, I'm there. I'm still awake, but I found my happy place.

"I'm not fucking helping you assholes. I don't care how much you try to convince me to come back. These games aren't fun anymore. Figure this shit out with Josh, or don't. Either way, I'm done." I slam the phone down on the counter.

Willa comes walking in with her hair bunched in a ponytail on the top of her head and she looks much better than she did before she fell asleep last night. At some point, we have to talk about what happened, but I'm giving it some time and hoping to make her smile today.

"How about if we do something fun today?"

Setting the glass down, she looks at me with her fluffy black brows pinched together. "Really? Like what? Board games and a movie? Oooh, ice cream. With a huge fudge brownie under it. That sounds like heaven."

My head shakes. "Nope. Something better. Pull your hood up, baby. We're going out." I snatch the keys off the counter and begin to arm the security system on my phone.

"Are you sure? What if someone sees us? We're so close to the end, why risk it?"

"Don't worry. I'll make sure you're hidden. We're taking

the backroads out of town and going someplace where no one knows who we are."

She seems reluctant to get excited, but once she sees what we're doing, I think her mood will change.

We get in the same vehicle we took yesterday and I make a mental note to fill the tank up before Anderson returns. "Buckle up and take a nap. We'll be there in about an hour." I toss a bag of cookies at her that I found in the cupboard. "In case you and the baby get hungry."

"Gee, thanks for the breakfast." She grimaces.

"Hey, it's something. Could have let you starve." I tease. "We'll get food later."

"Thank you." She holds up the bag. "This is actually really nice of you. I'm surprised."

"Surprised that I can be nice?"

"Well, yeah. You keep surprising me and I'm not sure what to think of it."

I flick the blinker at the four-way and take a left, heading out of town. "Are you thinking you might change your mind? Let me come with you? I'll give you cookies every day if it makes you happy."

Pulling her phone out, she holds back whatever she's thinking. She doesn't have to say anything. I already know it would be along the lines of, *please stop* or *don't do this.*

"Anyone tried contacting you yet?"

"Yeah, they've called and texted, but I'm not ready to read any of it. I've turned off my location, but I'm still too nervous to keep my phone on for long periods of time."

"Once you're out of town, you should probably get a new one with a new number." I wanna tell her to text me the new number, but she'll likely argue it and this will turn into a big thing that will ruin the day. I never thought that I'd be the one walking on eggshells here.

"Oh my god." She gasps, clapping a hand over her mouth.

"Pull over, Lars. Pull over right now." My foot slams on the brake in the middle of the road and I stretch my neck over to look at her phone. Her finger holds down the volume button, and the voice of a news anchor fills the empty space of the vehicle.

"Willa Jean Mack has been reported missing from the small town of Redwood. She was last seen by her stepfather, Pastor Rick Jeffries. Rick begins talking with just a headshot of him showing on the video. *"Willa is a good girl. Wherever she is, I don't believe she left on her own free will."* The news anchor appears again. *"Friends and family of Willa are very concerned that her disappearance is in some way connected to that of Josh Moran, who went missing only three months ago. Josh's car was pulled from Lake Ruin three weeks ago, but his whereabouts are still unknown."*

Willa and I look at each other when another familiar face shows on the video. "Is that Vi?" I ask, trying to get a better view.

"Shh. I need to hear this."

I can see Willa's heart palpitating through the thick fabric of her hoodie and while she should have expected this kind of public attention, I don't think she did.

Vi continues with her statement, *"It wouldn't surprise me if Willa and Josh just ran away together. If I had to guess, he made it look like he was a victim by pushing his car off the cliff and he was buying time so that him and Willa could run away together. It's not really my place to say this, but Willa is pregnant. Three months pregnant to be exact, and it's possible that the baby is Josh's. It wasn't until shortly after Josh left that Willa came to me and asked me to buy her a pregnancy test. I just hope that wherever they are, they are safe and the baby is safe."*

"What the actual fuck," I spit out. It's all I can say. I'm speechless. I feel like I was just slapped in the face with a gust of wind. A tornado swirls around inside my head while I try to grasp any sort of thought or reaction. "Did you and Josh—" I can't even say it. I shift into drive and peel out on the paved

HEATHEN

road. The tires spin relentlessly until they gain traction and a trail of smoke spits up behind us. Whipping the SUV around, I do a U-turn in the middle of the road.

"Lars, she's lying. I swear to God, she's lying." She cries out. "She's grasping for straws because her brother is missing. I hardly even knew Josh."

"What was all this for? Money? You wanted my money so you could leave town and raise your and Josh's baby?"

"It's not Josh's baby." She screams so loud that it echoes through my brain. Rattling shit up that was just starting to settle.

I need to get the fuck out of this vehicle. I feel like I'm suffocating in here. Willa and Josh? No fucking way. Vi has to be making this shit up. Like Willa said, she's grasping at straws. I should believe Willa over her. Willa has no reason to lie to me. Vi, on the other hand, is grieving the loss of her brother and hoping he's out there somewhere, alive. She has no idea that he's dead.

It's apparent in her behavior lately that Vi is having a hard time dealing with her brother's disappearance. She's done a one-eighty from a quiet girl to this goth chick who dyed her hair black and pierced her face.

Pulling down the two-track, I stop and shift into park then jump out and slam the door shut.

It's not long before Willa's door opens and closes. Dirt kicks up from my feet as I pace back and forth on the side of the SUV. "Lars, don't listen to her. She's not thinking clearly. Yes, she bought me the test. Yes, we sat together at lunch and we've talked, but I've never once even mentioned her brother during that time and neither did she. She probably just assumes because of the timing."

I throw my arms in the air. "Well, the whole world knows you're pregnant now, so I'm sure they'll be doing the math and making other guesses soon."

RACHEL LEIGH

"Ok." Her shoulders shrug. "Let them. It doesn't matter because I'm leaving."

I wasn't planning to tell Willa about the paternity test, but it's already done so no matter what the result is, I'll know soon. "The truth will come out. Don't you worry about that," I say, before pulling the handle of the door and getting back in.

Her body slides between the door and the seat, stopping me from closing it. "What's that supposed to mean?"

"It means that in about forty-eight hours, I'll know for sure if it's my baby. That blood draw you did was also a paternity test."

With pinched eyebrows, she takes a step back. "No?" she says the word like it's a question. "It was just early pregnancy blood work."

"That's what I told you. In case you've forgotten, my family has pull. One call and a stack of cash and our DNA was ran."

"You can't do that. That's illegal. You wouldn't do that." Her head shakes like not believing it might make it true.

"You obviously don't know me at all, Willa. Now get in, unless you wanna walk."

Three seconds later, she's back inside, and we continue to drive in complete silence. Willa stares out the window while I keep my eyes on the road.

"It's not your baby."

I look over and question what she just said. "What?"

"It's not Josh's. But it's not yours either."

Not mine?

It's not my baby?

She doesn't even look at me. She's too much of a coward. She didn't grow a backbone. She just learned how to manipulate.

I should feel a sense of relief. I should be happy. So why do I feel like I was just kicked in the stomach? Like I just lost

156

something that wasn't mine to begin with. Why do I feel like Colby is dying all over again?

At least I feel. It's a start.

I don't even raise my voice. "It was all a lie? All of it. Just a lie. Who the hell are you?"

"Who am I?" she shouts. "I'm the remnants of a winning bet. That's who I am." She continues, raising her voice with each word, "I'm the girl who was a stepping stool for everyone at Redwood High. The girl in the back row of the choir who was only up there to begin with because her stepdad was the boss." She stops shouting and looks back out the window. "I'm the girl who was called a slut because a video of my most vulnerable moment in existence went viral. Once I saw how you treated Trent in class, I knew exactly what I had to do. "

I catch a glimpse of her out of the corner of my eye and watch as a stray tear slides down her cheek. *Don't let it fool you, she's just as bad as you are, Lars.*

We pull up to Anderson's house and I'm still at a rolling stop when Willa jumps out of the SUV. She slams the door shut and runs toward the house. I sit there watching her, wondering how I ever fell for her bullshit sob story. My right foot digs into the brake so hard that I can feel it grind against the floorboard. *I'm such an idiot.*

Leaving this house today, I thought I was having a baby with a girl that I was pretty sure I could fall in love with if I was given the chance. I was planning to take her to a baby boutique in the city today. Wanted to buy her a car and fill it up with everything she needed for the baby. Once I got the results, I was gonna go finalize everything at the bank and set up an account for her that I could transfer money into when she needed it. I was prepared to take care of them, forever.

Now we're back and I've lost the baby, and I've lost Willa.

My palms slam on the steering wheel. "Fuck!" I shout. "Fuck. Fuck. Fuck." Slamming the gear into reverse, I back up and then pull forward into the garage, parking the SUV, just as it was before I took it.

My feet hit the pavement of the garage and I go inside with a heavy heart and an unclear head. As soon as the door shuts, I hear her. Whimpering, sniffling, and panting from the next room over. With light steps, I creep into the living room where Willa is sitting with her knees to her chest and her arms hugging her legs. She rocks slowly back and forth while she sobs with her forehead pressed to her knees.

Weightlessly, in an attempt not to startle her, I walk over to her. She doesn't lift her head, but she knows I'm here.

"The night the video surfaced, Rick raped me."

What did she just say?

I freeze. Unable to move. My heart drops deep into the pit of my stomach and I'm not sure that it's coming back up. I don't say anything. Wouldn't even know what to say.

"Every chance he got, he'd physically and verbally abuse me because of it." Her head lifts and her waterlogged eyes look back at me. "It's Rick's baby."

Drawing in a deep, yet unsatisfying breath, I close my eyes. "Shit," I mutter under my breath.

"Yeah. Shit is right. Now do you understand why I need to leave?"

Pressing my fingertips into my eyeballs, I rub aggressively as I try to comprehend what the hell I just heard. "He fucking raped you?" I deadpan.

She nods her head as tears slide onto the white sofa.

"He fucking raped you?" I say again, only louder. "Fuck." I scream.

My body turns around and I have no control over my feet as they take me out the door to the garage where my car is parked. My mind is in a constant state of fog.

"Lars. Stop!" Willa yells as she chases after me. "Stop! Don't do anything stupid. You'll make it worse. Please, I'm begging you." She sobs uncontrollably. The rest of it's a haze. I have no idea what she's saying as I get in the car, her words become muffled and strained. As soon as the garage opens up, I pull out, and this time, I'm out for blood.

WHAT I ONCE LOOKED AT as a home full of love, stands there as a broken house with rusted gutters, a cracked window, and cement slab steps that lead to walls full of secrets, lies, and abuse. Pastor Jeffries' white pickup truck sits out front, so I know he's here.

Ripping open the metal screen door, I turn the handle to the main door and push it open. His back is to me as he sits in a recliner with a newspaper stretched out in front of him.

Snapping his head around, he stands up, letting the paper fall to the ground. Long strides on both our parts bring us face to face. "I thought I told you to—"

One punch. Straight to his fucking nose.

"You raped her, you son of a bitch. You hit her and you raped her."

His hands cup his face and his eyes widen in fear. "Lars, let's talk about this."

Another punch. Same spot. Only this time, I hear a satisfying crack.

"I'm calling the—"

Curling my arm, I drive an uppercut into his stomach, feeling the bone of his rib against my knuckle. He balls over and drops to his knees and I use it to my advantage. Giving his head a push, I knock him down onto his back.

His cries ring louder as I kick him repeatedly in the head. One kick after another, assaulting his face with the toe of my boot. "You sick motherfucker," I scream at the top of my lungs. "Even God can't save you from what I'm about to do to you." I lose complete control of my mind and body. Adrenaline takes over and my leg lifts, ready to stomp on his face and end this madness once and for all. Squishing his face so hard that his brains squirt out of his eyes. He'll never be able to touch her again.

But a hand hits my shoulder. My body stiffens. Thoughts of a life in prison for attempted murder run rampant through my mind. Is it worth it? Yes. If it meant that Willa would be safe from this sick fuck forever. I turn, expecting to see a police officer, but instead, I see Zed standing there.

"No more. I have plans for him," he says with a calm and collected voice. It's almost like I'm looking at Zed from a year ago. A guy who was still an asshole, but someone I called a friend. I haven't seen this version of him in a while. Didn't think I'd see him ever again.

"You don't understand."

"I understand more than you think. If you want this to end, go to Talon's and lay low for the next forty-eight hours. Make some calls and help Talon invite everyone to his annual Ring in Christmas Break party."

Looking like him, like he's the complete dumbass that he is, I disagree. "We're not having a fucking party with all this shit going on."

"Yes, we are," he says sternly. "We need to carry on as usual. If we don't have the party, it could raise suspicion." He turns around and walks toward the door. "Come on, let's get the hell out of here before someone calls the cops."

In a state of confusion, I walk with him, but give Pastor Jeffries one last look. He's conscious now. His eyes look back at me and it takes all my willpower not to go back and end him. The screen door slams shut behind us and everything feels so surreal.

"That bitch of a sister of yours is stirring trouble. You ready to get your revenge and silence her once and for all?"

"Madison is a big inconvenience right now, but she's the least of my concerns. What do you have planned?"

"I'm handling things."

Leaning away, I look at him. "What do you mean you're *handling things?*" Zed is like a fucking reaper who holds all our secrets and watches from afar. He's constantly plotting and planning and comes out of nowhere. He never handles anything lightly and with Willa involved, questions will be asked.

Without a clue what he has up his sleeve, I nod in agreement. Madison is the least of my concerns right now, but she is a problem. "Stay away from Willa," I tell him with stern eyes and my fists at my side.

"Willa will be fine. You gotta trust me on this one." Stopping at my car, his body shifts to face me. "We good?" He holds up a fist.

I'm hesitant to trust Zed with my lunch money, let alone information that could destroy my life, but I knock my knuckles to his. "Yeah, we're good." I sure as fuck hope I don't live to regret this. I feel like I just made a deal with the devil. But what else could I possibly lose?

It's been twenty-four hours since my life unraveled. I haven't left this bed. I've just wanted to sleep it all away before I completely fall apart. The possibility that Mom heard the local news has crossed my mind. Thought maybe she'd return to Redwood in a panic and try and find me. She hasn't even tried to call, meaning she didn't hear or she doesn't care.

People will tell you that they have your back in good times and bad, but I've learned that people will drop me faster than they pick me up. No one cares. Not mom. Not Vi. Especially not Lars.

The entire town is probably rallying around Rick right now while he feeds them a sob story and plays the loving stepdad. Days and nights will pass by and no one will ever know who he really is. He'll take the bullets thrown at everyone, tell them God is their shield, but they'll never know he's the one who's been holding the gun the entire time.

It doesn't matter. I can handle the demons in my head as long as I never have to see Rick again.

Lars hasn't even called. I'm pretty sure he's given up on me, and why wouldn't he? I've been lying to him. I was furious with Lars for so long. If it weren't for what he did to me, Rick may have never started lashing out and staking claim in my body. This was the perfect plan to give Lars a taste of his own medicine while getting the money I needed to leave. The thing with perfect plans is, they usually fall completely apart before they come together.

Holding down the power button, I turn my phone back on. Mentally prepared for what's waiting for me, but also prepared to ignore it all. I'm sure the entire town is talking. Some worried. Some making their own assumptions, much like Vi did. Ugh, Vi! I'm so angry with her. I cannot believe she did this. Everything was going perfectly until she made that comment on national television. I'm not sure if she's upset because I haven't returned her calls, or if she truly thinks that I'm off somewhere with her brother.

Maybe it was Vi who has been stalking me. It would make sense because she knew about the pregnancy. Maybe she really does think I know where her brother is and she's been trying to get me to break.

Regardless, I've spent my entire life ignoring snide remarks from others; I have no problem doing it now. The one and only person whose opinion matters to me probably hates my guts now.

Unfortunately, he's probably going to hate me more after what I'm about to do.

Me: Can you still meet tonight?

Madison said she thinks we could help each other. For whatever reason, she has a vendetta against Lars and she's my only shot at getting him to give me the money so I can leave. There's a good chance that after the news interview, she's changed her mind, and if that's the case, I'm royally screwed. Desperate times call for desperate measures. Even if I'm doubting what I'm about to do, I have to try and get some leverage over Lars so I can take back the upper hand.

Madison: Yes, one hour. It will be dark by then. And Willa, it's all going to be ok.

My back drops back into bed and I breathe a sigh of relief.

One hour until my future is decided.

THE MINUTES FEEL like hours as I drive through town. I'm well-hidden and wearing a pair of black sweatpants and a black sweatshirt with the hood pulled up so I know that I'm inconspicuous. Yet, it still feels like someone is watching me.

I took the same vehicle that Lars has been using—the big black SUV with the tinted windows. Before I left, I looked up at the cameras and wondered if Lars was watching me. Then I remembered that I'm probably scum on the bottom of his shoe and shook that thought away quickly. It was all for the baby. As much I wanted to believe that he reciprocated my feelings, he didn't. Everything I felt was built on a lie. One thing I did learn is that he's going to be a good daddy one day and the mom to his child is going to feel so much love and protection from him. I felt protected. I felt adored and important.

Brushing away a tear, I say goodbye to this messy chapter of my life. The next one is going to be bumpy, but it's necessary to get to the end.

The SUV rocks as I creep slowly down the beaten path to the power lines. Panic ensues when the possibility of someone else accompanying Madison becomes a reality. No one knows I'm in town still and if anyone else finds out, Rick could find out. He could claim I'm emotionally unstable. Have me committed—or worse.

Headlines shine in front of me and I'm relieved when I see only Madison leaning against the door of a vehicle that matches the one I'm driving. That's not her car, but it's possible that she didn't want to risk driving it down this trail.

My anxiety hits an all-time high and I have to calm myself down before I get out. Feeling like I'm on the verge of a full-blown ugly cry, I pull myself together. I have to because there is so much at stake.

Take a deep breath, hold your head high, and do this.

Stepping outside feels like stepping into quicksand. A restless gnaw at my chest has alarms going off in my head.

"You made it. Nice ride." Madison shuffles to my side with a smile on her face. I hate that she's always so happy. I hate that she has reasons to be happy. Envy is a deadly sin, but with many other sins, it's crept into my soul and made a home there. Three months of pure hell will cause any sinner to beg for company. Is it so wrong to want what she has?

"It's not mine. It's…" I shake my head and stop saying too much. "You said we could help each other?" My legs quiver and that invisible quicksand begins sucking me in as I feel about two-feet tall in her presence.

"Come on." She nods toward the vehicle she came in. "It's cold out here and we have a lot to talk about."

I follow behind her like a puppy on a leash.

Once we're both in the SUV, I shift my body to face her. I have to be bold or I'll leave here with nothing. "I'm sure you saw the news. Just so you know, it's not true." I don't dare tell Madison the entire truth. If Lars decides to share that information, so be it, but the truth will never escape my mouth again. "I have no idea why Vi would—"

Madison holds up a hand stopping me. "Is it Lars' baby?"

I nod. "It is."

Her hands slap to the steering wheel and she squeezes it so tight that it looks like her knuckles are on the verge of breaking through her skin. Pressing her lips together, her head trembles. "Ok." She takes in a few heavy breaths. "Ok. This is fine. This is fine." Eyes lock on mine and chills shiver down my spine when I read the seriousness in her expression. "Willa. You don't want him and I'm not saying this to be mean, but he doesn't want you either. You see, Lars made me believe that he loved me, too."

"Of course he loves you." I chuckle. "You're his sister."

"No, sweetie. I'm his dad's stepdaughter. Lars played me the same way he's been playing you. I fell under his spell and fell in love with him. The sex was great, don't get me wrong, but then his friends started to interfere, without even realizing they were doing it. Josh went missing and everything changed."

Sex? Love? Madison and Lars, no way.

Looking at her with puzzlement, I'm not sure what she's even talking about. "What does Josh have to do with any of this?"

"Oh. You don't know? Yeah, Lars and his friends killed Josh."

Drawing back, I laugh. "Yeah, right."

Her head bobs up and down and she smirks cruelly. "Yes. They did. Lars swears they didn't, but I saw them loading Josh's body into a car in front of Marni Thorn's house. My guess is that they hit him on purpose and hid his body."

"This is ridiculous. Sure, they're all jerks, but they aren't killers."

"Josh was obsessed with Marni. Talon is obsessed with Marni."

I'm not sure if I believe what she's saying to me, but why would she make this up? If this is true, then I have my ammo. I have exactly what I need to get Lars to give me the money so I can leave.

"Prove it." I spit out. "If they killed Josh, show me proof."

"All the proof I need is up here." She taps a finger to the top of her head. "Lars knows what I saw. Even admitted to getting rid of the body. They pushed Josh's car into Lake Ruin, destroying evidence. Zed's the mastermind behind it all and I think he views you as a threat. I assumed you knew, but I guess he wants something else. He's going to help me make Lars fall in love with me. But that's not possible if you're in the picture."

"It was you, wasn't' it? You're the one who left the message on my phone and came to my house?"

She seems to be taken aback. "I don't know what you're talking about." Her expression goes blank. A dead stare at me that signals those alarms in my head again. "That doesn't matter. I love Lars and I know that one day he will love me, too."

Grabbing the handle of the door, I make no hesitation to jump out. I stumble over my feet and almost fall flat on my stomach, but Madison comes out of nowhere and catches my fall.

Her fingers tangle around my wrist and I try to shake her off to no avail. "Why are you doing this?"

"Love makes you do crazy things."

A damp cloth presses to my face and no matter how hard I try to fight, I lose the battle.

ROLLING MY HEAD IN CIRCLES, I fight to open my eyes. It feels as if I'm peeling my eyelids off from my eyeballs. So dry and heavy.

My head feels like it holds the weight of a bowling ball as I try to steady it upright on my neck. Smacking my lips together, I look around the dark room. The only sliver of light comes from a dim lantern on the wall.

Wriggling my hands, I gasp when I realize they are strapped to the arms of the chair. I look down and see that I'm bound. Only, it's not your typical chair. It's old. Very old, with wires attached to it and some sort of plastic egg over top of me that looks like a hair dryer from a salon. My body steels when I see him.

"Zed?" I mutter under my breath, but loud enough to grab his attention.

He greets me with a smile and stuffs his phone in his pocket. "Oh, good morning, Sunshine."

I fight again to free myself, but there is no point. Zed eats up the space between us and I continue to try because I'd rather cut my arms off than face whatever he has planned for me.

"Calm down, little one. You're not getting out of that chair." He breathes out a chuckle. "I won't hurt you."

Lies. All lies.

"Please, just let me go." I cry out. "I won't tell anyone, I swear."

"I didn't want it to come to this, Willa. You're a sweet girl. You don't deserve this." His expression twists and he grabs fists full of his hair. "But he's in my fucking head! He won't get the fuck out." His demeanor quickly changes again like his moods are snapping. Something I'm all too familiar with. "Always remember that behind every monster is someone who made them that way."

What does that even mean? Someone made him do this? I have no idea what he's talking about. I have to get out of here. My eyes skim the room and I wish they would have just stayed put on Zed, because fear thickens inside my stomach.

I'm at Briarwood. That mental hospital outside of town and this is a torture room. Is Lars behind this? Has he been planning this all along? Madison wasn't lying when she said that Zed felt threatened by me. But, I didn't even know anything until she told me. Maybe they really did kill Josh. Maybe they plan to kill me, too. I have no idea what's going on or what Zed's intentions with me are. I'm scared. Really, really scared. Not just for me but for my baby.

"You left the message, didn't you? You knew I was pregnant this whole time."

"I never left any messages. Didn't even know you were pregnant until that broadcast."

Of course he'd deny it. I have no doubt it was Zed this whole time.

Using my sweet voice in hopes of it buying his trust, I squirm. "I'm not feeling well, Zed. I think I'm gonna be sick. Can you please let me up?"

"Sorry. I can't do that. Not until I tell you what I want you to do for me."

"Do for you?"

"Mmhmm. Here's the thing, Sweater Girl, unless you want the entire town to think you were in cahoots with Josh and that you know where he is, you're gonna do exactly what I tell you to do. Am I clear?"

I could say yes. I could buckle and bow to him, but he doesn't hold all the power. I've got a little something up my sleeve, too. "But it won't be the truth. We both know that Josh didn't run away. He's dead and you know where his body is. Am I right?"

He laughs. He actually fricken laughs at me. "Good luck proving that. I know you've got connections." He holds up his hands and begins counting off fingers. "What, with the almighty Pastor Jeffries, the church board, and the drama club. I'm sure they'll all make my connections tremble." He laughs again.

He's right. No one would ever believe me. Right now, I'm a runaway. Half of Redwood probably thinks I'm with Josh, thanks to Vi. I've got nothing. I've got no one.

"What do you want me to do?"

Bending at the knees, he slouches down in front of me and begins trailing a finger up my calf. "First of all, you're gonna back me when I tell Madison Bishop she needs to leave town. I have a video of her holding a towel of chloroform over your face and knocking you out. She needs to think that you'll turn her in and tell the cops that she's held you prisoner this entire time you've been missing, if she doesn't leave and never come back."

"You want Madison gone?" I thought that Madison was on their side. She brought me to Zed, after all.

"Madison is a looney bitch who's obsessed with Lars. She's been making his life hell and no one fucks with my family. My boys are my family, whether they like it or not."

I can do that. I wouldn't even hesitate to actually go as far as turning her in. She did kidnap me. Zed is the one holding me hostage, but I have yet to hear what his endgame is. Whatever it is, it doesn't sound like I'll be leaving in a body bag. "Ok. Deal."

"Second, I need to know where something is in your house. And you will not tell a single soul about this. Do you hear me?" he raises his voice. "Not one person. If you do, it's game over."

"My house? What could you possibly want that I would have?" I live in a two-bedroom shack and the most valuable possession inside that house is my great-gran's urn.

"It's not something of yours. It's something of your step-dad's. It's a brown wooden box about as big as a Bible with a biblical scripture on it. 'But if you do not forgive others for their sins. Our father will not forgive you for your sins.'"

I side-eye him with a raised brow. "Rick used to say that to me all the time. How do you know that verse?"

He ignores my question completely. "It would be hidden. I want you to go there and find it."

I shake my head. "No. I can't ever go back there. I just can't. Why can't you go?"

Standing up, he screams, "You *will* go and you *will* find it!" His words cause my body to wince in fear.

"Why can't you go find it?"

"I've been there three times and came up empty-handed each time. You've lived there for years and should know every crack and crevice in that place. I'll be watching to make sure you're safe."

"But Rick will see me. He'll turn me in."

"Rick won't be there. You're going tomorrow during the morning service."

It seems that I have no choice. But I do have some leverage, and a way to leave Lars out of it. "If I do this, I want enough money to leave Redwood and never come back."

"Deal," he spits out, like it's nothing for him to hand over a hundred grand.

"I didn't say how much. I need enough to last me for a while. Like, thousands."

"You get me that box and if you still want to leave come Monday morning, I'll give you the money to go. In fact, I'll even book your flight. But there's one more thing. Don't you dare open that box. If I even suspect you've tampered with it, it's also game over."

Curiosity is really getting the best of me. I can't even try to guess what this box could have in it that Zed wants. But, if this sets me free, I'm on board. "Ok. I'll do it."

"Good." He smirks. "Now that we have that taken care of, whose baby are you carrying in there?" He points to my stomach. "We both know it's not Josh's. Is it the pastor's demon spawn?"

Completely taken aback, my eyes pop wide open. "What?"

"You don't have to answer me. I just hope that one day the memories escape you. Holding that shit in can really fuck a person up."

I don't say anything at all. I'm not sure how he knows, but he does. I'll never admit it to anyone. I'd die first.

"You're a good person, the baby will turn out just fine." He begins to walk away from me, leaving me strapped to the chair.

"Hey, Zed?"

Glancing over his shoulder, he looks at me.

"Don't tell anyone. K?"

He zips his lips up and tosses the invisible key into a hole dug in the cement slab of the floor.

I shouldn't believe him, but I do. Something tells me that Zed has secrets of his own.

LARS

My mind is completely blown that these guys are putting together a party right now. Talon paces back and forth in front of the fireplace with his ear pressed to the phone. "Yep. Just bring friends. That's all we ask. See ya then, man."

It's true that Talon throws a few annual parties, but when they are this forced, it can only mean one thing—someone's planning on fucking some shit up and needs an alibi.

The Halloween party was the night that we were trying to frame Marni. Now, here she is, making calls and helping these guys throw this thing together at the last minute. She's still pissed at me for telling her dad the truth, but she's also relieved that he's no longer implicated. She said they had a talk and she told him that she's ok with waiting for her trust fund until she's married. I mean, why wouldn't she be ok with it? Talon has enough money to buy the entire town. She's set for a while.

"Lars." Tommy angles his head to the door. "You've got company."

My feet carry me quickly to the window and I look outside and see Madison walking up with a fucking basket of cookies. She's wearing a pink dress that barely covers her ass and heels as long as my cock when it's hard. "Great." All eyes shoot to me, but no one says a word. "I'll be back," I tell them.

Pulling the door closed behind me, I stand under the neon glow of the porch light. "What are you doing here?" I sigh.

"Baked you some cookies." She hands me a basket and I snatch it from her hand and look inside at the perfectly rounded cookies and there is no way in hell that Madison made those.

I drop it down at the side of my foot. "You need to leave."

"Listen Lars, I know things have been weird lately, but it's going to get better soon, I promise."

"What's that supposed to mean?"

"It means that with Willa gone, we can finally be together."

My heart jumps into my throat. "Willa's gone?"

"Yeah. She's gone for good. At first, I thought that maybe you and I could raise the baby together. I mean, it's a part of you, so I thought that I could love it no matter what. But then I realized, I'll never be able to love a child that was conceived between you and another girl, so I let him get rid of her."

My legs buckle and I lean back against the door to brace myself. *Get rid of her?* "What are you talking about?"

"Zed. He came to me and told me that he would take care of Willa if I brought her to him." Her shoulders rise as my heart drops. "So I did." She says the words like we're talking about a fucking basket of cookies.

I spin around so fast that my brain gets dizzy. Ripping the door open, I leave Madison standing there and I go inside. "What the fuck did you guys do?" I shout so loudly the words reverberate through my own ears. "Tell me, dammit!" Everyone shares a glance, but no one talks. "You tell me where WIlla is right fucking now or I'll go straight to the cops and confess everything."

"She's ok, Lars. I made sure of it. Willa is back at my dad's house," Marni says, as she walks toward me.

In an attempt to pacify me, she places a hand on my arm, but I swing it off. "Don't touch me. I want answers."

Talon joins her side, like the pussy-whipped bitch that he is. "Marni and I were watching the entire time. We wouldn't have let anything happen to her."

My hands fly all over the place as if I have lost control of my body. "Watching what? Watching who?" I wail with anger and intense agitation.

"Zed. He just needed to talk to her. He did, and now she's safe."

The door behind me comes open and I don't have to turn around to know who just walked in. "Leave Madison," I say, while I stare straight ahead at the empty space over Talon's shoulder.

"Don't just leave, run," Marni tells her. "You kidnapped a pregnant girl and Willa is prepared to go to the cops if you don't get the hell out of Redwood and never come back."

Turning around, I look Madison dead in the eye. "If you hurt her, I swear to God."

"I didn't. I swear. But, Zed said—"

Talon chimes in, "Zed lied."

"Come on, Lars." Madison takes hold of my hand. My eyes shimmy down her arm to where we're connected and I snarl. "Get your fucking hand off me."

"Lars. I love you. Don't do this."

Talon steps closer. "You better go, Madison. They don't play games. You *will* be convicted of kidnapping. Your pretty ass won't survive prison."

She tugs at my arm. "Don't make me leave you. We belong together."

Gripping her by the wrist, I lead her outside. "Go to your dad's in Colorado. One day, we will see each other again."

She falls into my arms and I hold my hands out behind her. "But. I'll miss you."

"Just go," I tell her again, before I spin her around to face her car.

I don't even wait for her to leave; I just walk back up the steps to the porch. I hope Madison gets the help she needs before she royally fucks someone up. As for her leaving, I know this was Zed's plan. He always has a plan. I'm pretty pissed that no one filled me in because I would have never let it happen. Which is exactly why no one filled me in.

Without saying a word to anyone, I snatch my keys off the couch and leave. I'll be back for the party tomorrow night because I always stick to my end of the deal, but Zed better stick to his. Come Monday morning, all this shit better be laid to rest.

I'm sure it won't be long until Lars tells everyone the truth about the baby. Hopefully when that time comes, I'm far away from here.

It hurts really bad. Worse than I could have ever imagined. I knew it wouldn't be easy to lie to him, but I also never anticipated falling in love with him all over again. So much for sticking to the plan.

My tears have run dry. Even if I wanted to, I'm not sure I'm capable of crying anymore. This day—this month—has been so emotionally draining. Marni and Talon let me go after Zed left the room. I have no idea where he went, but they told me everything would be ok. Marni was actually sweet, unlike past encounters with her in school, or lack thereof. Marni never took notice of me, so she never had an opportunity to tease or ridicule me. She's one of the popular girls, so I always assumed that if she had noticed me, she would have jumped on that train. I was proven wrong.

Throughout life, we encounter people and draw judgments of them based on who they associate with. One might look at me and automatically assume that I'm a sweet girl, but if they see me with Lars, they'd probably think he drained me of morals. I'm starting to learn that people aren't always what they seem. Because Lars isn't just this savage bully who likes to wreak havoc, he's got depth and heart. He has a past and a future and he's just trying to survive, like I am. Like we all are.

Curled up in a ball on the bed, I jolt upwards when I hear someone coming down the hall outside the door. "Marni?" I say loud enough, so that whoever it is can hear me.

The door opens and Lars walks inside. Once again, without knocking, but this time, I don't even care. My heart melts into a puddle in my lap and those giddy butterflies mixed with that agonizing fear of the unknown return. "You're here," I say, trying not to be too obvious that I'm over the moon excited to see him.

"Are you ok?" He remains at the door and doesn't even bother to come closer. His arms are crossed over his chest and eyes twinkle in the dim light of the room.

"I'm ok. I take it you heard?"

"I had no idea they were doing this. I'm sorry."

"It's ok. Everything is starting to make sense now. Well, most of it, anyways."

His head tilts to the side and he cracks that sexy smile that turns me to mush. "I'm glad that it's making sense to you because I have no clue what's going on. Seems I'm out of the loop on this one."

"Well, I don't know what Zed's plan is, but he says if I help him, he'll help me leave."

"You don't have to help him if you don't want to."

"But Marni said that it's the only way that you can all be free from this mess with Josh."

"Ah, you know about that. Why am I not surprised." He begins walking toward me, my heart jumping with each step that brings him closer.

"Madison actually told me that part." I bite back a smile. "Heard you two are in love?"

"Madison needs serious help. Hopefully she gets it when she's in Colorado."

"She left already?"

"Let's just say she's on her way out."

Thank God. I really didn't want to deal with that girl. "I'm sorry I lied to you, Lars. For what it's worth, I felt like I didn't have many options."

"You don't have to apologize. Everything that happened to you is because of me. I didn't deserve your truth. Still don't."

"Well, if it wasn't for you, then it would probably have been one of them who took the bet. I'm glad you took it."

He takes a seat on the bed and drags his teeth over his bottom lip. "I never would have let anyone else have it. Probably would have beat the shit out of them for even suggesting someone else do it."

I feel like I should be mad even talking about this, because the bet was the first flip of the domino, but the way his words warm my insides makes it impossible to be upset about it anymore. "I hope we can move on from this all and I know we'll never see each other again, but…" I begin to choke up and take a long pause. God, it hurts so bad. "You'll always be my first."

"I didn't deserve to be."

"Not my first, first. I'm talking about my first love." It's always been Lars. Ever since his brother's funeral, he found his way into my heart. I'd forget about him for a while, but then he'd pop up somewhere, like church, and I'd feel him knocking at the walls inside of me again. It wasn't until freshman year that my crush developed. By sophomore year, he visited me in every dream. Junior year, I fell in love. Senior year—I lost him. "Can you promise me one thing?"

"I can probably do that."

"Wait until I'm gone before you tell everyone the truth about the baby. It's only a couple days."

I watch as his fingers trail down my bare leg. Sending goosebumps in their path. "I wanna go with you, Willa."

My head shoots up. "You what?"

"Let me leave Redwood with you. I know you said that it won't work and that I don't want that life. But, that life is all I want. What I don't want is a life without you in it."

I'm pretty sure my heart just stopped beating. "But the baby, it's not yours."

"She's always been mine. I don't need a DNA test to tell me otherwise." He reaches into his pocket and pulls out a piece of paper. "That reminds me, the results came in. At first, I wasn't even going to pick them up because I knew all I needed to, but then I remembered they ran some genetic bloodwork to make sure everything is ok. Good news, the baby is healthy."

I'm not even sure what he said after she's always been mine. Obviously, I know he's metaphorically speaking. We both know the baby is Rick's. But, in his heart, it's his baby.

He hands me the paper and my eyes skim over it. Everything looks good, and it's confirmed that there was not a match between the fetal fragments in my blood work and the blood work Lars had done.

He reaches into his pocket and pulls out a separate piece of paper. "Apparently they also do a gender test. Do you wanna know or should I let it be a surprise?"

"Oh my gosh, you better tell me!" I drop the results in my hand on the bed then snatch the paper from his hand. "It's a girl!" My hands fly up and the paper falls beside me.

"See. That's another reason I have to go with you. She's gonna need a dad to protect her from assholes."

As much I want this. It's a fantasy. It's not real. Lars thinks he wants this life with us, but how could he really? He's only eighteen years old. Hasn't even graduated yet. Letting him go with me and raise the baby would be selfish. It hurts fiercely to have to do this, but I can't let him throw his whole life away. Climbing onto my knees, I sit in front of him on the bed. Tears sting the corners of my eyes and threaten to break free while a ball lodges in my throat. "Lars, you're going to be the best daddy in the world someday. But, it's not time for that, yet. You still have so much living to do before you settle down."

"No." He shakes his head. "No. I want this. More than anything in the world. I want you. I want our baby."

"No you don't. You just think you do. You want out of this town. Away from your idiot friends and away from this mess." I think very clearly before I say what's coming next, but it needs to be said. "Loving this baby won't bring Colby back. You're feeling the emotions you've been searching for, Lars." I smile through the pain that's eating away inside of me. "Let that be enough."

Taking my hands in his, he lays them on my lap and stands up. "I'm feeling emotions because of you. This has nothing to do with Colby." He bends down, pressing his hands on either side of my head with his face mere inches from mine. "I love you, Willa." His mouth meets mine and tears slide down my cheeks. Falling onto my lips, I can taste the saltiness of this heartbreak.

Sweeping his thumb underneath my left eye, he breaks the kiss. "I'll follow you wherever you go."

A life with Lars would be a dream. He's standing here telling me he loves me and my baby and he wants to be with us. Why am I fighting it? I don't have to leave my heart in Redwood; he can come with me.

Kissing his lips gently, I smile. "Ok."

"Ok?"

"Yeah. Let's run away."

"You're serious?"

"You didn't give me much of a choice. You said you'd

follow me and I've had enough stalkers the past couple days to know I don't want more. So, yeah. Come with me. There's just one thing."

"You name it."

"I'm still helping Zed."

He grows weary and I can tell he's not pleased. "What's he want you to do?"

"I can't tell you, but it's not as bad as what you're probably thinking. It's tomorrow morning and should only take me an hour tops. It's not just for me; it's also for your friends. And for Zed, too. I'm not sure why, but this is important to him. I can't leave Redwood with a guilty conscience, knowing that I could have helped them and I didn't."

"Alright. I made a promise that I'd be around tomorrow with the guys, so we'll plan on leaving Monday."

I stand up and jump into his arms. "I can't believe we're doing this." My arms hook around his neck while my legs latch around his waist.

"I never planned on letting you leave without me."

Willa and I laid in bed for hours talking. I told her all about the pact and what happened with Josh. I offered her a stamp as one of us, but she immediately declined. Willa doesn't want her revenge because she thinks that revenge hurts the victim more than the assailant, but one day, Rick will pay for his sins.

When I look at her sleeping peacefully, I see the Willa that wears her heart on her sleeve. The girl who'd give you the skin off her bones, the blood from her veins, and a chunk of her heart, just to be accepted. I would have taken it all and dressed myself in her broken pieces just because I could. My entire life I've been nothing but a boy crying out for attention. Whether it was making another person the butt of my jokes, feeding my ego with a win from a bet, or using my brother's death to be noticed by my parents. Willa didn't deserve it and I never should have used her just for kicks with the guys.

"What time is it?" Willa stretches with a yawn.

"It's early. Go back to sleep." I kiss her on the cheek. "I have to go to my house and see my dad and I'll be back before you need to leave."

"Hurry back," she mumbles, as she tugs the blankets around her.

As much as my old man pisses me off, I've gotta see him before I go. I also need to make sure that Madison followed through and left Redwood.

Once the alarms and cameras are set, I go to my car. Christmas is only four days away and there's a nip in the air that has me cranking the heat up. There's a real possibility that I'll get to see my first white Christmas. Willa chose New York. She said that she's always had big dreams of a city life. It'll do for now, but as the baby grows up, we'll need a big house and a yard.

I know that Willa wants to leave Redwood and never come back, but I can't make that same promise to myself. There will be times that I'll come back and visit. I've got my boys here. We're all a little dysfunctional, but that's what keeps us together. I don't have a clue what Zed's plan is, but the closer he gets to his revenge, the less evil I see in his eyes. I'm not sure that any of us will ever forget what he did. Taking advantage of Marni, blackmailing me so that he could get to her. But, for his own sake, I hope he gets what he wants out of this day.

I pull up to the house and it looks like Cruella had someone turn it into a Christmas Candy Land game in the yard. There are blow up decorations covering the entire lawn and lights strung on every inch of the house. There must be some sort of contest going on because she's not exactly the warm and joyous type.

As soon as I get out and notice movement going on inside the house, rage consumes me. Through the picture window, I can see Madison sobbing into her mom's shoulder. Dad stands by idly with his hands in the pockets of his black Kiton suit.

Just when I think I need to get the fuck out of here, Madison looks at me. Raising her hand, she points her finger and begins crying harder. Her mom peels Madison off of her and disappears from my view.

When the front door flies open and Lynn comes running at me in a pair of heels and a coat, made from at least forty white rabbits, wrapped around her, I take a few steps back and hold my hands up. She tears one shoe off and raises it in the air as she charges me, though it actually slows her down because she's wobbling all over the place trying to balance herself with the missing six inches on one leg. "Woah," I hold my hands up. "What are you doing?"

Before she gets to me, her red pump flies through the air and lands about six feet to my right. Terrible throw. "Have you lost your damn mind?" I holler.

She grabs her other shoe as my dad comes rushing out the door. "Lynn, stop." He makes it just in time to grab it from behind, before she drills the heel into the top of my head.

"Lars. Inside," Dad says as he holds Cruella in place.

"Nah, I'm good." I shoot a thumb over my shoulder. "I'll just go."

"Inside. Now!" he shouts with an authoritative voice that I've grown accustomed to.

Really don't wanna go in there with Madison. She's standing in the window with tears streaming down her face, playing the victim. I'm not sure what she told them. This could be really fucking bad.

But, I do as I'm told and head for the door. I don't dare walk in alone, though. Being alone with Madison never goes well and I'm not sure I'll be able to refrain from losing my temper and making things worse than they already are.

Standing at the front door, I wait for Dad while he tries to reason with Lynn. His hands are braced on her shoulders and the way his jaw is ticking leads me to believe that his irritation doesn't only sit with me.

Pulling out my phone, I check the time: 10:16. Willa said

she needs to leave at eleven o'clock and I told her I'd be back before she heads out. "Come on. I don't have all day," I holler across the lawn.

Both heads twist and look at me and I probably should have just kept my mouth shut. Dad comes stalking toward me, huffing and puffing, while Lynn trails slowly behind. She hugs her rabbits closer to her chest with her eyes laser-focused on me. "Get the hell in the house." Dad grabs me by the arm and drags me like a ragdoll. "You've got some explaining to do, young man."

"Whatever she told you, it's all lies. She's a fucking psycho, Dad."

"Yeah. No kidding," he mutters under his breath. Is he taking my side? Do they both finally see what a nutcase Madison is?

We step into the living room and Madison's frown quickly diminishes. "You came for me. Like you said you would." She begins walking toward me, but Dad sticks his arm out to stop her from coming any closer.

I look from Madison to Dad. "What's going on here?"

"Madison claims that you two were in a relationship, but you cheated on her and knocked up the pastor's daughter and recently told her to go wait for you in Colorado."

My head drops back and I let out a dramatic sigh. "Fuck. You said that, Madison?" Her smile only grows. She's either pleased with herself, or she truly believes her own lies. I turn to Dad, lean forward and whisper in his ear, "Can we talk in private?"

Dad nods in response and I follow him down the hall into his study. When the door closes, I lay it all out. Well, not all of it. "She's lying, Dad. She's fucking obsessed with me and I think she needs some serious help."

"Is that baby yours?" Dad spits out. When I don't respond, he raises his voice. "Is it yours?"

"Yeah." I nod. "Yeah, the baby is mine."

"Damnit, boy. Do you have any idea how bad this looks for our family?"

"Our family?" I huff. Is he serious right now? "Our family? You mean my dad who's never home. My stepmom who only wants your money. My stepsister who is three seconds shy of a complete mental breakdown. Or my mom who moved three states east because she couldn't stand living with a man who refused to acknowledge that her youngest son existed and died. Do you even remember your other son, Colby?"

His jaw locks and his eyes narrow in on the wall behind me. "Don't you talk about him."

"Why the fuck not? Isn't it about time that we start talking about him? It's been nine years, Dad. Stop pretending that he was never a part of our family."

"Get the hell out of here," he shouts, pointing to the door. Normally, I'd go. I'd drop it and move on. Not this time. After nine years, I'm ready to speak my truth.

"No," I tell him. "I'm not leaving until you hear me out." I click the lock on the door and walk back to the center of the room. "He was born in January of 2013. It was the first time I had ever seen a snowflake fall in all my years of living in Redwood. It was rare, but it happened. Mom said it was God's way of welcoming Colby into the world. You brought me to the hospital and I sat in the corner and didn't even wanna look at the little thing. But you forced me to hold him and when I did, it was reaffirmed that I didn't want a little brother. Everyone was so caught up in Colby being here that it felt like the world forgot about me."

"Stop right there." Dad holds up his hand, but I don't stop.

"Two days after he was born, I sat outside the school for an hour because you guys forgot to pick me up. One week later, you missed my first basketball game. At this point, I hated that baby even more. I just wanted him to go back to wherever that snow fell from."

"Enough!" Dad screams.

"Four years later, he died, and it was all my fault."

Dad's feet sweep the room, back and forth. "No, Lars. It wasn't your fault."

"You can't keep blaming Mom. How would she ever know that I'd ignore him while he wandered outside."

"It wasn't your fault. It wasn't your mom's fault. It was my fault, dammit. Your mom had an important business meeting that day. We both knew it for weeks. I was supposed to be there with him, but I never came home the night before. I was at a hotel in the city having one of my dozen affairs while I left your mom to take care of you boys. She did what she had to do." His face drops in his hands and for the first time in my entire life, I watch my dad cry. "I should have been there. It was always easier to blame your mom."

Dad is not the affectionate type. I can count on one hand how many times I saw him kiss my mom. He rarely smiles. Doesn't speak from the heart and bottles up his emotions. We're similar in that aspect. I stand here with my hands at my sides unsure whether to comfort him or to give him his space.

When his head lifts and his tears are apparent, he makes the decision for both of us. Eating up the space between us, he slaps one hand around my back and pulls me to his chest. "Don't blame yourself. You loved Colby and his death was an accident that I should have prevented."

Did I though? Did I love Colby? I'm not so sure I did.

"It's not your fault, Dad. Like you said, it was an accident. It's time for us both to move on from it. Start talking about him more. Remember the short years we had with him."

He steps back and a smile breaks on his face. "He sure did love you. Thought you were the best brother in the world. Wanted to be just like you."

My heart twinges at his words. I was far from a good brother. I was awful to that little boy. But Colby didn't see it that way. That sweet little boy didn't know any better. He always wanted to play video games with me, but I always gave him the dead remote. Never once let him try for real.

"He was a good kid," I say. He really was a good kid.

Breaking the tension, Dad wipes his tears away and straightens up. "So, a baby? This is a big change, Lars. You sure you're ready for this?"

"I am. I've had a lot of time to think about it and I'm ready to step up to my responsibilities. It also helps that I'm pretty drawn to the baby's mom."

"So, what? You been hiding this girl somewhere? She better have consented or I'll kick your fucking ass."

"She just needed some time alone to think about things. She never actually ran away. And no, she has nothing to do with that Josh kid's disappearance."

"Willa Mack, huh? Never would have guessed that one. After that whole scandal that you took part in, I thought for sure the girl hated your guts."

"She did. But, we've moved past it."

"Pastor Jeffries sure as hell hasn't. That must be why he stopped by the other day looking for the two of you."

Not surprised.

"Madison is just jealous. You can't take anything that girl says seriously."

Dad slaps a hand to my back. "I believe you."

"You do?" I question, feeling my forehead wrinkle in surprise. Dad's actually taking my side over Madison and Lynn's.

"She came onto me a few different occasions. Caught her naked in my bed once and told her that if it happened again her and her mom were both out on their asses." He snatches some papers off the desk and looks them over awkwardly, like this entire conversation is making him uncomfortable

"Holy shit." I laugh. Though, it's not funny.

He drops the papers back on the desk. "I'm walking them both out this afternoon. Lynn and I were never in love. It was all her own fantasy. Much like Madison's with you. Lynn is planning to take Madison to her dad's in Colorado where he's enrolling her at some academy. Apparently this isn't the first time she's had an unhealthy obsession. Of course, Lynn will place most of the blame on you, because that's how Lynn is. But we all know that Madison needs help."

"Be prepared for an all-out war in the courtroom."

Dad chuckles. "I'm the best divorce lawyer on this side of the country. I covered all my tracks before I even proposed. She won't get a penny."

There's a long pause while I try and figure out how to tell Dad that I'm leaving Redwood. In the end, I play it safe for the time being and tell him I'm just leaving for a few days and he gave me his blessing.

Today was good. I'm walking out of this house feeling like I can finally fully breathe.

Now, I just need to haul ass and get back to Anderson's to see Willa before she goes on her secret mission for Zed.

23

WILLA

Silence engulfs the vehicle as I sit inside. Once again, I borrowed Anderson's SUV. I make a mental note to thank him for all of his help this week. He didn't have to agree to let me stay in his home, but he did. Although, I'm pretty sure it wasn't just a kind gesture like I want to believe it was.

I shoot Lars a quick text and tell him I left early and I'll be back soon. I really didn't want to see Lars before I came here because I knew there was a chance he'd follow me just to make sure I'm safe. Zed is parked directly across the street from me and I made a promise that I'd keep everything between us. These guys might play dirty, but I don't.

His eyes bore into mine as I stare back at him. He's sitting behind the wheel of a black Escalade, wearing a pair of sunglasses and a black beanie on his head. Zed wears so much darkness and although rumors have it that his heart matches the shade of his clothes, I truly believe that he has the ability to feel very deeply. He's just chasing monsters like the rest of us.

When he gives me a thumbs up, I open the driver's side door and feel like I'm stepping out into the gates of hell. It's been over a week since I've been in this house and to say I never wanted to return is an understatement. I don't even want my belongings inside. Nothing in there is of any value to me.

One step after another, I find myself at the door. My fingers wrap around the old, rusted handle of the screen door and when the familiar scraping sound of the bottom hits the metal of the frame, my stomach turns. I push open the main door that is never locked, nor latched, all the way and step inside.

The smell immediately brings back traumatic memories and I realize that I need to make this quick or I'll be leaving empty-handed.

With my phone gripped tightly in my hand, I pay close attention to make sure it doesn't vibrate. Zed said he'd text me if I needed to hurry and get out. Let's hope it doesn't come to that because I panic under pressure.

Zed said there is a box somewhere in here, but I have no idea where this box could be. The house is only about twelve hundred square feet, so it can't be too hard to locate.

I start with the kitchen, opening and closing cupboards and drawers, but I find nothing.

My heart rate excels when I eye Rick and Mom's room. Well, Rick's room now. The door is closed and if Rick is hiding anything, that's where I'd expect it to be. I turn the handle and push the door open. It looks the same as it always does. Full-size bed in the middle of the room against the wall. A floral comforter laid on top with decorative throw pillows that match. His dresser sits on the right side and holds different biblical figurines such as a candle that he lights during his prayers. I pull open the top drawer and shuffle through his endless amounts of socks. Nothing.

Second drawer, just folded T-shirts. Nothing.

Third and fourth drawers, more clothes. Nothing.

Next, I try the closet, but that also leads to a dead end.

192

"Where could it be?" I mumble, beginning to feel anxious and agitated. I turn my phone on and text Zed.

Me: I can't find anything. Are you sure there's a box? Maybe he got rid of it.

He immediately responds.

Z: It's there. Keep looking.

"Damnit." I spit out. I rarely swear, but I'm finding that the use of swear words does actually help to relieve stress.

I head out of the room and an unwanted realization sweeps over me when I eyeball the basement door. If I had my way, that whole basement would be filled with cement and cease to exist. There are so many awful memories of that small space. Rick would only go down there when he'd take me with him to catch a feel or relieve some of his own pent-up tension. It's pretty empty, aside from some old boxes and shelves.

The clear plastic handle feels cold against my skin. The edges digging into my hand because I'm gripping it with enough force to snap it off. Taking in a deep breath, I open it. The musky aroma immediately hits me, but I hold my breath and take a few steps down the old rickety wooden staircase.

It's damp and pretty much what you'd expect to find in any old basement of a house built in the early nineteen-hundreds.

Still standing on the steps, I scour the room, hoping I don't have to go any farther. I really don't want to see anything worth checking out down here because I can already feel sweat dripping between my boobs.

I swallow hard when I see an old bookshelf perched against the very back wall of the basement. *Just ignore it, Willa.*

My phone vibrates, causing my body to jerk.

Z: Hurry up.

"You come down here and I'll tell you to hurry up. Asshole." I should send that to him, but I don't. Instead, I creep farther down. Standing on the last step, I lean forward to try and get a better look, but it's too dark, so I flip on the flashlight on my phone and shine it over toward the shelf.

It's packed full of dusty old books. If I run over, skim through them quickly, I can be out of this basement in two minutes tops.

So, that's what I do.

With my flashlight on, I tear the books off the shelf, one by one, letting them fall to the floor. There are at least a dozen different Bibles. Christian books. A few old romance novels that were probably Mom's.

Once the first row is cleared, I move onto the second, pulling books and dropping them over and over again, until one drops with a hollow sound against the cement.

Bending down, I pick it up. It looks like a book, but it's not. It's a wooden box with a small clasp on the side. The spine looks like that of a Bible and on the top it reads, *'but if you do not forgive others for their sins. Our father will not forgive you for your sins.'*

This is it! I send Zed a quick text telling him I have it and then I bolt to the stairs, making no attempt to slow my steps. Once I'm at the top, I push the door open and don't even bother shutting it.

Gripping the box tightly to my chest, I go back outside and stick to the promise of not looking inside the box. As curious as I am, I get the feeling that looking inside would be a death wish that Zed would grant me.

His vehicle begins creeping down the road and his arm is stretched out the driver's side window. I jog over to him, place it in his hand and with his eyes set straight ahead on the road, he doesn't say a word, then he's gone.

I sure hope whatever is in that box brings him peace and not more war.

✝

Lars' car is parked in front of the garage, blocking the entrance, so I pull up behind him and turn the ignition off.

Going through the side door of the garage, I flip the light on, so I can see, then enter through the mud room. I kick my shoes off before opening the door and I'm immediately hit with the overpowering and ever so satisfying aroma of garlic.

Lars is standing over the stove, wearing an apron, while the heavy metal lyrics of Slipknot blast through the speakers in the kitchen.

I'm pretty positive that he has no idea I'm here, so I make no attempt to be known. Taking soft baby steps behind him, I pull out a stool and sit down. Resting my chin on my fist with my elbow pressed against the marbled center island, I observe his cooking skills. Once he starts jamming out, I observe his singing skills, too.

He's got water boiling in a pot while he browns meat in a pan, and if I had to guess, he's making spaghetti.

"I'm impressed," I say loudly, so that my voice carries over the music.

He spins around quickly and grabs his chest. "Shit, you scared me."

"I didn't know you got scared. It's enlightening." I smirk. "Whatcha making?"

He walks over to a deck placed under one of the cupboards and stops the music. "I call this my 'don't be mad that I have to leave for a while tonight' offering."

"Ahh, so you're leaving me again?" I tease. I already know that there is some party that he has to attend. Marni and Talon had mentioned it yesterday. My feelings aren't even hurt that I wasn't invited because they all know that I can't go. Aside from this circle of people, everyone assumes I've run away. Which, I prefer because come tomorrow, I am running away. I'm technically an adult, so I'd prefer to call it moving.

"It's just for a couple hours and you won't even be alone. Marni said she'd come keep you company."

I've grown pretty used to being alone, and being the intro- vert that I am, I actually prefer it. But I do know that Lars' friends are important to him and recently Marni joined that list, so there is no harm in trying to get to know her a little better. "That's nice of her."

"Yeah, I figured you two could watch some chick flicks, paint your nails. Ya know, all that stuff chicks like to do."

I've never done those things. I don't even know how to paint my nails without them looking like a toddler took a bottle of polish and slopped it on my fingers. Marni is going think I'm this sheltered girl who just lives in the church and has no life. The truth is, that was my life. I am that girl.

Water begins bubbling over the pot, causing the burner to sizzle. I jump up to help, because one thing I can do is cook. It's sort of a gift Mom left me when she fled. The responsibility of tending to her soon-to-be ex-husband's needs and desires. Anger begins to boil inside of me, much like the pot of water. Snatching up the box of spaghetti noodles, I push the thoughts from my head. I snap a handful in half and drop them into the boiling water, while Lars stands next to me draining grease into a can. "I'm pretty impressed that you know how to cook. Don't you have people who do that for you?"

"Well, yeah. But it's spaghetti. Everyone can cook spaghetti and garlic bread. Shit." He snatches an oven mitt off the counter. "The garlic bread." He moves me to the side and pulls the oven open, only to find some burnt bread sitting on the rack. "Ok, everyone can cook spaghetti." He closes the oven back up and shuts it off. "Who needs garlic bread anyways." He gets behind me and nuzzles his face in my neck, tickling me with the short stubble on his face. "I can get used to this. Cooking with you. Kissing you."

His hand sets on my stomach and he turns me to face him. "Everything I want in life is in this room right now."

My eyes widen. "You're surprising me again. I had no idea you could be so sweet."

His neck stretches, and he sets his chin on top of my head. "I'm surprising myself. You make me wanna be better, Willa."

My head presses to his chest, snuggling in and feeling so safe and protected in his arms. This is my happy place. "I'll never understand why you want to be with me. I'm a mess."

"From one mess to another, we've got this." He kisses my forehead and I believe him. Everything is going to be ok. This fairy tale might not last forever. No one falls in love and keeps it at our age. It would be a rare gift that I'd gladly accept, but I have to be realistic. This life isn't going to be easy. We have a lot of bumpy roads ahead. But for now, I'm living in the moment and holding on tight.

24

LARS

"How hungry are you?" I grumble into the crease of Willa's neck. Now that she's mine, I can't keep my hands off of her. Pure perfection, inside and out.

"Not at all."

My hands cup underneath her ass, and I hoist her up. With her legs wrapped around me, I carry her into the living room, slightly nervous of how this could play out. She has scars inside, naturally so. She's been tormented by a lion who bared his teeth and threatened to feed on her soul. It's going to take a lot of time and patience on my end before she ever fully lets her guard down.

But the way she's kissing my neck as I carry her through the living room leads me to believe she wants this just as much as I do. "Are you sure?" I ask her, taking the steps upstairs. Her grip around my shoulders tightens. "I won't let you fall." I chuckle.

"If you drop me, so help me God."

"Listen girl, I work out for a living. I've been on break for a couple weeks, but there is no way I'm dropping your one-hundred pound ass down the stairs." When we get to the top, she sighs in relief. "Did you seriously doubt me?"

"Not one bit."

"Liar." I kick open the door to the room she's been staying in and lay her down on the bed. "I don't like to be lied to." My lips slam into hers as I seduce her tongue. Her legs bend at the knees, inviting me between them. I take the empty space, without putting my full weight on her, grinding my throbbing cock at her entrance through her pants.

Gripping the bottom of my shirt, she rips it over my head and flings it to the floor. "Take my pants off." Her voice is grating and full of demand. I do as I'm told. Who am I to argue with a pregnant girl. I have yet to see mood swings, but I'm sure they're coming at some point. I only hope her stamina doesn't decrease because I'm loving this wild side of her.

Pushing myself off her, I slide her pants down, along with her panties, while she takes her hoodie off. Her bra follows suit and her perky breasts and hard nipples greet me. Her silky smooth skin is entrancing and does indescribable things to my insides. I drop my pants in one swift movement. With her legs dangling over the edge of the bed, I push underneath her knees and bring them halfway to her head, taking care not to squish her belly.

My tongue covers her pussy, licking in long strides and tasting her sweet juices. "Mmm," I hum against her entrance. She's so fucking wet. I drop one foot down, but she grabs ahold of it and pulls it back up herself, spreading her legs wide open for me. Circling my fingers at her entrance, I flick my tongue against her clit, causing a vibration that has her shuddering. My eyes skim up and I see her watching me, watching us.

Curiously, her mouth forms an O. Suddenly, the shy girl is gone, and I'm staring into eyes full of wonder and lust. Taking her into a whole new world of consensual pleasure where shame has no business being present.

I slide one finger inside of her, twisting it around like a key in a hole. Then another, spreading her open wider and feeling the warmth of her walls around me.

My eyes return to her pussy and I watch as my fingers slide in and out of her. Her arousal runs down her ass, and I dart my tongue out and lick her clean. Dragging it up to where my fingers press inside of her, I pull them out and flex my tongue muscle inside, while my fingers caress her sensitive nub. When she quivers and whimpers, I know that's the spot she likes.

"Lars." She moans. "I'm—" She begins crying out in heavy breaths of pleasure. "I think I'm gonna come."

"Don't fight it, baby." I stick my fingers back inside of her. Gliding them deeper and in quick movements. When I feel her clench around them, I know she's close. Taking her to the height of her orgasm, I dart my tongue repeatedly at her clit.

"Oh God," She bellows, followed by a drawn-out breath. Evidence of her orgasm spills around my fingers. I ride her out until her body relaxes on the bed. She jolts like her body is being zapped by a current and slaps a hand over mine. I pull my fingers out and climb back between her legs.

My cock finds her entrance like he knows right where to go and I slide inside. So tight and dripping wet. Being inside her is what I would imagine heaven is like. I glide in and out from the tip of my head to the full length of my cock. Our pelvic bones collide then separate in a continuous motion.

Watching her expression as her mouth hangs agape and her nostrils flare, I feel mine do the same as I slam into her. 'You ok?" I ask, making sure that she's not feeling an ounce of pain.

"Yes. Don't stop." Her fingers dig into my shoulders and I'm pretty positive she's about to have her second orgasm. I come up on my knees and grab hold of her legs, letting them drape over my forearms. In short and rapid thrusts, I pound her pussy with my pelvis. With my free hand, my fingers lap around her clit.

My tongue sweeps out, licking my lips and catching the bottom one between my teeth as I drive into her. "Mmm, you feel so good." Her tits bounce up and down and just watching them sends me over the edge.

She lets out a muffled groan and curves her back. "I'm gonna come again."

I push harder and faster. Mimicking her heady breaths and then losing myself inside of her. I don't stop pumping until I know she's finished. Once I'm sure and she cracks a sly smile, I stop moving. After a few seconds, I pull out and drop to the side of her.

Pushing myself up on my elbows, I hover my face over hers. "I can get used to this." I kiss her lips and feel her smile against mine.

TALON WASN'T KIDDING when he said this party would be raging. The lawn is plastered with stumbling bodies and a mixture of cans and red plastic cups.

There's sparks of fire and ash, followed by a cloud of smoke, coming from the side of the house. Guys are chanting around a keg while they tip a girl upside down.

Her feet hit the ground and she begins gagging before puking up everything that just went down. When she turns her head just a tad to the right, she lets more out on top of one of the guy's shoes.

"Titan!" The guy with vomit on his shoes hollers. "Long time no see." He slaps a hand on my back, and I look down at his shoes.

"Wish I could say the same." With my eyes on his feet, I scowl. "You fucking wreak. Take those nasty things off before you go in the house or Talon will have them up your ass." I keep walking, leaving him hanging.

I spot Tommy and Talon standing around the fire. Tommy's double fisting drinks and having a few choice words with Wyatt McCoy. Some things never change. Wyatt has been on the receiving end of harsh words and torment from all of us, but Tommy really lays into him hard. I suppose it's easier to push around someone who doesn't push back. It was a fun game for a while, but lately, I'm not about that bullying shit.

"Woah, woah, woah." I grab ahold of Tommy when he tosses both bottles to the side and bumps his chest against Wyatt's.

"You wanna fucking go. Let's go," Tommy bellows. Wyatt brushes him off then turns to walk away. "Yeah, that's what I thought."

"Dude. Chill the fuck out. What's your problem?"

He points over the fire where Wyatt stands with his love interest, Shane. "He's my fucking problem."

"Whatever it is, just let it go. Has anyone heard from Zed?" I look from Tommy to Talon who both shake their heads simultaneously.

Tommy looks at his Apple Watch. "He should be here soon. Did you guys bring your repentance?"

"Got mine." I pat at my front pocket. Every year at this annual party, we have a little ceremony. We all bring something —or write it out on paper—that has weighed heavily on us this year. It's usually something we either want kept a secret or left in the past. We burn that bitch and let the smoke carry the burden of it away. We walk into the new year with a fresh start and clear head, even if it's only that one problem we're stepping away from, every bit of reprieve helps.

"Yep.

Tommy staggers away and I'm really starting to worry about him. He's been distant. Drinking heavily and slacking in school. It's not like him. "I sure hope he's able to walk away from whatever's weighing him down lately."

Talon stuffs his hands in his front pockets and looks over his shoulder. "Yeah. Something is going on with him. He won't talk about it. Gets all defensive."

"He'll come around eventually. Maybe after this mess with Josh is behind us, we can all breathe a little easier."

Tommy returns with two fresh drinks in his hands. "He's here."

I turn around and look over my shoulder and see Zed strolling up to the fire. His hands are stuffed in the pockets of his black jeans and he's sporting a shit-eating grin. People clear his path and chicks snicker while whispering into each other's ears. I'll never understand why girls are so drawn to his bad boy persona. Then again, I could say the same for Willa.

Zed points a finger at a few stragglers around the fire. "You and you. Leave." The guy and girl walk away immediately, leaving just the four of us around it. "Let's get this shit over with. Talon, you start."

Normally we'd all be laughing and reminiscing about the year. This time it's different. We're miles apart, even though we're standing right next to each other.

Without even questioning him, Talon reaches into his pocket and pulls out a box of matches. He doesn't have to say anything, but he does. Looking through the fire, he glances at all of us and holds up a small box. "This box is one match short. We all know where the missing one went. I got my revenge with the help of you all and I sleep better at night because of it. Don't let anyone tell you that it's not worth it. Inner peace is worth every strike you have to make." He tosses the box in the fire.

Zed side-steps to the left toward Talon and holds his fist out. "Happy for you, man." They bump fists and Zed returns to where he was standing. "Tommy. Go."

Tommy pulls something else out of his pocket. It's not a piece of paper; it's something small and black. He doesn't hold it up, he just tosses it directly in the fire and keeps his eyes on the blaze. He doesn't have to say anything, but we're all curious.

"Do you have anything to say about that?" I ask him.

"It's a card from a camera. It doesn't matter what's on it because it's gone."

We all share a look, all but Tommy, who is watching intently as the plastic melts on top of a smoldering log.

"Alright then. Lars, you're up."

Reaching into my pocket, my fingers grip the folded-up paper. I pull it out and unfold it. Looking one last time at the results before I let it float over the flames. "Congratulations boys, you're gonna be uncles." The guys don't know the truth. No one does and no one ever will.

They don't question it. Even if they had their suspicions, they'd never share them.

"Alright, Zed. Looks like you're the last one," Tommy says as he tips back his bottle.

Zed pulls something out from his back pocket. It looks like some old pictures—three, maybe four— but he makes it a point to hide whatever is on them.

He steps up to the fire and tears them in half. Again and again. Dropping piece by piece into the burning flame. One stray square picks up in the wind and blows over to my foot. Zed throws the remaining pieces into the fire and his eyes shoot to mine. A look I've never seen before holds tightly to his gaze.

Fear. Shame. Humiliation. I bend down and pick up the puzzle piece that holds his ten-year-old face and walk over to the fire and drop that son of a bitch in. "Alright. Let's get a drink." I beam, giving Zed an out from questions. He cracks a half-smile and nods. It's his asshole way of saying thanks.

"You boys enjoy. I'm leaving town for a while, maybe forever. Who the fuck knows." Zed peaces us out with two fingers then turns to walk away.

"Woah. Wait a minute. We had a fucking deal." Talon jogs over to his side and grabs his shoulder. "Where is he?"

Zed's hands hit his chest. "Hey, now. I'm a man of my word. In time, you'll get what you want." He smirks, before continuing on his way.

"Motherfucker," Talon shouts from the other side of the fire. "I say we kill his ass right now. Toss him in the fire and let the smoke carry his ass away. Revenge for all of us on that fucking pussy."

My fists ball at my sides and the savagery I've tried to push down for the last week returns with a vengeance.

With my feet escaping me, I hurl at Zed from behind. Slamming into his body and taking us both straight down to the ground. We crash into a couple guys who lose their drinks, one spilling down my back, but the ice-cold beverage feels refreshing against my fired-up flesh. Someone tries to pull me off of Zed, but my arm flails freely as I shove them back then drive my fist straight into the back of Zed's head.

Tucking his hands behind his back and underneath my legs, I grab him by the throat and shove his face into the dry grass. "You fucking played us. Had Willa do your dirty work and for what? So you could escape town and leave us to clean up your mess?"

"I said in time." He chokes out as his body wiggles to try and break free.

"How much fucking time?" I'm grabbed from behind again, and this time, I'm jerked off from Zed and dropped to the side.

"Enough!" Tommy shouts. Coming down next to me, he gets close. "Everyone is fucking watching right now. Let this go."

I brush myself off and get to my feet, and by time I turn back around, Zed has disappeared into the crowd. "You idiot!" I scream. "You just let him go?" I give Tommy a shove and walk away before I do something I'll regret. Like burn this whole place down.

"**P**ack your shit. We're leaving tonight," Lars growls, as he comes storming into the kitchen. I'm mid-chew on a piece of pizza.

Choking it down, I drop the slice onto a paper plate. Marni is sitting right beside me with raised brows and the same look of confusion I'm wearing. "Are you drunk?" Stupid first question, but he's clearly not thinking straight.

"No, I'm not drunk. I'm fucking pissed." With one swipe of his arm across the counter, the box of pizza goes flying to the floor. "I should have killed his ass when I had the chance." He begins pacing the length of the kitchen. Steam rolling out of his ears while he rubs his knuckles.

I push off the stool and walk over to him, placing a hand on his shoulder to stop his movements, but the lack of intensity in my touch has him keeping on his path. "What happened?"

When he responds with only a grumble and a huff, Marni pulls out her phone to call Talon, I assume.

Standing in the middle of the kitchen, I watch Lars but listen to Marni.

"Hey, what happened tonight? Why's Lars so pissed off?"

RACHEL LEIGH

There's a beat of silence and her eyes shoot to me. "He did what?! We all had a deal. He got what he wanted." Another pause. "Alright. Well, I'm leaving. I'll be there in a few." She ends the call and stands up. "I've gotta go. You good here?"

"Yeah. We'll be fine. Thanks for hanging out with me tonight."

"Of course." She pulls me in for a hug. "If you ever need anything, just let me know. You're one of us now." She nods her head toward Lars with a smirk. "And if this one starts acting up, call the guys, they'll handle him."

"I will." I chuckle. When she starts picking up the pizza on the floor, I stop her. "I'll get that. And I'll make sure the house is in tip-top shape before we leave. Tell your dad I said thank you."

"When I see him again, I will." She leaves the kitchen and I take over cleaning up the mess.

A rapid thud against the back wall has me jumping up. "Lars!" I gasp when I see blood running down his hand and a dent in the wall.

"Fuck!" he screams, before slamming his fist into the same exact spot. If he was expecting a smooth blow through drywall, he was sadly mistaken, both times.

"Stop it!" I hurry over to him, grabbing a hand towel on my way. "Would you calm down. This isn't helping anything."

"He played us. He used you, used us, and he's leaving town without giving us any answers."

Just as I finish wrapping the towel around his hand, a sharp nudge in my side has me grabbing my stomach.

His eyes widen, and suddenly he's forgotten all about Zed. "What's wrong? Is it the baby?"

I shake my head. "Just a weird dull pain." I cringe when the stabbing sensation happens again. "Ouch." I take a few steps backward and Lars helps me over to the stool. "Maybe it was the pizza." But the next jab has me second-guessing that possibility. "Ahh." I curl over, holding tightly to my stomach. "Lars, I think something's wrong."

"Come on." He scoops me up in his arms, cradling me like a baby.

"Where are we going?" I ask, as he carries me out of the kitchen.

"To the hospital."

"No! What if Rick finds out I'm there. He'll track me down."

He sets me down on the couch and goes to the door to grab my shoes. Sliding one on then the other. "He won't know we're there and even if he does, I'll never let that son of a bitch near you again."

Another stab to the side and I whimper, "It hurts." It's not an uncontrollable pain, but it's nothing I've ever felt before and that worries me. Lars is right; I need to get checked out. Even if it's just for peace of mind.

Once he has his shoes on, he lifts me up again. "I can walk."

"No, you're not." With me still in his arms, he crouches down and turns the handle on the front door. "I'm parked out front. You ok?" He looks at me, and I can see the worry in his eyes.

"I'm ok." I assure him, in hopes of assuring myself at the same time. *Please, God. Don't let anything happen to my baby.*

We arrive at the hospital in record time. Lars pulled right up front and had a few choice words with the valet when he ordered him to get a wheelchair. I told him I didn't need one, but he insisted. Then he threatened some donation to the hospital and went as far as threatening the guy's job when he said there weren't any available. Lars made him go to the second floor to find one. Five minutes later, I'm climbing into it. "I've got this. Get your hands off of her." He swats the guy's arm away. "Go do your fucking job."

"Lars! Stop it. He's trying to help the best he can."

"Well, he needs to try harder." Once I'm in the chair, he pushes me through the doors himself, tossing daggers at the valet. "You fuck up my car and I'll do the same to your face."

My face falls into my hands while I try to hide it, hoping that no one sees me. Not because I'm in hiding right now, but because Lars is so embarrassing. As crazy as it is, a small part of me is attracted to his bad boy persona. But being a straight-up jerk isn't necessary.

Lars checks us in, and once again, I'm feeling like a small child having him always do the adult stuff for me. When the receptionist tells him it will be a few minutes, I immediately grab him by the shirt as I sit in the chair next to him. I shake my head and mouth, "Don't!"

His eyes narrow as he searches my face for how angry I'll be if he does.

Then he does it anyway.

"If you don't get my girlfriend into a room right now, that new wing that's being built in the ICU will be postponed until twenty-thirty. Kick someone out, clean a bed—I don't fucking care. But I'm not leaving this desk until we have a room. And it better be sanitized."

My eyes pinch shut and my chin drops to my chest. Another jab has me grabbing my side again. It's this tugging and pulling sensation. Like someone is trying to pull my ovaries right out of my stomach.

He catches me holding tightly to my stomach. "Now!" Grabbing the attention of every person in triage.

Three minutes later, we're in a room and a nurse is taking my vitals. "Well, your vitals look great. We'll get you in a room right away," she rolls her eyes at Lars, but he seems pleased with himself.

"Appreciate that." His voice is now unfazed and polite. He sticks close to my side and though, I'm in pain and unsure what's going on, it feels good to have someone in my corner who wants to be there. It's in this moment that I realize how safe me and my baby will be because we have him. I feel cherished. I feel loved.

When the nurse takes the handles of the chair, Lars steps up. "I'll push her. You just lead the way."

I bite my bottom lip, trying to hold back from swatting him with the back of my hand, but I wouldn't be able to reach him anyway.

We travel down a narrow hallway where the nurse scans her badge and two large doors open. She leads us into the first room on the left. Lars pushes me next to the bed and I stand up to get on it.

"You'll need to put this on. The radiologist will come for you in a few minutes for an ultrasound."

My heart begins to twitch. A pang of excitement overpowers the shooting pain beneath my rib cage. "We get to see the baby." I look at Lars who cracks a smile.

Lars doesn't hold the same enthusiasm as I do. And that would be because Lars is a realist. Me? I'm the dreamer. We balance each other pretty well, but in this moment, I need his optimism. Deep down, I know the baby is fine. I can feel it in my heart. If something were wrong, I would know, wouldn't I? Mother's instinct or something like that.

The nurse opens then closes the door and once I'm sure she's gone, I stand up. "It's gonna be ok," I reassure Lars, once again.

"Yeah. Everything is fine." He forces a smile. I pull my shirt over my head and Lars wraps the gown around me. I leave my bra on because I'm not having a mammogram or anything, so all they need is access to my stomach.

We both sit in complete and utter silence. I never knew the sound of nothing could be louder than the sound of everything.

There's a subtle knock at the door and a girl walks in. She's young, probably early twenties. A nice tan, dark chocolate-colored eyes and jet-black hair. "Hi, I'm Mary and I'll be taking you down the hall for your ultrasound. Do you prefer the wheelchair?" She looks from me to Lars and I'm not really sure who she's asking. She must have caught wind of Lars' outburst minutes ago.

"Yes. She'll be in the chair," Lars says as he takes my hand and stands me up. I'm trying really hard to hold back an outburst of my own. It's great that Lars is trying to be so help-ful, I really appreciate it. But my entire life, I've done every-thing for myself and I'm going to need him to allow me to make some decisions on my own if this is going to work out in the long run.

I take a seat in the chair and roll my eyes at Lars. He squints his brows. "What?"

"You know what." I leave it at that and let him push me while Mary walks a few steps ahead of us.

"Do you know how far along you are?" Mary asks, without looking back at us. She scans her badge at a door and pushes it open, holding it with her hand so Lars can wheel me into the dark room.

"Umm. Yeah. I'm about ten weeks. I think." Originally I told Lars I was eleven weeks, last week. I know exactly how far along I am because I started my period two days after Lars and I slept together. It wasn't until last month that my period never came and I took a test.

"Nice. Congratulations," Mary replies. She begins punching some stuff into a screen then instructs me to lie flat on the table. Lars lingers right next to me. He's so close that I can feel his breaths hit the bare skin of my stomach. Mary squirts some gel on my stomach then flips on a large projector on the wall in front of me.

She begins moving the wand all around my stomach and I watch the screen intently, not sure what exactly I'm looking at.

"Alright. We're going to have to do a vaginal ultrasound because you're still just a bit early for the abdominal scan."

I push myself up on my elbows. "Is that normal?"

"Absolutely. It's very rare that you'd be able to see a ten-week gestational sac through the abdomen. No worries, hun. We'll get you all checked out. I'm going to step out and you'll need to take your clothes off from the waist down." She looks at Lars. "Just push the door open when she's all set."

Folding my clothes in a neat pile, I realize that the pain has subsided. It's been minutes since I felt the sharp twinges. Lars holds out his hand to take my clothes from me. "I think I'm ok now."

Lars goes over and pushes the door open a crack then returns to my side. "You wanna leave?" Because I'm not too keen on them shoving a wand up your pussy." He grabs ahold of a wand about the length of a ruler and holds it up. "You'll never enjoy my dick again."

Bursting out in laughter, I snatch it from his hand. "Put that down."

"You sure you don't want me to loosen you up a bit with it before she rams it in? Ya know, a little foreplay?"

"Stop it." I blush.

"There might be some extras in the cupboards. We can bring one home for later."

I shoot him a stern look when extra light breaks through the room from the open door.

"All set?" She asks as she takes her place by the monitors. Tearing open a plastic wrapper, she pulls out a condom and proceeds to roll it onto the wand. My first time using a condom and it's not even on a penis. That's about as backwards as this entire situation. "Ok. Legs up. You'll feel some slight pressure and let me know if you feel any pain." The wand rolls in and I try hard to focus on the screen and not what's going on beneath the sheet.

"Is that her?" I ask, pointing to the screen at a tiny little lima bean.

"It sure is."

It's moving around. Not much, but tiny little flutters. A few seconds later, Lars' phone begins vibrating loud enough to catch my attention. At the same time, a swooshing sound rings through a speaker connected to a monitor. It's fast and strong.

"That's your baby's heartbeat."

Warmth radiates through me. A happiness that I didn't even know existed. That's my baby's little heart. I look up at Lars, but he's nose-deep in his phone. "Lars. Did you hear that?" He doesn't lift his head. His eyes are wide and his face his pale. "Lars," I say again.

"Hmm?" He lifts his face from his phone and looks at the screen. "Ah, yeah. Nice and strong heartbeat." He kisses my cheek. Though, his expression doesn't change. He's here, but he's not really here.

"What's wrong?" I whisper when he presses an elbow next to my head and watches the screen with me.

"Not yet," he mumbles.

My phone begins vibrating in my pants on another chair and we look at each other. Lars probably knows what it's about. I, on the other hand, have no clue what's going on.

After Mary snaps a few pics, she pulls the wand out and I pull the sheet down over my legs. "These are for you." She hands me a couple pictures of my little lima bean. "Go ahead and get cleaned up and I'll be back in a minute to take you back to your room."

I hold my breath, counting the seconds in my head until she's gone. "What happened?" I spit out as soon as the door latches shut.

"Holy shit, Willa. You're not gonna believe this." He hands me his phone. "Read that."

December 22, 2020

BREAKING NEWS

Josh Moran, 18, of Redwood, AZ, has been found deceased in an apparent murder-suicide.

Chills circulate through my entire body. I slap a hand to my mouth and look at Lars who has returned to his pale ghost-like state.

Josh Moran went missing sometime at the end of October. His car was pulled from Lake Ruin, just east of Redwood three weeks later. Though, foul play was suspected, his family held out hope.

"He's a good kid. Smart. Funny. Everyone loved him." His sister, Vi Moran, seventeen and also of Redwood, told authorities.

"Well, that's a lie. Even Vi knew her brother was a sicko."

"Keep reading. It gets crazier." Lars moves his eyes from me to the phone.

Authorities were called to the two hundred block of West Elm when Pastor Richard Jeffries was found deceased with a self-inflicted gunshot wound to his head. Beside him, they found dozens of photographs in a biblical box containing child pornography of male and female children that stem back to as early as 2010. The children range in age from only eight-years-old to an estimated sixteen years of age.

"No way!" I choke. "Oh my God, Lars. Kids? There are more kids?" My heart breaks in two. Wait. A box. I stop reading and scroll down a bit at the collage of photos. There's my house with caution tape surrounding it. And the box. There are no pictures, of course. But that's the box Zed had me get. "Lars. I think that Zed was a victim of—" I can't even stomach the words.

Lars nods. "I think you're right."

Oh no. Poor Zed. I'm not sure how old he was or when this could have happened, but if he was a victim, it explains everything. Especially his behavior these past years.

I continue reading...

After a thorough search of the residence, Josh Moran's body was discovered in the basement of the home. His body, badly decomposed, will be taken for an autopsy, but authorities have every reason to believe that Josh was, too, a victim of the late pastor's.

"I can't read any more of this. I feel sick." I hand him back his phone and get up to get dressed. I feel faint, but I also feel this surprising sense of relief. As I'm unfolding my clothes to get dressed, my phone falls out and I remember that I had some sort of alert as well.

Turning it on, I see a text from Zed. I swipe the phone open and read it.

Z: You can stay in Redwood now. You're welcome.

There's a knock at the door, but we both completely ignore it. "Lars. Read this." I hand him my phone and pull my underwear and pants up.

His eyes flash to mine. Big and broad. "He did it. It was him."

Another knock has Lars walking over to the door. My body visibly shakes as I follow behind him.

The next few minutes are a daze as I process everything. Rick is gone. *Rick is gone.* And I'm free. We don't have to leave Redwood. I don't have to hide. Lars and I can still be together. Assuming that's what he still wants. I look over at him as he sits slouched in the chair, texting at rapid speed in his phone, while we wait for the doctor to come in. He's so strikingly handsome. Everything about him makes my heart skip and my knees weak. But, what if he doesn't want me or the baby anymore now that we'll be staying? Would I still ask him to go? I don't want to lose him. But, I'm me. An embarrassment to most. Unnoticed by many. Unwanted by all.

My soul aches at the thought of losing him forever.

The doctor comes in, but Lars' eyes never leave his phone.

"Good evening, Ms. Mack. I'm Doctor Shell." The polite older gentleman extends a hand. "I've had a look at your ultrasound and everything looks great. Are you still having the pain?"

"Actually, no. It stopped all of a sudden," I tell him, but I'm so focused on Lars right now as he stands up and walks out the door without a word. "Well, what you're feeling is pretty normal. At this stage of pregnancy, things are shifting and making room for the growing uterus. Ligaments tug and pull and sometimes, they can be pretty painful. But, I assure you, your baby looks great. If you have any more concerns, just give us a call."

A sense of relief unravels through me.

The doctor walks me out and I look up and down the hall for Lars, but he's nowhere in sight. "I think my...friend is in the waiting room. Thank you so much," I say, before going through the exit doors. When I reach the lobby we entered in, I still don't see him.

"Excuse me. Have you seen the guy I came here with?" I ask the receptionist. The same one that checked us in. She points to the exit and rolls her eyes.

"Thank you," I tell her before walking through the self-sliding doors.

It's dark and cloudy and there's a weird mood in the air. A feeling of dread and the unknown. Lars has his foot kicked up on the side of the building and a cigarette hanging from the corner of his mouth. This is the first time I've ever seen Lars smoke. Never even smelled it on him, so I never suspected he did.

In a state of frustration, I walk over and snatch it from his mouth and drop it to the sidewalk. The heel of my foot digs into it, extinguishing the red cherry. "You left me. Didn't even stay to hear what the doctor said." My arms wrap around me as the wind picks up.

"I knew everything was fine. Baby was moving on that screen. Heartbeat was healthy."

"You left me!" I shout again. The realization that we're having our first real argument comes to light, but is it really an argument if it's one-sided? Because he doesn't even seem to be paying attention to what I'm saying. "You know what, forget it. Just take me....just take me somewhere." I almost said home. But where is home. I'll never go back to that house. Still, don't have any money. I'm homeless. I'm pregnant and homeless. A stray tear slides down my cheek.

Lars glances at me for second, giving me that sliver of a moment while he takes a break from his phone. I guess this is the end. He really is giving up on me. "Hey," he drops his hands to his side, "what's wrong? Why are you crying?" Pulling my lips between my teeth, I pinch my eyes shut, not allowing any of my tears to fall. "Willa. I'm sorry. This is just really big and I needed to talk to Tommy and Talon and see what the hell is going on."

"It is big. But, so was this visit." Maybe I'm being overly emotional. Lars is right. This is huge. Zed murdered Rick and sent him straight to hell. Josh's body was found and everyone thinks Rick killed him. Maybe he did kill him. Maybe Josh was a victim, too. "You're right. The baby is fine. We need to find out what happened. Let's just get out of here."

No longer needing the wheelchair, we wait for the valet to bring the car around. Instead of shutting his phone off for a few minutes, Lars makes a call through his Bluetooth as soon as we get inside. "You cold?" he asks as the sound of ringing surrounds us through the speakers.

I nod and he cranks the heat all the way up.

"Dude. This is unreal. Un-fucking-real," Tommy says.

"I'm on my way over. You guys stay there," Lars tells him then ends the call. Instead of dropping his hand in his lap, he places it on my leg and gives me a squeeze. "I'm sorry."

"It's ok. I'm just glad the baby is ok."

About five minutes into the drive, I break the silence. "Has anything changed, Lars?" I freeze as I wait for his response.

"Everything's changed, babe. We don't have to leave anymore. We can stay in Redwood. That son-of-a-bitch is dead." He shouts all too excitedly, "He's fucking gone."

I nod with a sly smile. "Yeah. He's gone. But what about us?"

"What about us?"

"What happens now that we're staying? People will judge you—judge me."

Cocking his head to the side, he looks from me to the road. "Is that what you're worried about? Willa, it's you and me. You, me and our baby. Fuck everyone else."

I smile again, and this time, it's not sly, forced, or fake. "Yeah. Fuck everyone."

"Willa Jean Mack. Did you just say fuck?"

"Yeah, and it felt really fucking good." I slap a hand over my mouth and giggle.

"You naughty little Christian," he teases.

Switching to a more serious note, my smile fades. "We still don't know who left that message or came to my house." I look at Lars who glances back and forth from me to the road. "Do you still think it was Zed?"

He takes longer than I thought to answer, which leads me to believe that he doesn't think it was Zed. I almost feel like I would have been more satisfied if he said yes. At least that way I would know.

"Honestly, I don't think so. For whatever reason, Zed wanted to help you. I'm not sure why. Don't think he knew about what happened to you, but it's like he empathized with you. I could see it in his eyes—heard it in his voice—when he found me at your old house."

"Well, what's your guess then? Rick?" My shoulders shrug.

"Maybe Madison was lying?" It's more of a question than a statement because he'd know better than I would, the lengths that girl would go to.

"It could have been any of them. Even Vi. Apparently you can't trust her as much as you thought you could."

I nod. He's right. It could be anyone and there's a good chance that I'll never know who it was. Doesn't matter anyways. I'm putting the past behind me and moving forward.

Willa Jean Mack is gone. I'm not the same girl I used to be. Lars changed me that night three months ago and every night after that. I'm learning that it's ok to say fuck off. I don't have to be a doormat or hold back my feelings. I'm allowed to push back and when the world wants to know why I'm so quiet, I'll scream in their face at the top of my lungs. I have a voice now and you can bet your ass that I plan to use it.

Two weeks later

There are three things that I know for certain: the pastor is dead. Zed killed him. Now Zed is gone.

We thought it would be best to attend school like usual. Treat the day normally and relinquish all suspicion. It would be totally feasible for Willa to take some more time to mourn the death of her stepdad and his actions, considering no one knows what she went through with him, but she's here. She's wearing a smile with her head held high.

Willa and I have been staying at my dad's house. Even spent Christmas with my dad, and to my surprise, it was pretty laid back and I actually enjoyed his company. I can't even remember the last time I sat down and had dinner with the old man.

After Margo, the housekeeper, cleared the table, Dad brought out gifts. And when I say he brought out gifts, I mean for his granddaughter. Mountains of clothes, and pretty much anything a baby needs that isn't a necessity. To say he's excited is an understatement. I know he didn't personally pick any of it out, but he's making an effort.

The cafeteria is exactly how I remember it. Crowded, loud, and smells like ass. The walls in this place hold some good memories, but going virtual was the best choice I ever made.

Truth is, I was failing. Fucked off at school, fucked off at home, and I needed to get my head on straight. Granted, staying with Talon didn't give me that boost of motivation I needed, but the lack of distraction helped.

Talon and I had the grand scheme to try and do better so we could get into a good school with Tommy. We knew that Zed would be working for his dad and staying in Redwood. At least, that's what we all thought. Talon and Tommy are smart as hell. My grades are mediocre, so chances are, Willa and I will stay local and raise the baby in Redwood.

I can see that Tommy heeded my advice to befriend Willa. Didn't want to force him because she'd think I was trying to make her friends, but I pretty much told him to take her under his wing. They're sitting at the same table I sat with the guys at every day for lunch. Willa is sandwiched between two of the biggest full backs the Ravens have ever seen. Tommy says something that makes her laugh and I feel myself smiling along with her. She's so fucking cute. How I never saw it before boggles my mind. Maybe I did and I just never allowed myself to explore it because she was an outcast—the quiet girl who was sheltered. I know now that she put her walls up so high because she didn't want to be seen. At least, not in the way people were looking at her. But, I see her now, and I love what I'm looking at.

As if she senses my presence, her head slowly turns to face me. The way her eyes light up does something funky to my chest. Her chair slides back and she walks hastily over to me. "What are you doing here?"

The chattering voices fade away and all I hear and see is her. Willa is my calm in this chaotic world. She drowns out the noise and brightens the darkest day.

I wanna kiss her, but I also know that all three aides are watching me because, technically, I'm not supposed to be here. "Wanted to surprise you."

"Well, you did. I've missed you."

"Me, too. Crazy how just a couple months together every day can make one day apart feel like an eternity."

"Come sit with us." She gestures toward the table where her food is sitting.

"Actually, I wanted to give you a little high school experience that no one should ever miss out on. Finish eating then meet me in the hall."

Walking away, she leaves me standing there. But, instead of sitting back down, she says something to the guys, picks up her tray and goes to the trash and dumps it. "Hey, you need to eat."

"I did. Now give me this experience that I *can't* miss."

Taking her hand in mine, we leave the noise and static and step into the empty hall. "This way." I lead her down the hall past the senior lockers. Looking both ways first, I push open the janitor closet.

"No. Uh uh." She pulls back, but I pull harder, getting her into the closet and closing the door. "Lars, we cannot have sex in here."

"I know. We can do that at home. I just wanna make out with you."

"And that's an experience that I don't dare miss out on?"

"Mmmhmm." My lips shadow hers. "All the cool kids are doing it."

"Just how many girls have you brought in this closet?"

I don't answer, I just kiss her. Hard, passionate, and with

enough tenacity to make my dick instantly harden. Maybe this wasn't such a good idea.

"Well?" She pulls back, awaiting my answer.

"The truth? You're my first." It's not a lie. I'm not even sure that this a thing; it just sounded fun. I figured, we only have six more months until the baby comes, so we need to do all the youthful shit while we can. This is our last chance to be reckless and immature before we have to buckle down with responsibility.

"Liar."

"I'd never lie to you." Another truth. Willa is probably the only person in the world that I care enough about to give all my truths to.

Finally, she gives in and her body relaxes in my arms. My hands slide down to her ass and I give both cheeks a firm squeeze. We're just making out, but that includes copping a feel. She must have read my mind because she shoves her hand down my pants. "Willa, you dirty girl. We're at school," I tease.

"Don't you know that we only live once?" She pops the button on my jeans and slides my zipper down. My pants linger around my hips as she begins pumping my cock with her hand. Grazing her thumb over my head, she rubs the bead of pre-cum then resumes stroking.

I grab her face and pull it back to mine. "That feels so good, baby," I mutter into her mouth. "I'm getting you back later, promise."

"You better." She strokes my full length faster and my head falls back. My eyes close and my mouth forms an O as I feel myself fill up. Throbbing and ready to release. "God, I love you," I say in a breathy moan before I spill into her hand. She keeps jerking me off, sloshing my cum all over my dick. When my head comes back up, she stops.

"What do I do with this?" She laughs with her hand still wrapped around me. I slap around the pitch-black closet until I find a rag to give to her. I tug my pants back up and wait until she tosses the rag before opening the door.

Voices begin to carry down the hall and I don't even have to ask or hear her say it to know that she's nervous about walking out there. "Like a band-aid," I tell her. "We open the door quickly and shut it just as fast then walk down the hall normally."

"Everyone's gonna know."

"What's our motto?" I ask her, as I grip the handle, ready to escape.

"Fuck everyone." With my free hand, I pull her mouth to mine for one last kiss before I swing the door open. Laughing, she stumbles out into the hall. I slam the door shut and take her hand in mine. "I'm going to wash my hands then I have to get to class. I'll see you in drama, later?" She stops in front of the girls' bathroom.

"You can count on it." I flash her a smile and release her hand.

I MET Willa at her locker for all three classes. There was no sense in going home for just a couple hours. I played around in the library on the computer for a bit. Tried to get into my old locker to no avail. Went out in the parking lot for a smoke. It's a nasty habit that I kicked a while ago, but once in a great while, I still indulge. "I'm so nervous," Willa says as she swings her locker open and drops her books inside.

"Don't be. I told you before, that part is yours."

"I really wish that you would have accepted the role of Beast."

I let out a laugh, then another. "Not a chance in hell. I'd do just about anything for you, but I won't do that." After I say the words, I break into song, shouting out the lyrics of "Anything for Love" by Meatloaf.

"Stop it!" Willa swats playfully at me. All it does is make me sing louder. Everyone looks but since when do I give a shit about making a scene? "Lars!" She grits through her clenched teeth. A few passersby laugh and I finally give in and stop. "You're so embarrassing."

"Get used to it." I give her a smack on her ass.

We stop outside class and Willa pinches her eyes shut in front of the board that holds the chosen roles for the play.

"You got it!" I shout with excitement before she even has a chance to look. Grabbing her by the waist, I spin her around. "I fucking knew you'd get it." I mean, honestly, who else would have gotten it? Madison is gone and no one else wants it. Either way, Willa is really good and I knew she had it in the bag.

"Yay. Let's celebrate tonight."

Flinging an arm over her shoulder, I lead her into class. "You got it. Butt sex all night."

"Not a chance. I would do just about anything for you, but I won't do that."

I break out in song again, and this time, she just walks away from me with pink cheeks and a cute ass.

Trent joins her side and when he wraps his arms around her, something twitches inside of me. I saw that Willa got the part. I also saw that Trent is playing her beast. Taking in deep breaths, I attempt to calm myself while his crummy hands rub up and down her back. She breaks away and looks back at me to make sure I'm behaving. I smile and wave then quickly drop my courteous expression when she turns back to Trent and he looks my way. With two fingers, I point to my eyes and then direct one finger at him. His eyes widen and he takes a step back.

He can be her beast in the play, but I'm the beast that lives in her heart.

It's the coldest day of the year, so far, which doesn't say a lot, considering it's the first week in January. Willa is sitting in the front seat of my car—in the dark, at a cemetery—with the heat on full blast.

I walk through the maze of stones like I know exactly where to go, even though it's been five years since I've even been here. Somehow, though, I end up right in front of Colby's gravesite.

Slouching down, I don't say anything for at least five minutes. I just stare straight ahead reading the engraved words on his headstone. *Beloved son and brother.* Mustering up the courage, I try to talk to him. Although, it feels weird at first. "Hey, Colby. How ya doing?"

Stupid. How do you think he's doing? He's dead. I drop down on my ass and try again. "I'm sorry I haven't been here to see you in a while. Things have been busy."

It's a lie and he knows it. Fuck it, it's time to be honest. "Look, I know that I sucked as a brother. I was always so mean to you. Never let you hang out with me and my friends. Even locked you in a closet once. Ok. Twice. The truth is, I didn't know how to be a brother. I didn't know how to be much of anything but a selfish spoiled asshole. I was just a kid, too."

Looking down at my hands at the PlayStation controller I brought, regret floods through me. I set it down in front of his stone and begin picking at the grass at my side, pulling piece by piece and dropping them back down. "I'm sorry, Colby. You didn't deserve any of that. You loved me. You looked up to me and I just pushed you away any time you came close to me." I choke down the lump in my throat. "The thing is, I didn't know how to love, so even if I did love you, I didn't know what it felt like. I've always thought that because I didn't feel it while you were here that it meant I never loved you at all. The truth is, I do love you, Colby. I'm just now learning that love isn't always black and white. There are times you think you hate someone you love, but you don't really hate them, you're just angry. That love is still there; it's just masked by other emotions. So yeah, I love you little brother and I'm sorry it took me so long to tell you that."

I go to push myself off the grass, but I stop myself and get on my knees. "You're gonna be an uncle. I'm having a little girl." The wind picks up and I laugh. "Yeah, I know. Me? A dad to a little girl. Shit man, I'm gonna need some guidance on this one or I might end up burning this whole town down just to get rid of the asshole teenager boys." I hear the car door shut, so I wrap things up. "I'll make sure she knows who you are and maybe bring her to visit sometime. You would have been a good uncle." I kiss my fingertips then touch his stone. "Later, little bro."

When I stand up and turn around, Willa is standing there. I give her a smile to tell her that I'm ok. And, for the first time in my life, I actually believe it.

"How do you feel?" she asks, nuzzling her face into my chest. My arms wrap around her back and I hold onto her tightly.

"I feel good."

Her delicate fingers graze over the infinity tattoo on my neck. "So, you got your revenge on Madison, what's next for the rebels?"

Pulling back, I brace my hands on her shoulders and look into her soft glowing eyes. "Actually, Madison was never my revenge. It was me all along. I was fighting against my own inner demons. I think I finally won." I press a chaste kiss to her forehead, holding my lips still and thinking about what is next for me and the guys. Tommy's next. He's been fighting something of his own and I think we're all ready to see him happy again. "Come on," I take her hand, "let's get out of here."

We walk away and I feel like the weight of the world has been lifted off my shoulders. My heart is full, my head is clear, and the woman of my dreams is carrying our baby. Come what may, I'll give my last breath to protect my girls.

The End.

EPILOGUE

LARS

We're headed over to Marni's house for a surprise birthday party that her dad is throwing her. Apparently he's been kissing her ass to make up for selling her to the devil—the devil being Talon. I think Anderson is starting to learn that we're not all as evil as he took us for. We're just loyal as fuck to each other and we prefer to eliminate toxicity. I mean, only two out of the four of us are murderers, so we're not all that bad.

We're creeping down the driveway when Willa stops me halfway down. "Hey, back up."

"Why?"

"Just do it."

I shift into reverse and roll the car backward. "Stop! That," she points up, "is that a camera?"

Leaning forward, I get a closer look. "Yeah. It looks like one, why?"

"If Josh was hit right in front of the house, shouldn't there be some kind of footage on that camera?"

"Hmm, I guess. Maybe. But if Anderson thought he killed Josh for months, I'm sure he's checked into it."

"Yeah. You're probably right."

Shifting back in drive, we keep moving forward. There are only a few cars here. Probably just Marni's close friends and family. Wouldn't be surprised if that shithead Axel and his nitwit friends are here. Still can't stand those guys, even if they did help us out when Zed lost his mind a couple months ago. They weren't there to help us—they were there for Marni.

They actually remind me a lot of us. They're tried and true, we're ride or die.

Memories of my stay here with Willa hit me as soon as I walk through the door. From bickering to mental breakdowns to making up and making love. It's been a whirlwind, but the future is looking bright for all of us.

Tommy and Talon are sitting on the couch, and when I spot Marni, I realize we're late. "Shit man, you said eight. Happy birthday, Marni." I swat Talon on the back of the head. He actually said seven, but I won't admit that. Willa and I had a hard time getting up today and spent most of the day naked in bed. It definitely beats yelling surprise to someone who probably already knew she was having a party. Talon's a whipped little bitch, and there is no way he kept it from her.

I take a seat next to Tommy and pull Willa down on my lap. "What are you guys talking about?"

Talon looks at the older group across the room who must be friends of Anderson's, then he leans forward, bringing his voice down a few octaves. "I was just saying that someone out there is wondering how the fuck Josh's car went into Lake Ruin and how his body ended up in the pastor's basement. I mean, they've gotta be shitting balls right now."

"No kidding. I was thinking the same thing. We're clear for now, but someone out there knows something."

"Is it possible that Rick really is the one that hit him?" Willa shrugs her shoulders and looks from person to person.

"Nah, too obvious. And it certainly wasn't an accident.

When we found Josh, it looked like he had been mauled to death. Like someone ran him over and backed up a few times to finish him off. Then, of course, Marni's dad came flying down the road and smooshed his ass even more."

Willa cringes. "Ugh, that's disgusting."

"You should have seen his face, it was—"

"No." I shake my head to Tommy. "Don't go there."

Willa gives me a nudge. "Ask about the camera."

"What camera?" Marni asks.

It's probably a dead end, but what the hell. "There's a camera about halfway down your driveway facing the road. I'm sure your dad already checked it, but it could have caught something."

Marni taps her finger to her chin. "Hmm, I don't remember a camera in the driveway. Hey, Dad?" she hollers across the room, "come here."

Anderson makes his way over to us with a glass in his hand. The ice clinks against the side of the glass sloshing the caramel-colored liquor. "Is there a camera in the driveway?"

He raises a brow and thinks on it. "Tiny white camera?"

Marni looks at Willa. "Yeah, it was white," Willa says.

"Oh yeah. It's from the old system. That cheap piece of shit that wouldn't pick up a pack of wolves coming down the driveway."

"Is it armed?" Talon asks.

"Nah, I don't think so. That system was set up through a third party. I'm pretty sure we dropped them when we switched to a private system."

"What's the name of the company?" I ask, pulling my phone out, ready to search the company name.

"Umm, Whitlock Security."

"We're gonna look into," Marni tells him. "I'll let you know if we need anything to log in."

He nods and walks away, but not before giving Talon a death glare. Some things never change.

In a matter of seconds, I've got the company pulled up. "It looks like they have an online system where you can see all saved footage from the start of service. Doesn't hurt to try. Go ask your dad what his log-in info is."

Marni jumps up and goes to talk to him.

"It could be nothing. But it could be something." I shrug. "Good catch." I nudge Willa.

Fifteen minutes later, she returns with a piece of paper. "Holy fuck, what did you have to do, track down the software developer?" Tommy teases.

"Sorry. My dad doesn't know this shit. I had to search his office. Call his former assistant. Anyways, I got it." She hands me the paper and I log him in.

"Bingo. We're in." I scroll down and there are at least a thousand pages of motion-activated footage. "Holy shit. These have today's date on it." I click on one clip and it shows Tommy's truck coming down the driveway only seventy-two minutes ago. "Fucking-A dude, we got it!"

"No way!" Everyone gets up and hovers around me. "There's one clip clocked in five minutes before Tommy and Talon would have gotten there. This has to be it. The other ones are all after we arrived. This is some serious shit, we need to delete this when we're done."

"What are you waiting for? Play it." Tommy bumps me from behind the couch.

I tap play on the forty-two second long clip. It's not very good footage and I can see why Anderson switched companies. A car flies by, but it goes as fast as it came. There isn't a chance in hell we'd be able to make it out.

"Wait, go back," Marni says, after another car is shown on the screen.

Dragging my finger back, I take us to the thirty-one second mark. "There it is again. Anyone recognize that car? It's blurry, but it's something." I pause the video on a black shiny little car that tapped his brakes right around where Josh would have been lying.

Marni slaps a hand over her mouth and takes a few steps back. "What's up, girl? You look like you've seen a ghost."

She shakes a finger at the phone. "Zoom in on those tires."

Pinching my fingers together on the screen, I drag them to zoom in.

"Shit!" Marni huffs. "I know who that is."

"Who? Who the fuck has neon pink hubcaps?" *Holy shit! Of course!*

"Wyatt McCoy." Tommy snaps his fingers. "I'm gonna fucking kill his ass."

"Like hell you are. Wyatt's my best friend!" Marni snaps back. "You better not lay a finger on him."

This is like a fucking dream come true for Tommy. For some reason, he can't stand Wyatt. Poor boy isn't gonna know what's coming when Tommy gets ahold of him. I'm not sure Marni, or anyone for that matter, will be able to stop him.

Vandal is coming March 25th! Preorder Now: http://mybook.to/vandal

MESSAGE FROM THE AUTHOR

Readers! Thank you for giving Heathen a chance. I hope you enjoyed Willa and Lars' quest to find happiness.

Carolina, you have been such a blessing in my life and I appreciate all you do for me.

Amanda & Aurora, thank you so much for beta reading and giving your feedback and thoughts. I love you both!

Sara, once again, thank you for being my go-to-girl and dealing with my constant randomness.

Talk Nerdy PR, thank you for helping get the word out about my books. You've been wonderful to work with.

Kate, thank you for this gorgeous cover. You rock!

Becky, thank you for another beautiful edit and for being so flexible. You're amazing!

Thank you to all the bloggers who like, love, share, and review. I appreciate you all so much.

My amazing street team, thank you for your daily support and shares! I couldn't do this without you all.

I'd love to hear what you thought of Heathen by leaving a review. I'd also like to invite you to join my readers group Rachel's Ramblers.

xoxo-Rachel

ABOUT THE AUTHOR

Rachel Leigh resides in West Michigan with her husband, three kids, and a couple fur babies.

Rachel lives in leggings, overuses emojis, and survives on books and coffee. Writing is her passion. Her goal is to brighten at least one person's day with the worlds she creates between the pages of her books.

f facebook.com/rachelleighauthor

🐦 twitter.com/rachelleigh_1

📷 instagram.com/rachelleighauthor

a amazon.com/author/rachelleighauthor

g goodreads.com/rachelleigh

BB bookbub.com/profile/rachel-leigh